FINDING OUT

A Novel

Sheryn MacMunn

DEDICATION

This book is dedicated to all the grandmothers and friends who teach us about life, love, and how to grow up

ACKNOWLEDGMENTS

I am deeply grateful to all those who helped me along the way while I wrote this book.

I am especially thankful to Liz Beckwith who was the first person to read this and offered help while I edited and re-edited, plus she's been a great friend in every way.

Kia Heavey, my writing partner, who kept me going with great advice and stories about her publishing experiences.

Angela Haskell who told me for years to write a book and was the best roommate ever.

April Kihlstrom for her 'Book In A Week' course where I learned about character development, plot structure and how to be a better writer.

The following people offered invaluable advice and encouragement: Merry Conway, Joy Breed, Theresa Federici, Katrina Garrier, Maura Phelan Murnane, Laura Londin, Ruth Sanzari, Lisa Smith, Victoria Lyons and my fabulous editor, Meredith Hays.

To my Mother, who stayed up all night reading and editing the second draft. My Dad, who gave good advice about how the men in the book should act.

To my Nana Virginia, and my Grammy Rose, who loved me, always made time for me, and passed on a love of books. I miss you both every day.

Ruth, who mentored me for many years, becoming a third grandmother. I still think of you every day and now understand the things you taught me all those years ago.

Last, and most importantly, my husband Matthew, who gave me a notebook and pen when I first told him that I wanted to write a book and said 'start now.' Thank you for inspiring me to keep going and waiting patiently to read it. Your support means everything.

And for my wonderful children. This book is for you so you remember to never, ever give up on your dreams.

FINDING OUT

Sheryn MacMunn

1

"I can't believe my friends were right," was all Sheila Davenport could think as she stared at Joe. After seven years of defending him and being so sure their relationship was solid, it turned out her friends were, in fact, right.

"What do you mean you're moving out?" Those last words weren't registering in Sheila's brain. She was exhausted from her trip to Boston as the Senior Account Manager of *Goodliving.com*. Although the train ride home to New York should have been three and a half hours, freezing snow had delayed the train making the trip almost six hours long. Adding to the stress of travel was the fight she and Joe had on the phone yesterday when Joe accused her of not caring about his needs. But to discuss this on the sidewalk in front of their co-op building was too much.

"I'm leaving, Sheila. In time you'll see this is the right thing." He looked at her warily repeating the words he had read on the Internet about how to have a 'great' break-up. What Joe didn't understand was that those break-up lines were created for people who had dated casually or maybe a few months. So he was a little surprised that Sheila was having a hard time understanding him.

"Joe, I know you're upset. Let's go upstairs and talk over dinner. We'll order from -" Sheila began.

"No!" Joe practically yelled, then turned away as Rudy, the evening doorman, suddenly appeared.

"Hey, Sheila, can I take those bags for you?" He reached for the bags with his usual smile. Freeing herself of her heavy bag loaded with what had to be fifteen pounds of paper from every meeting she had during the week, her leather purse and suitcase, Sheila sighed with relief and started to smile. Until she caught the quick, pointed glare Rudy shot at Joe and a small pain started in the left side of her stomach.

Not knowing what to say, Sheila stared at the man she had loved for the past seven years as he gazed across the street at Gramercy Park. The chilling February air went right through her, but she honestly didn't know if she was shivering because of that or because Joe wouldn't even look at her.

"It's freezing, Joe. I need to go inside. We can't solve this on the street," she said.

"There's nothing to discuss. I moved out." Joe stared at the ground with his hands in his coat pockets.

Moved? Did he just say moved? Sheila opened her mouth but quickly snapped it shut as the full reality of the situation hit her, almost draining her of breath. Joe had actually moved out while she was on her business trip. Past tense. He was not coming upstairs and, in fact, she was being dumped on the street.

"Joe, we've been together for seven years. You can't break up with me on the street!" One of their neighbors hurried past with her head down, embarrassed to have overhead the comment.

"This is why I'm not coming up. I don't want to be yelled at. I'm not happy and I moved out. My key is upstairs on the kitchen table." He started rubbing the back of his head in that nervous way that always aggravated Sheila; now it infuriated her.

She wished she still had her computer bag so she could swing it at his head. "When exactly did you make this decision?" She stared at him, trying to have some dignity.

"Last week."

2

"And that's it? This is all I get after seven years? A goodbye on the sidewalk? No real reasons or any chance to work it out?" She couldn't figure out if crying would be a good or bad thing right now, so she kept it together until he answered.

"There's nothing to work out. I found someone else." He said it so quietly, she thought she misheard him.

"What?" All her energy slipped to her feet and left her body. She quickly stepped to a bench along the sidewalk and slumped onto it. Unable to even look at him, she leaned forward to stop her head from spinning. Who? When? She wanted to ask but the words couldn't make it out of her lips.

"I'm sorry," he said. "I've got to go."

The pressure in her chest kept her from calling out to him. It was all she could do to drag the breath into her lungs. When Sheila finally looked up, all she saw was Joe getting smaller and smaller against the black iron fence of the park. He never even looked back. It was the end of the greatest love affair of her life and the beginning of incredible pains in her stomach.

2

The apartment looked like a jigsaw puzzle with some of the pieces missing. Sheila walked into the apartment, large by New York standards, expecting to find a jumbled mess. But as she looked around the room, confusion replaced her fear. The furniture was still in place, the apartment was actually very neat, but as she sat on the sofa in their living room to take it all in, she noticed that Joe had taken various paintings and photos off the wall, leaving large spaces that disrupted the symmetry of the room.

She stared at the spots of butter colored paint, trying to remember what photos were missing, but for some reason, she couldn't place them. Maybe it was the shock from Joe leaving, though that hadn't really sunk in. Or maybe it was because the walls had been the same for years. When they painted the walls years ago, they put up the photos and some paintings and just left it. Now she had spots of paint staring at her in a color she had always disliked — she preferred a muted blue or something more modern but Joe had insisted.

"It's classy. My boss' living room is this color. It goes with everything. We'll never have to go through this again." he had

4

said, referring to their fights as they renovated the apartment. And Sheila gave in, happy at the thought they would never again have to argue over carpet samples or faucets or paint colors. Now as she sat and stared, it was as if the color mocked her. *Joe is gone, but I'm still here.* She shook her head and turned away.

Their shelving unit also looked strange since he had removed college trophies and all photos of him, his friends and his family, but left all souvenirs from their trips and all photos of them. Sheila looked back to the wall again and sunk deeper into the sofa, the tears starting down her cheeks as she realized he had only taken mementos that didn't represent their life together.

Why did he leave the furniture? She wondered, looking at the brown sofa that Joe had picked.

"It's a great designer. It's in all the magazines. Look." He had held an issue of *Architectural Digest* in front of Sheila.

"But it's so traditional. And ugly." Sheila said.

"I can't have nouveau furniture if I need to entertain my colleagues; I need to have what they have. We can't look like kids experimenting with a crayon box," Joe said.

And that had been that. They set up their house and went on with their lives.

Sheila wiped the tears from her face with her hands, not bothering to get a tissue as she looked at the club chair. Of course he didn't take it. To move any of the furniture would require a moving van and a special permit from the doormen, plus he only really loved the antique bedroom furniture. Remembering Rudy's look, Sheila sprung off the sofa stopping short at the bedroom door, unable to step inside.

She stared in shock at the empty space that had once been her bedroom. Joe had not only taken the bed frame, he had taken the dresser and armoire, leaving the mattress and box spring with her clothes neatly folded in piles on the floor against the wall. The wall that used to hold their fifty-two inch flat screen TV. This was one purchase they agreed on because Joe and Sheila loved curling up in bed to watch movies and their favorite TV shows. When Joe decided to pay with his corporate card, he was very nonchalant.

"We need the points for a nice trip. We'll go someplace warm this winter." he had told her as he handed his card to the cashier.

And Sheila dreamed of the trip they would take instead of the fact that they usually paid for all house expenses from their mutual account. Oh no. The bank account.

Sheila and Joe had a mutual bank account and deposited money every month for expenses and miscellaneous things like trips, entertainment and furniture. They contributed equal amounts each month, which had been a sore spot as Joe's income surpassed Sheila's at least threefold. But, he reasoned, Sheila owned the co-op, so on paper she had more than Joe. It was true; Sheila had bought the one bedroom co-op in 2000 before they had met. She had been young and rich, thanks to an Internet IPO. Being from a humble background, she originally looked at studio apartments and one-bedrooms in the up-and-coming areas of Brooklyn until her then boss got hold of her.

"Are you crazy? The commute to Brooklyn will kill your social life. And why are you looking at studios?" her boss asked when he picked some listings off the printer. "Sheila, you need to set your sights much higher. You're a millionaire now. You need to go big and stay big. I'm sending you to my broker."

That broker took her financials and showed her the types of apartments she could now afford, which were in some of the best buildings in Manhattan. When Sheila found the gorgeous one bedroom in the neighborhood of her dreams, Gramercy Park, she rushed to sell her company stock for the fifty percent down payment. Then she sold more to furnish the place and began to live larger than large with her new wad of cash. Being young, Sheila never thought she'd earn any less and the remaining stock would keep climbing in value. By the time the market collapsed at the end of 2001, the company was sold to the biggest competitor, she was out of a job, and the rest of her stock options were worthless.

She quickly found another ad sales position for less money, but she was able to pay her mortgage and have some left over. Enough to do a summer share in the Hamptons, where she met Joe.

It had been an easy beginning to their relationship. Every weekend they were in the same place with the same group of friends getting to know each other. When the summer ended Joe had called and asked her on a proper date and the rest, as they liked to tell their friends, was history.

By the time he moved in a few years later, the economy had picked-up and they were both doing well in their careers again. So they renovated the co-op and refurnished it together. Well, Sheila actually took a HELOC on the property and then used some of the money for Joe to finish grad school full-time. She had looked at the HELOC as a solid investment in her future. The co-op would definitely increase in value and Joe's MBA would provide more income. Much better than investing in another company that would go bankrupt. So over the past five years of living together, they had managed to amass almost one hundred and fifty thousand dollars in their shared account.

She ran to her desk and quickly logged into the online banking system. Sheila froze and stared at the screen. There was less than twenty-five thousand dollars in the account.

As she slumped into her chair, she saw a letter with her name on it in Joe's handwriting.

Dear Sheila:

By now I've told you it's over between us. To help you ease into the transition of living alone, I left the apartment virtually the same with the exception of some items I brought with me and some things I bought with my own money.

In lieu of disrupting your life by dividing our assets, I totaled their worth and deducted that amount from our mutual bank account. I thought the furnishings would bring you greater comfort than money.

If you need anything else, you can send an email and I'll respond in a timely manner.

I'll always think of you fondly and wish you the best.

Joe

* * * * *

The rest of the night was a blur. Sheila called her best friend, Jenn, who stayed on the phone with her for hours, dissecting the scene over and over while Sheila drank glass after glass of wine. Jenn knew Joe was a shit but not this much of a shit. Jenn ended the call promising to be at work early so they could talk more. Then she turned to her husband.

"Did you know about this?" she asked.

"He didn't say anything to me, but let's face it, they weren't married. After seven years, you know it's going to end at some point. I just didn't think he'd have the balls to do it. I always thought it would be her," he said.

That had been Jenn's hope all along, but that didn't help her friend.

After drinking more wine, Sheila called Morgan, a friend she had set up with Joe's best friend, Dylan.

"No!" Morgan was sitting in bed with Dylan by her side. She smacked him on the leg as she listened to Sheila. "No, Dylan never said a word. You know I would have told you." She was looking at Dylan. *OMG*, she mouthed. "Sheila, I'm so sorry. I'll try to get any information but you know guys, they don't talk, so Dylan probably doesn't know anything."

That call lasted for an hour, with Sheila drinking a second bottle of wine and promising she wouldn't call Joe. But drunk, lonely, and sad, Sheila fell onto the mattress with the phone and dialed Joe's number. He didn't answer so she hit cancel and redial over and over again until she finally fell asleep.

3

Returning to work after the breakup was torture. Sheila woke at the usual time but when she looked at Joe's pillow and found it empty, she was momentarily shocked until the memory of last night exploded into her brain. Unfortunately, a massive hangover struck at the same time so Sheila lay in bed staring at the ceiling, which was much farther away since her mattress and box spring were on the floor, and let the tears slide down each of her temples.

She should call in sick, Sheila decided, to give herself a chance to find out what other things Joe may have taken and try to talk to him. But when she picked up her cell phone to call her assistant, two calendar alarms showed two big sales calls. She groaned and covered her eyes with her arm. Maybe that would be best after all, she reasoned. Keeping busy might help her think more clearly, which would be helpful when she talked to Joe.

Jenn had come in early as promised and sat in Sheila's office replaying Joe's words over and over. They hadn't even noticed that the office was filling up so they continued talking as they walked out to the support area, only to be overheard by Stacey, the most obnoxious of the support staff, thereby dashing any hope of Sheila finding solace at work.

"Oh! My! God! Did you really just say that Joe broke up with you?" Stacey stood in her cubicle positively giddy at the thought of a new office drama unfolding.

"Stacy, lower your voice." Jenn had a problem with Stacey, as did most people, but unlike most people, she wasn't afraid to put her in her place. "We're in the middle of the office."

"So it's true? He really dumped you on the sidewalk?" Stacey practically screamed.

"Who got dumped on the sidewalk?" Susan Lynd, the willowy Southeast Rep, came out of her office.

"Sheila!" Stacey shook her head in shock.

Susan gasped. "I don't think you want to tell that story to too many people."

"Yeah" chimed Melissa Hellman, Sheila's Assistant, as she put her bags on her desk outside Sheila's office. "Being dumped is humiliating enough, but on the street - that's really bad." She looked at Sheila with pity.

"He's the jerk, not Sheila. It's not her fault." Jenn said defensively.

Susan and Melissa rolled their eyes at each other. It might not be her fault but why would anyone admit to being dumped on the street?

"All I know is I would die if that happened to me," Melissa offered. The last time Melissa had been dumped was in college and when he broke it off, she ate nothing but ice cream for a week and gained ten pounds. Melissa shuddered to think about it.

"Ditto," said Susan. "That's one good thing about a pre-nup. If my fiancé did that to me, he'd be paying through the nose."

Sheila winced a little at that. Susan had just met her fiancé six months ago and was already engaged with a huge rock and a pre-nup. He was loaded, divorced and hung onto Susan's every word. As a result, Susan didn't care much about work anymore. All she did was plan her wedding, which would be in September, and then she'd go off into the land of ladies who lunch.

"Has he changed his Status on Facebook? Did you change yours?" Stacey asked.

"I've got more important things on my mind than Facebook." Sheila realized that she should have called in sick.

"I don't think so. EVERYONE's going to go to his Facebook page and yours. One of my friends got dumped on Facebook by her boyfriend of three years!"

"See why you don't want to tell that story?" Susan said. "You're now on par with Stacey's friends."

"Screw you, Susan," Stacey lobbed at the sales rep. "What's his name again? Joe Allen?" She went to her computer and started typing.

Just then, Scott Majors entered the office. "What story?" Scott was a big teddy bear of a guy who everyone just loved.

"Sheila's boyfriend broke up with her on the sidewalk yesterday," Stacey shouted a little too enthusiastically, typing away. "And now, I'm trying to find him on Facebook to see if he changed his status."

"Oh. Sorry." He looked at Sheila with genuine concern and walked into his office. Even though he was a nice guy, he had no desire to get in the crossfire of what would surely turn into an "all men suck" conversation.

"What? Say it's not true!" Mark stood behind the group with his jaw to the ground. The out and proud assistant to the group had just arrived to work. "I know exactly which self-help books you need. I'll bring them tomorrow."

"Nice of you to join us." Jenn looked at her watch.

"Are you still wearing that? It makes you look fifty." He shuddered and sat down.

"I hate to say it, but Stacey's right," said Melissa. Melissa and Stacey had a love/hate relationship that only fixed itself when they wanted to get out of the office early or screw someone over. In this case, they obviously wanted to avoid work and screw Sheila, so this was going to take some time. "If he changes his status first, everyone will see his post first and they'll know he broke up with you. You could make everyone think you broke up with him if you change your status first."

"Well, we just broke up, so I'm sure he hasn't changed it," Sheila said as calmly as possible. Since Joe was dating someone else, his status wouldn't change anyway, but she didn't want to explain that right now. She had given them all enough to gossip about for at least a week. "Don't bother looking, Stacey. It doesn't matter."

"Yes, it does. Jesus, there's like, hundreds of Joe Allens and they're all ugly. We'll have to look at your profile. Come here and login." Stacey typed away.

"Wait. I'm friends with Sheila, I'll check." Melissa chimed in.

"What? I sent you a friend request weeks ago," Mark snipped. "What's with the diss, girlfriend?"

Sheila was losing patience. "I don't check Facebook that often," she said as she walked into her office.

"Are you kidding? I'm on it all day!" Mark offered.

"Yes, we know." Jenn glared at him. He shrugged and turned back to his computer.

Melissa suddenly gasped and the group rushed to her computer. There on the screen was Sheila's Facebook Wall. Sheila didn't see anything unusual, just a bunch of posting about the things her friends had done last night.

"What is it?" Sheila asked. "This is what I always see."

"He's not in your friends list anymore." Melissa looked at Sheila sympathetically. "He defriended you."

The group stood silently as Sheila took the mouse and scrolled through her friends list looking for Joe, but he wasn't there. She looked at her wall which usually had a bunch of postings from Joe since he was the Mayor of Dunkin' Donuts and went there at least three times a day. Those postings were gone too. Everyone looked from her to the computer, waiting for a reaction. She leaned forward and typed his name, "Joe P. Allen", in the search box. Her stomach turned when his profile appeared. Sheila couldn't see anything on his page, not even his photo. Joe had not only defriended her, he made his profile private.

"I'm sure if I login as myself, I can connect with him. But in the meantime, since no one can see his page it doesn't matter what he does with his status. Guys, it's just a stupid website." She stood straight and walked into her office without shutting the door to show she wasn't upset.

But she was. She sat in agony as her computer booted up. As soon as her browser opened, she tried to go to Facebook, but her hands shook so badly she mistyped it three times. She finally found the page and logged in as herself. She still could not find Joe in her friends list and when she searched for his page, it was the same page she had seen. No photo, no information. Just a message that he was only sharing information with people he knows. It's only a stupid website, she kept telling herself, trying not to cry. But the fact that Joe had shut her out on this very public website hurt almost as much as the break-up itself. After a few minutes, she quietly shut her door.

Like all office gossip, this flew around quickly. An hour later, Sheila was called into her boss' office.

The space was quite large with windows on two walls which could have provided some wonderful sunlight except Alessandra Arrugio, SVP of Sales, kept the blinds shut all morning, making the office dark and cold. It gave Sheila a little chill every time she had to enter. It didn't help that Alessandra's desk sat less than six feet from the doorway, confronting everyone who entered. Actually, it sort of blocked the doorway, sitting back just far enough for Alessandra to place two uncomfortable chairs and still allow the door to shut.

The desk was another matter. It was a sleek, cold table with a massive LCD screen to the left, blocking Alessandra from view if she worked on her laptop. Most of the time, all a person could see from the doorway was the LCD screen and the edge of Alessandra's massive chair, which enveloped her petite five-foot, two-inch frame. The rest of the desk was an empty surface which further blocked entry to the office by stretching approximately ten feet from the wall.

Other than the desk and a filing cabinet, there was a couch and club chair in the far corner with a small coffee table in front. Alessandra had tried to get rid of them when she first started at *Goodliving.com* but the maintenance department wouldn't remove them.

"Sorry, Ms. Arrugio. The furniture has to stay as is. Its company issue for executives and this is an executive office," Rick Smith, the head of Maintenance who had been with the company for over twenty years, told her.

"Come on, Rick. I'll deal with management this afternoon. I'm not having meetings in my office, so I don't need the furniture," Alessandra cajoled. "Plus it's ugly. When did they buy this stuff? 1990?"

"Just about." Rick said. "But I can't take it. If you have any luck with management, you tell them to call me direct and I'll take it." And the furniture stayed in the corner unused.

"So, your boyfriend's gone." Alessandra said without bothering to look up from her computer.

"Yes, he is." Sheila winced as she sat down.

"Did he really break up with you on the sidewalk in front of your building?" Alessandra continued typing on her keyboard intently, barely visible behind the LCD screen.

"Yes." Sheila sighed. The morning had already been a disaster and having her boss ask personal questions while practically ignoring her was a little more than Sheila could stand.

"Did he find someone else?" Alessandra finally looked at Sheila with her deep blue eyes that were actually pretty when not terrifying the hell out of someone. "They usually do. My ex had been having affairs for years."

"I don't think so," Sheila lied.

"Well, at least you didn't marry him." She looked back to her screen which usually meant the conversation was over, so Sheila got up to leave.

"Wait." Alessandra took her time typing and then looked back at Sheila. "Are you going to be OK?"

Sheila was startled at the question. Alessandra was not a nurturing type of boss. In the three years they had worked together, Alessandra has never so much as said 'Bless you' after someone sneezed. In fact, Alessandra once infamously asked someone at her former company to come back to the office four days after having a child to help with a presentation. Did Alessandra actually care?

"Well, I'm still kind of shocked -"

"No. I'm talking about work." Alessandra looked evenly at Sheila. "Are you going to freak out? Start losing business? Become a Buddhist?" She rolled her eyes. "Do I need to start looking for a senior seller or are you going to stay focused and handle your job?"

"Of course I'll be fine. It won't be a problem," Sheila shot back, worried by the accusation. "I knew it was coming," she added. She had already lost her boyfriend; she couldn't lose her job too.

"Good. That's what I want to hear." Alessandra smirked at the obvious lie. "The best way to beat a man is with your wallet, my dear. Is he fighting for any assets?" Sheila shook her head, not wanting to tell Alessandra about the hundred and twenty-five thousand dollars missing from her bank account.

"Good. Then out-earn the fucker. That's the only way to get back at him." She turned back to her computer again. "Show him your life didn't fall apart. Be smart and buy more real estate."

"Whose life is falling apart?" a man's voice came from the doorway.

Sheila's stomach dropped as she turned to see Baxter DeVry, President of Shearson Media's publishing division, standing behind her. He never visited this floor, preferring to make everyone come to him.

"No one's. Sheila and her boyfriend broke up so I'm dispensing a little life advice this morning as well as running your number one sales team." She slid her chair from behind the LCD screen to face Baxter but didn't get up.

"Well, Sheila, you are getting help from the best of them. Alessandra certainly knows how to live." Baxter smiled tightly and continued looking at Alessandra. "However, I need to discuss actual business. Sheila, could you excuse us?"

"Yes, of course." Sheila tried to gracefully maneuver her way out of the chair without bumping into Baxter, who was too busy staring at Alessandra to move. His six-foot frame loomed behind Sheila, making her feel very small and extremely uncomfortable as her boss and her boss' boss stared at each other with an animosity they tried to keep hidden. It didn't work.

Baxter's father had once run Shearson Media and gave Baxter his first job at the company thirty years ago during the golden age of nepotism and good old boys clubs. It had been a great ride until the damn Internet came along in the nineties and the board decided they needed someone running the company with a pulse on "new media". Things changed rapidly. The board went through a number of heated battles over the direction of the company. When a new CEO was needed, they unexpectedly voted to hire Ann Joyce, a high profile outsider, instead of promoting one of Baxter's closest friends who had been with the company for more than twenty years.

It had torn Baxter to pieces as more of his friends were either pushed out or resigned. The company had been a place where people could stay their entire careers, creating deep bonds among the men and their families.

About five years later, Ann Joyce hired Alessandra without asking Baxter. Although Alessandra officially reported to Baxter, the Digital division was the wave of the future so Alessandra had direct contact with Ann Joyce. Baxter hated her for it.

He knew Ann didn't like him and had wanted him to leave. But with Baxter Sr. still on the board, no one would vote for that. So he stayed.

Sheila finally extricated herself from the chair and said her good byes. She was barely out the door as it closed behind her.

4

Thank goodness this day is over, thought Sheila, walking the thirty blocks home. The pain from her shoes kept her mind in the moment and off the fact that her house would be empty when she got there.

Standing at the corner of Park Avenue and 50th, she surveyed the crowds of people rushing all around her. Some were running to Grand Central to catch a train. Why run? Sheila wondered. Another train will come. What's the rush? Yet she wished she had a reason to rush home.

As Sheila walked through the underpass to 44th Street and turned left for Lexington Ave, the pain in her feet became too much and she hailed a cab.

"Gramercy Park South," she told the driver and promptly fell back in her seat as he sped off like a madman.

"Hey! Slow down!" She glared at him in the rearview mirror. He returned the stare. When Sheila didn't flinch, he slowed down and muttered to himself. Settling into the cab, Sheila turned off the requisite TV installed in every cab in the city. Peace and quiet, that's what she needed. Why anyone needed to stare at a TV when they had all of New York City outside the window was beyond her.

As the cab turned onto her street, Sheila closed her eyes, envisioning Joe standing outside her building, waiting for her just as he had last night. Only this time, he had a bouquet of red roses and a smile. Of course, when the cab stopped Joe wasn't there. She stared at the stone columns surrounding the black lacquered door to her building until Rudy came out to open her door.

"Hi, Sheila. How was your day?" Rudy asked while offering his hand to help her from the taxi.

"It was good. Thanks, Rudy." Sheila walked up the stairs and across the pre-war lobby to her mailbox, hoping not to bump into too many people. Already bruised by the reaction from her co-workers and horrified that Baxter had learned about her personal problems, she could only imagine what her neighbors would do.

Sheila had not been entirely welcomed at Twenty-Four Gramercy Park South. With only twenty-eight units in the building, the co-op board had a strict qualification process to be sure they were getting someone who would respect the quiet tone of life in the building. As a young Internet millionaire — who was single — she didn't fit with the old money crowd in the building and the co-op board almost rejected her. But some members of the board felt that the building needed new blood and a debate ensued for days about whether a single woman would be able to lead a decent life or traipse a parade of men through the building, putting them all at risk, like those girls from *Sex and the City*.

Before the final vote, Sheila had been invited to tea with Ruth Grey, the President of the Co-op Board, and a friendship had been born. Shortly after, Sheila moved into the apartment across the hall from Ruth. Ruth was now eighty-six years old and the oldest tenant in the building. She had bought her unit in 1962 with her husband and raised her son here. Joe had never really warmed to Ruth but Sheila found her delightful. Other residents in the building slowly came to accept Sheila, especially since Ruth liked her so much. But still, she wasn't sure how they would feel about having a single woman in the building again.

Sheila glanced through her pile of mail as she continued through the lobby to the elevator. Joe had been the one to grab the mail each night and deal with the bills. It was obvious that he hadn't done it for a few days because there were a lot of letters from her mortgage company. As the elevator doors opened, Ruth stepped into the lobby with her new cane.

"Hello, my dear." Ruth's smile caused her face to swallow her eyes as the skin crinkled at the corners. But the shocking blue color still shone through as she looked at her young friend brightly. "And how are you today?"

"I'm fine, Ruth. How are you? New cane?" Sheila stopped, not wanting to be rude, but today she really didn't feel like chatting.

"Nuisance is more like it," Ruth said, holding the cane in front of her. "Getting old is for the brave, my dear."

"Well, have a great night." Sheila smiled and stepped into the elevator.

"Oh, Sheila?" Ruth called after her.

"Yes?"

"What are you doing on Sunday? I would love it if you would join me for dinner." Ruth smiled again.

Sheila tried to think of an excuse, not ready to explain to another person that Joe had left, but Ruth beat her to the punch.

"Dear, I saw Joe moving out last week and I'm sure you're very upset. Why don't you come over for dinner? I always found Sunday nights to be the saddest of the week and I'd hate for you to be alone."

Sheila's shoulders slumped. Of course Ruth would know. "I'd love to join you, Ruth." They settled on a time and Sheila rode the elevator to her floor.

As she entered her apartment, Sheila threw the pile of letters on the dining room table and fell onto the couch in tears, not only because she could finally relax after a horribly long day, but picking up the mail made her realize that she was truly on her own. She sat up and looked at the pile of bills on the table. She didn't even know where to begin. She got up and put the letters in the bottom drawer of her desk. She couldn't deal with it now. It just didn't make sense. Maybe dinner with Ruth would be a good opportunity to get details about Joe's departure. She needed more information to put the pieces together.

In the lobby, however, Ruth was shaking her head. Her young neighbor had no idea that her whole life was really in front of her, and thinking of the past was only valuable if it could teach you something.

5

The week had passed in a blur with no more surprises and no word from Joe, even though Sheila had left a few messages. The only calls Sheila seemed to get were from a telemarketer, which she promptly sent to voicemail every time.

Normally, Sheila would have been thrilled that it was late Friday afternoon, but this was her first weekend alone. Thankfully, she already had dinner plans with Morgan for Saturday night and Ruth on Sunday, but a Friday night alone made her want to cry again.

Friday was the night that she and Joe spent together curled up on the couch eating take out and watching T.V. Joe had to get his fill of flipping between CNN and ESPN, and then it was movie time. She thought of all those times they had fought about which movie to watch and how she usually gave in because Joe

22

didn't do chick flicks. Now she scanned her computer looking for a movie she could download onto her iPad to watch in bed, but nothing looked good.

"Sheila!" Alessandra's screech rang through the office. "Come in here!"

Even after three years, Sheila wasn't used to being screamed at and she jumped.

"Hey. How are you?" Sheila sat in one of the uncomfortable chairs.

"Hey?" Alessandra rolled her eyes in disgust. "Doesn't anyone know how to be professional anymore?"

Sheila shrugged, knowing silence was best for this type of mood.

"We found a new sales person. She starts Monday morning and you are in charge of training her." Alessandra didn't once look at Sheila as she continued typing.

"Oh. Shouldn't I have met her?" Sheila said.

Alessandra sighed heavily and looked at Sheila. "Shut the door," she instructed.

Once Sheila had closed the door and sat down again, Alessandra said, "She is a family friend of Baxter's. Her father and Baxter were fraternity brothers or some bullshit. So make sure you're nice and everyone else is, too. She's never been in sales before, so she's going to need a lot of training. And you have to share Melissa with her." Alessandra went back to her emails.

"She never sold before? How much work experience does she have?" Sheila asked.

"Practically none." Alessandra continued typing. "It is up to you to make sure that she gets up to speed quickly and makes money. Do you understand?" Alessandra looked at Sheila evenly. "Baxter's going to have his eye on this, so you better stay on top of her. Plan to have lunch with her on Monday. Someplace nice. It sounds like she's used to the finer things. I suggest you spend the weekend putting together a list of accounts for her."

Sheila walked back to her office and crashed into her chair. Well, at least she had something to keep her occupied this weekend.

"And what are you doing tonight, Miss Lonely Heart?" Mark breezed into Sheila's office and draped himself across a chair.

"Why are you here?" Sheila hadn't seen Mark in the office past five o'clock since he started a year ago.

"Answer my question and then I'll tell you. If you're worthy." He stared at his nails which Sheila noticed were buffed.

"Did you get a manicure?"

"Sweetheart, I'm gay and it's Friday night. Of course I got a manicure. You should have gotten one too, now that you're single."

Sheila turned back to her computer.

"Now, we both know why you're here late on a Friday night, so I'm going to be your Prince Charming and rescue you." Mark said.

Sheila started to laugh.

"No, really. This is just too sad for me." He motioned to her, sitting at the desk. "Shut down the computer, we're going out. I'm feeling a Pretty Woman moment for you."

Sheila looked at him quizzically.

"I'm not going to pimp you out. Geez, you're so uptight. I'm taking you out to have fun. No work. No talk of Asshole Joe. Just fun with young, hard bodied men who won't break your heart. But first, we really need to get you some clothes." Mark said.

"Gee, Mark. As fun as it sounds to get a makeover and hang out with you and your friends, I do have things to do—" Sheila said.

Mark came to look over her shoulder. "You're looking at rom-coms on iTunes. Oh, honey."

"I'm done." Sheila shut her lap top quickly. As she packed her bag, Mark stood in front of her.

"Sheila. I don't bite and you're alone. My boyfriend of six months dumped me a few months ago so I know you're hurt.

Why can't you just come out and have fun? Does everything have to have a purpose?" Mark said.

Sheila thought hard to find an excuse and couldn't.

"Come on. We'll get you dressed and get you a manicure. We'll probably need a pedicure too, from the look of it. Chop, chop!" He clapped his hands and Sheila got her coat. Maybe this Friday night wouldn't be so bad after all.

*****

Oh, the pain. What the hell happened last night? Opening her eyes slightly, Sheila squinted at the ceiling. Ugh, the blinds were open and it was too bright. Reaching for her cell phone caused another groan which hurt her head even more. Right. She was alone. And she went out with Mark last night. Closing her eyes again, Sheila tried to remember the previous evening.

*****

"We are celebrating!" Mark had yelled to all his friends at Cheeks, the hottest gay bar in New York. "My gorgeous friend, and boss, got DUMPED by her man." Boos erupted from the crowd, making Sheila feel some camaraderie with the men. "On the SIDEWALK!" Sheila smiled bravely as the group gasped in horror.

"Oh, honey!" A gorgeous blond named Tom gave her a hug.

"That's cold!" yelled someone else. "He sucks!"

Maybe hanging out with gay men will be an option to being single, Sheila thought, accepting all the hugs and condolences.

"So now it's up to us, my dears, to make sure our friend regains her faith in men. Cheers!" Mark raised a shot in the air as one was placed in Sheila's hand. "Let's get drunk!" He downed the shot.

"Hey, sister. You need to drink all of it," said another gorgeous man in the crowd. He couldn't have been more than twenty-five.

25

"Oh, I haven't done a shot in ages. I'll just take my time." Sheila smiled.

"Sipper alert! She's not doing her shot!" he yelled.

"Shoot it, shoot it, shoot it!" Suddenly Sheila was surrounded by a group of chanting men – all gorgeous, all young and none of them interested in her. Maybe they're right; maybe I do need to lighten up. So she smiled and gulped the drink and promptly choked and coughed, causing a great round of laughter.

Mark came over, "I guess it's been a while since you've had Patrón." He handed her a napkin. "Sorry. But in about thirty seconds, you'll feel fabulous."

He was right. The warmth quickly spread through her body and suddenly everything was okay. She was happy.

*****

Getting out of bed, however, was as far from happy as she could get. Trudging to the bathroom set off a pounding in her head. What had made her think drinking with twenty-somethings was a good idea?

Suddenly, Beyoncé's *Single Ladies* was blasting through the co-op, almost causing Sheila to fall off the toilet. Was someone else here?

She went into the living room. Her clothes were all over the place, but where was the song coming from? She went through the clothes, getting more frustrated by the second. She finally found the sound coming from her boot, but it stopped. She shook the boot and her Blackberry fell into her hand. The sound started again, almost making her drop the phone.

Sheila answered it. "Hello?"

"You sound like hell!" It was Mark, laughing. "Did you have fun last night? My friends loved you!"

"Oh, yeah. I think so. I'm a little hung over. Why are you so happy this morning?"

"Morning? Honey, its 11:30. I've already been to the gym and now I'm meeting friends for lunch. You either need to start drinking heavily or never drink again. Either way, you're still a blast. But I'm mostly calling to make sure you actually got your phone."

"Thanks. Why was it in my boot?" Sheila asked.

"Oh my. You don't remember?"

"Remember what?" Sheila's stomach slid, waiting to hear while Mark laughed loudly.

"You called Joe! Like four times from the bathroom! And sweetheart, the bathroom in Cheeks is not a place someone like you wants to be for any extended length of time. When I found out, I took away your phone, but you insisted that you needed to talk to him. Do you remember any of this?"

A weak shake of her head was all Sheila could manage.

"So we made a deal; you could contact him using my phone and when you did, I took a picture of me and my friends and texted it to him, telling him he's a loser for dumping you! Isn't that a riot? Then I kept your phone so you wouldn't call him anymore and I hid it in your apartment. Oh, and I changed your ringtone to *Single Ladies* for certain callers. Hope you like it," Mark said.

Sheila got off the phone and lay back in her bed, completely sick at the thought of Joe getting calls and pictures of a bunch of guys from her last night. But then she laughed, imagining Joe watching ESPN or CNN while she was at a bar having fun. She smiled, admitting to herself that last night had been fun. She and Joe hadn't had much fun in the past. She stopped to think about the last time they did have fun and realized she couldn't. The relationship had been steady and reliable. They had their routines and each had their duties. Joe handled the finances, maintenance on the co-op, and planned the vacations while Sheila dealt with the groceries, cleaning lady, and their social life. "Like married people," they used to say and smile at each other.

And then she was asleep again, working off the hangover so she could be fine for dinner with Morgan, where hopefully she'd get some more details about Joe's new life.

6

"Hi!" Morgan rose from the table to hug Sheila. "How are you?"

By this point, the hangover was gone, but Sheila was still exhausted. "Fine, fine. What about you?" She wasn't going to start badgering Morgan about Joe just yet, but the waiting was torture.

"I ordered a bottle of wine for us." Morgan started to pour a glass for Sheila.

"No, thanks. I drank enough last night to last a month."

"Yeah, I heard." Morgan looked anxiously at her menu.

"From who?" Sheila looked at her friend.

"Let's just get this out of the way. Okay?" Morgan put down the bottle.

"Yes." Sheila sighed with relief. "Tell me everything, please."

"Okay. But first, here's your wine." Morgan spilled some of the Merlot as she passed the glass to Sheila.

"No, I can't drink, really. I have the worst hangover—"

"Joe's dating Taylor."

"Taylor? His Assistant?" Sheila digested this information. "He always said she was a mouse and kind of dim." She fell back in her seat.

"I'm so sorry. I've already told Dylan I'm not going out with them. But we went out with a group from Dylan's work last night and they were there," Morgan said.

"What work event? He's been gone four days. I would have known about it." Sheila leaned forward again.

"It wasn't a real work event. Their boss, Tom, had a dinner party at Recette. Joe brought Taylor. Apparently, Tom knew and wanted it in the open." Morgan said.

"Stop. Wait." Sheila shook her head. "Are you honestly telling me that Joe left me for his twenty-six year-old assistant and Tom knew?" Sheila prayed she wasn't hearing this right.

"I'm sorry. I swear I didn't know until last night. Dylan thinks Joe sucks too." The two women sat in silence. "Do you want to leave? We can go for a walk?"

"No." Sheila grabbed the glass and gulped the wine. There had to be a mistake. Sheila and Joe had been to Tom's house more than once. She had even been to their baby's christening last year. Now Tom was throwing Joe and Taylor a dinner party?

Morgan lifted her drink, too, which is when Sheila noticed the sparkle. "Oh my God! Morgan, is that an engagement ring?"

"Yes." Morgan had no idea what to do with Sheila so devastated. She just stared at Sheila, waiting for a reaction.

"When?" Sheila said.

"Tuesday." Morgan replied.

Tuesday. That was the day Joe left. Now it was Saturday and in the past four days Joe had moved on with his assistant and her best friend got engaged. Everyone's life was moving forward and she was back at step one.

Sheila smiled brightly and held her wine glass to toast her friend. "That is wonderful!" She would not fall apart now. She would not ruin her friend's good news. She refused to be one of those women. For the rest of the night, they talked wedding plans and honeymoons and Sheila kept the focus off of herself. After dinner, Morgan reached across the table and took Sheila's hand.

"Sheila, there's one more thing." Morgan said.

"What?" Sheila couldn't take any more surprises so she begged God to let this be good news.

"I want you as my Maid of Honor. And I'm really sorry the timing is so bad. Before you say 'yes,' you should know that Dylan asked Joe to be the Best Man before Tuesday and Joe said "Yes." I told Dylan he needed to take back the offer, but he can't. They're best friends. Will you still say 'yes'?"

"Of course I'll be the Maid of Honor. I'm delighted you asked." Sheila looked at her friend and smiled. And it'll give me something to focus on, she thought to herself.

They parted ways and Sheila held it together in the cab, through the lobby, and even after she shut the door to her apartment. Then she cried just as she had cried every night since Tuesday but this was worse. How long had her life had been a lie waiting to end? While she was making plans and working on their life together, Joe had been plotting to leave with someone eleven years younger. Someone he had always said he could barely stomach at work. Sheila sobbed, wondering how many other lies she had believed while she wasted the past seven years of her life.

7

"Come in! Oh, this will be lovely!" Ruth stepped back for Sheila to enter her apartment with a box of cupcakes. Sheila always liked coming to Ruth's. It was the type of home she imagined her grandparents would have, if she had grandparents.

"Make yourself at home," Ruth called as she shuffled through the living area, past the dining room table to the kitchen. Sheila sat on the red velvet couch against the far right wall and stared across the room at the Manhattan skyline.

Ruth's apartment was a duplex which had been created by combining a two bedroom co-op on Sheila's floor with the two bedroom co-op above it. Being on the other side of the building from Sheila, Ruth had a fabulous skyline view of the Empire State Building to the north and the NY Life Building's gold pyramid to the west. Directly below her windows sat Gramercy Park in all its glory. Sheila's own views faced the buildings on the north and east sides, though she could see Gramercy Park from a certain angle.

The credenza to her left was crowded with photos and beautiful knick knacks that Sheila had never seen. In fact, now that Sheila looked around the room, there seemed to be a few differences from her last visit.

"Redecorating?" Sheila asked when Ruth returned.

"Yes." Ruth sighed. "Since my hip has stopped behaving, I'm moving my most important things downstairs, which is now my living space. The upstairs is now storage space."

"Well, I'm glad you chose to stay on this floor." Sheila smiled.

"And so am I. Now, let's eat," Ruth said.

As the two women sat at the dinner table, Sheila was dying to ask Ruth what she had seen when Joe moved out while Ruth, like all good mothers, wanted to be sure Sheila ate a good meal. The poor girl looks lost, Ruth thought, as Sheila pushed her food around her plate making small talk about current events.

"So, how are you?" Ruth finally asked.

"I'm okay. I've been busy at work and went out with friends the past two nights, which has been nice. My friend, Morgan, is engaged. She asked me to be maid of honor." Sheila smiled lamely.

"But that doesn't tell me how you are." Ruth looked intently at Sheila. "That just tells me what you've done. Have you taken any time for yourself since Joe left? Or talked to anyone?"

Sheila sat in a swirl of emotion. It had occurred to her to take time off but sitting in the apartment would have driven her crazy. And no one at work really wanted to hear about the break up since the day it was announced. In fact, no one, except Jenn, really seemed to think about it at all.

"It's been hard, especially since it was a surprise. I had no idea it was coming. You knew before I did, since you saw him move out." Sheila sat looking at the plate of homemade food, losing her appetite.

"Well, that is sad," Ruth said. "He didn't say anything to you about being unhappy?"

"No." Sheila looked despondent. "That's why I'm so confused. And hurt. We were together for seven years and now I'm alone." She fought back the tears.

"I am sorry he was so cruel to you," Ruth said, truly concerned. "But you do know this isn't your fault or anything that you did, don't you?"

"I don't know anything. He won't even return my calls. And—" Sheila stopped, not wanting to give Ruth any more reason to think Joe was cruel.

"And?"

"He's with someone else." Sheila couldn't control the tears any longer. "His twenty-six year-old assistant!"

Sheila let it all out. She had stayed strong at work all week, been a good friend to Morgan, and exhausted herself in the process. Coming home alone every night with no one to talk to was hard. She was used to sharing her day with Joe and getting his advice. She didn't know how to be single and she didn't like it.

Ruth listened as Sheila poured her heart out. The poor girl was so upset. Ruth had never been a fan of Joe's. He was polite enough but it was apparent to her anyway, that he would never commit. He didn't have to. Sheila gave him everything he wanted and never asked for anything in return.

"Well, of course you're upset, Sheila. He wasn't forthright with his intentions and was really quite low to end things the way he did. But you have to keep living. Move on," Ruth said.

"How? I haven't been single since I was twenty-nine. I don't even know how to date anymore."

"Dating will come. Right now, you need to do something to make yourself happy. Create the best life possible," Ruth said.

"How? Half of my life is gone." Sheila wiped her eyes. "Have you ever felt like everything was just upside down?" Sheila looked past Ruth to the photos on the credenza. "You were married. You grew up with a close family. Can you imagine coming home and no one is there? It's like someone vanished."

Ruth smiled knowingly. "My life had ups and downs, I assure you."

Ruth turned to look at the credenza full of items from her life. How she missed her family. Bill, her husband of forty years, most of all. That emptiness was almost all she had now. But she shook her head to push the memories away. This was about Sheila. Ruth knew she was suffering, yet in so many ways, she was better off. But who could tell Sheila that right now?

After a few moments of silence, Sheila looked at Ruth then followed her gaze.

"You have so many nice things." Sheila's eyes fell on a blue vase on the coffee table. "That is gorgeous."

"Thank you. My grandmother gave it to my mother as a wedding gift. It's my favorite thing in the world. I've been putting things in boxes, but I can't bear to shut that away. I think beautiful things should be seen and touched. Though sometimes thinking of the past too much is like looking into the sun. It can hurt." Ruth saw the confusion in Sheila's face. "There were many dark times in my life. Some things I don't care to remember, especially during the war."

"Did your brothers fight in Germany?" Sheila asked.

"No." Ruth smiled. "We were in Germany."

"You mean after the war?" Sheila said.

"No, during. We went to visit my grandparents and had to stay." Ruth rested her eyes on a photo of her with her parents and younger siblings. "That photo was taken right before we left for Germany. There were rumors of Hitler, but we didn't know how bad it was."

"How could you not know? Everyone knew, didn't they?" Sheila asked.

"My dear, your education has been neglected." Ruth smiled lovingly at the girl. "It was 1938. The government didn't want to publish stories. Remember, we weren't far along from the First World War."

"No one in your family wrote?" Sheila asked.

"The mail was searched. Nothing could get through. Father did hear something, but the government didn't confirm it, so we went." Ruth shrugged.

"This is like a movie. How long were you there?"

"Seven years." Ruth answered.

"Seven years? Why didn't you leave?"

"My father was a scientist who had information that the Nazis wanted. We were held there." Ruth said.

"Held? No one came to get you?" Sheila's jaw dropped.

Ruth chuckled. "Who could come? The Nazis weren't exactly letting people travel through Europe easily. Plus, we were hiding."

"Hiding? You mean like Anne Frank?"

"Sort of."

"Did you see soldiers and bombings?"

"Yes, I saw soldiers and bombings and things no one should see." Ruth spoke sadly.

"I'm sorry. I didn't mean to upset you."

"No need to apologize." Ruth shook her head. "People are titillated by the horrors of war but it's devastating. It's not something to be taken lightly. I haven't thought about the war in a long time."

"I can't believe you were in hiding. You never mentioned it in all the years I've known you."

"What good would it do? Living in the past can sometimes make things seem worse than they were. And it's not healthy. Everyone today wants to talk about their past as if it's the most fascinating thing. It's not. The war happened. We got on," Ruth said.

Sheila looked back at the picture of Ruth's parents surrounded by six children. "The baby was beautiful. Is that you?"

"No. That's Annabelle. I'm the oldest, with the long hair. I was twelve."

"You were adorable!" Sheila searched for a resemblance.

As Ruth looked at Sheila, she realized that Joe's leaving had been the worst thing to happen in Sheila's young life. She truly didn't know any other hardship. Sheila may not know how to move on, Ruth considered. Although Ruth didn't like to talk about the past, she wondered if her friend might learn something from it.

"I tell you what. If you bring the tea to the coffee table, we'll sit on my old red couch and I'll tell you a little of what happened while we eat those cupcakes."

8

Twelve year-old Ruth König couldn't wait for school to end. For the past two weeks her Mother, Eliza, regaled her with stories of Germany, her beloved homeland, and all the family and friends they would see during their summer trip. Being the oldest, Ruth helped her Mother with the chores and the past few weeks had been wonderful as Eliza sang songs from her childhood and glowed with excitement, sharing memories about each family member. Plus, most of the regular chores were forgotten as Ruth helped get all the clothes ready for the seven children and her father. The family was to set sail in one week, the day after school ended for summer break, and the excitement made it difficult for the children to concentrate at school.

"Tell me again what Opa and Oma will be like, Mama." Three year-old Greta asked.

"Your grandparents are the kindest people I have ever known. They will love you so much," Eliza told the beautiful blond girl.

"Will we see the house where you and Papa lived when you first married?" Ruth, ever the romantic, asked.

"Yes. It is also the house where you were born." Eliza smiled at her eldest daughter.

"How many cousins do we have again?" Dieter, her rambunctious eight year-old, was already planning teams for kick ball.

"Seventy-two."

Eliza answered each question, never tiring of talking about Germany and the family they had left behind so long ago. She never intended to be in the United States this long. Franz, Ruth's father, had been sent to America for a joint project between Columbia University and the Humboldt University of Berlin. It was supposed to be a two year project but they were still here, eleven years later. Eliza hoped when they returned to Germany this summer, Franz might decide to stay. He had said his skills might be needed more in Germany than America, which gave Eliza hope.

*****

Finally the last day of school came and Ruth fidgeted in her seat watching the clock painfully work its way to three o'clock wondering how time can move so slowly when you are waiting for something glorious. When the bell rang, Ruth sprang to the front of the school to gather her brothers and sisters. She called 'good bye' to her friends, promising to write. Ruth had already made a list of addresses so she could send letters to her very best friends. After all, being away for the entire summer was a lifetime for a twelve year-old girl.

"It will be over before you know it," her father often said teasing her with his smile.

When the children got home, however, there were no smiles. Their parents sat in the parlor, looking grim.

"Good afternoon, Papa. Mama." the children greeted their parents.

"Hello," Franz answered. "Mama and I need privacy. Please go outside and play."

"Yes, Papa." they murmured. As they passed through the room, Eliza lifted Annabelle, the baby, for Ruth to take. At four months, little Annabelle was the heart of the family and Ruth was clearly her favorite.

They ate a snack in the kitchen with Silke, their housekeeper, until five year-old Tomas crashed through the kitchen door. Being the youngest boy, Tomas was usually the last to know anything and often laughed at when he said something he thought was quite smart. But today he had a secret and he was eager to share what he knew.

"You'll never guess what happened! Go ahead! Try!" Tomas jumped up and down.

"Not so loud," Sarah whispered.

"Tell us!" Dieter demanded.

"There's a problem in Germany, so we may not go!" His eyes shone with excitement at this news.

The children erupted at the thought.

"Children, hush!" Silke admonished. "Tomas don't spread half-truths. Your parents will tell you what you need to know when you need to know it. Now finish your snacks and go play. I'm making a special dinner for tonight and packing food for your trip."

But the children couldn't play. They asked Tomas questions but it was clear that he didn't know much. He began to cry as Dieter told him he was useless. Ruth sat and hugged Tomas while Annabelle slept on her shoulder.

Something must be wrong if Papa was home in the middle of the afternoon and Mama was crying. Ruth hoped he would explain at dinner because asking wasn't an option. But her Father said nothing and the next morning, they boarded the steamship

New York to Europe. The family arrived in Hamburg, Germany in July 1938.

9

Summer in the German countryside was wonderful. An endless stream of relatives had been visiting and the children were having a great time on Uncle Peter's farm. Ruth especially loved the gardens and volunteered to pick vegetables every chance she could. Now, as family gathered from around the country for a massive reunion, Ruth was in the kitchen as the women laughed, talked and created a feast that would feed two grandparents, twenty-four aunts and uncles and seventy-two cousins over the weekend.

The party started on Friday and by Saturday morning, it was as if Ruth had known her extended family all her life. What a joy to be near those who looked like her and hear others talk in German. Her mother screamed excitedly as each car pulled onto the farm and another person ran to hug her. Yes, it was a magical vacation.

"Ruth, go play outside with the children. Your cousin, Heidi, is arriving any minute. She is your age. You should have lots to share. Go play, child. You'll be an old lady who spends all day in the kitchen soon enough." The group laughed as her grandmother led her by the shoulders toward the kitchen door.

Ruth walked through the crowd looking for the other children. With so many people around, Ruth didn't have to watch her brothers and sisters so closely. She stopped and listened for their yells, which led her to the front of the house. Sure enough, Dieter was leading a game of kick ball for the boys and arguing about whether Cousin Georg was out on second base.

"He was out!" One of the cousins yelled. "My foot was on the base!"

"No, it wasn't!" Dieter replied, stepping closer. "Your foot was over here." He stomped on the ground.

Normally, Ruth would have intervened but with so many cousins around, including those who were now in the middle of the argument, she didn't have to worry about it. So she joined her female cousins sitting on the lawn, waiting for Heidi's arrival. A sudden glare of sunlight blinded her momentarily. Raising her hand to protect herself, she peeked from behind her hand to see a car had approached unnoticed because of all the yelling and arguing. The front doors were open, reflecting the sunlight. The glare even stopped the argument as the children excitedly watched to see which relative was here now. It must be Heidi, Ruth thought. No one had mentioned that her family had such a fancy car. Anticipation turned to confusion as two men exited the car. The boys nudged each other, while the rest of the group stood in total silence staring at the men, who stared back.

Each man wore a gray uniform with jacket, trousers and calf-high boots that also shone brightly in the sunlight. The black belts around their waists had what looked like a bird on the silver belt buckle. Ruth remembered seeing many of these uniforms when she got off the boat in Hamburg.

"Papa, who are those men?" she had asked.

"Don't stare, Ruth. And do not speak to them," was all he said.

As Ruth squinted in the sun, she noticed a patch on the left arm of one man that matched a badge on his cap but Ruth couldn't see the details. The man on the passenger side opened the rear door and another man stepped out. Dressed in the same gray uniform, he looked like Ruth imagined a movie star would be. He stood ramrod straight, his black hair perfectly sleek under his cap. His piercing blue eyes scared the children into silence as he looked evenly at each, one by one. Finally, he spoke.

"And how is the party?" He smiled, waiting for their response. "Which of you are the König children?"

The children looked back and forth nervously amongst themselves. He had spoken English. As Dieter stepped forward to answer, Ruth ran and grabbed him.

"We don't know these men," she whispered, staring back at the leader. Even at this distance his eyes shone brilliant blue as his face broke into a smile. Ruth put her other arm around Dieter protectively as he continued to smile broadly.

"Go inside, children." Uncle Peter's voice rang suddenly from the front porch. He quickly descended the stairs, followed by a few of Ruth's uncles.

The children filed into the house except Ruth who stayed on the front porch, straining to hear the conversation.

"Ruth, go in the house!" her Uncle Norman demanded as he passed her to join the group.

"That man asked for Father" she whispered. "Should I get him?"

Grabbing her arm, he shoved her through the door. "Do not say another word. Do not say your name. And for God's sake, do not speak English!" Norman hissed.

The scene Ruth found in the kitchen was completely different from just ten minutes earlier. Oma cried while Opa argued with his grown children that he should be the one to speak to the men. A few moments later, Uncle Peter came into the back yard and whispered into Franz's ear. Franz pulled back, locking eyes with Peter, who nodded his head, confirming Franz's thoughts without hearing them.

Eliza approached and Franz whispered in her ear. He grabbed her arms and held her up as she digested his words. Her face paled but she didn't react. She simply nodded her head in agreement. Then Peter and Franz signaled to the aunts who quietly began rounding up the König children, bringing them into the house, through the kitchen and up the back stairs.

"What are we doing?" Dieter demanded, upset at leaving his cousins.

"Quiet," Mother whispered urgently as Aunt Marta dragged a ladder to the hallway, climbed up and pushed open the hatch in the ceiling, revealing a dark attic. She stepped down quickly and ushered each child up the ladder into the attic one at a time. Ruth sneezed in the dusty space which held trunks and old boxes that took on odd shapes in the dark. Mother stuck her head through the hatch and turned to Ruth.

"Keep them quiet and have them sit on the ground." She handed Annabelle to Ruth. "All of you obey Ruth. Stay here and someone will get you when it is clear." Eliza looked at her children and smiled bravely. "Don't worry. Everything will be fine."

Then she pulled the access panel in place, enclosing her children in the sweltering, dark heat.

"When what is clear?" Greta whimpered. No one answered. The children simply sat quietly, waiting to be released.

"I want to see what's going on," Dieter said.

"Quiet." Ruth looked at his silhouette.

"Don't be such a ninny, Ruth," Dieter said, crawling across the floor to the small window on the other wall.

Ruth grabbed his ankle. "Mother said to sit and you will." She twisted his leg with one hand while holding the baby.

"Get off!" he cried, kicking at her.

"Stop it!" cried Sara as Annabelle started to whimper. Suddenly there were footsteps and murmurs in the hallway below. All the children froze. The heavy footsteps moved from room to room slowly. Ruth couldn't make out the words but the voices were clearly male and unfamiliar. Fear swept through her, replacing the nausea from the heat with a cold sweat. She looked to Sara for some sort of reassurance but could only make out a lumpy shadow as Sara comforted Greta.

The voices were raised for a moment and the entourage clamored down the stairs abruptly. The wait during that silence seemed forever. In the distance, they heard car doors shut and the start of an engine.

Ruth looked down to see she still clutched Dieter's leg and let go. Even in the darkness, a perfect white handprint remained. They all stared at it, mesmerized until the attic hatch pushed into the space, releasing the hot air. They didn't dare move but all eyes were on the light coming from the floor below.

"Papa!" The children scrambled to the opening as Franz's head popped up. He looked at his children. Just fifteen minutes ago, they had been a happy, smiling bunch at play. Now they sat terrified.

"You can come down now," he said and smiled briefly. Then he turned and waited at the bottom of the ladder, helping his children climb down and giving each a hug as they landed on the ground.

"Papa!" Greta clung to him. "Why did Mama put us up there? I didn't like it. Please don't make us go up there again!" Her face was nuzzled in his pant leg.

Father reached and picked up his young daughter, lifting her chin to see her eyes. "Mama did what was right, Greta. And you must, too." He kissed her cheek and looked at all his children. "It was an unfortunate experience, that's all. Papa has fixed it and now, we can enjoy the party. Next week, I'll take you to the picture show!"

The children cheered but as they walked down the stairs, Ruth was uneasy. Her father was her hero and always told the truth. She had always felt safe knowing he was near. But something in his smile felt odd and it wasn't until she went into the backyard and looked at the faces of her relatives that she knew for certain he had lied.

10

On Monday morning, Sheila was happy she didn't have to find ways to entertain herself. She just had to go back to work. Considering the weekly sales meeting was at 9 a.m. every Monday that was saying a lot.

"Mark's out today with the flu," Stacey announced. "But he did say that he and Sheila had a great time Friday night. You know, you'll need to hang out with straight guys if you're ever going to get laid again. Scott, you must have some friends Sheila can date."

Jenn chimed in to change the conversation. "So, you had a good weekend?"

"Yes. I had dinner with Morgan. She's engaged." This brought a round of 'oohs' from the women in the group.

"Thank God she sealed the deal. Two years is long enough without a ring," Susan said, adding "Sorry," when she saw Sheila's face.

"No, it's fine. You're right." Sheila was not going to let anyone see her down. "The rest of the weekend was good. I had dinner with my neighbor. Get this, she's eighty-six and was actually stuck in Germany during World War Two. She was telling me—."

"Wait a second." Stacey wasn't buying Sheila's good mood. "You mean you hung out with gay guys, talked about someone else's wedding, then learned about ancient history with an eighty-six year-old? That was a good weekend? Don't you think you should have been out looking for a boyfr —" Stacey stared at the door as Alessandra walked into the conference room with a young woman close behind.

The woman was dressed impeccably in a clingy lavender cashmere dress with gray suede open-toed booties. A matching Hermès belt accentuated a tiny waist. Her caramel-colored hair was pulled into a low bun with just the right amount of tendrils hanging by her face. All the women stared, suddenly self-conscious about their outfits.

Alessandra stood by her seat at the head of the table and smiled. "Everyone, please welcome Crystal Warren, the new Sales Rep on our team. Crystal, would you like to say something to your new teammates?"

Crystal smiled at the group. "Hello, everyone. I'm so happy to be here and look forward to learning all I can from the team and sharing my experience with you." Then she turned to Alessandra. "I'm also so excited and humbled to work with you, Ms. Arrugio. I look forward to learning a lot from a legend."

Alessandra smiled graciously. "You can call me Alessandra. We're one happy family here. Let's get started."

The meeting was basically the same as any other Monday morning sales meeting but Crystal's appearance had thrown everything off. Sheila couldn't get comfortable. There was something about Crystal's smile that didn't sit well. Plus, she knew the girl had no experience and was Baxter's hire. And Alessandra was actually nice.

"Okay, that's it. Sheila, I need to talk to you for a minute. Everyone else, go," Alessandra said.

"I need you to make sure Crystal has an easy time acclimating. As you can see, some people may not like the competition, but I don't care. You need to show her the ropes, take her on some calls this week and get the others to do the same. We got more than we bargained for with this one." Alessandra said.

"I'll make sure she gets it right."

"No. Don't give her too much advice. She comes from a privileged world, so let her make her own mistakes. Got it?" Alessandra walked out the door.

Not really, Sheila thought as she walked to Crystal's office. Fraternity brothers? Privileged world? When she got to Crystal's office, Melissa was already helping Crystal.

"Hi, Crystal. I'm Sheila Davenport. Are you finding everything okay?" They shook hands and Crystal smiled.

"Well, I think this place needs some decorating before I can get comfortable. How can anyone work like this?" Crystal looked around the office in disbelief.

"Well, most sales people don't have offices, so we're pretty happy not to be in cubicles," Sheila said. "In the meantime, I'm going to put together a list of meetings you can join to begin to learn our pitch. Why don't you and I go to lunch this afternoon and —"

"Sorry. I'm having lunch with Uncle Baxter." Crystal rolled her eyes and laughed at her goof. "I mean *Baxter* to celebrate my coming on board. I'm not sure what time I'll be back. Why don't I check my schedule and get back to you?" Crystal turned her back to examine the office.

"Sure." Sheila forced a smile, remembering Alessandra's words. "I'll schedule meetings for you to join with the other reps. Do you have any questions?"

"Yes. Can I paint my office?"

*****

The next morning, Alessandra trudged through the freezing cold wondering how she was going to get through the day. Her hangover was usually manageable by the time she got to the office but today it was unbearable.

Walking through the building lobby, the doorman jumped to open the turnstile for her. There was no one in the elevator when she got on. It was 7:45 in the morning. It was pathetic that no one else was there. What happened to the days of being at your desk before your boss got in? She snorted out loud, banging the button for fifteen.

Granted, she got emails all hours of the day from her sales reps, but the support staff just made her sick. She seriously wondered what was going to happen to American business in the future.

Her husband, ex-husband, she reminded herself, always got a kick out of the antics of the young people in his office. She found them, and him, annoying.

To start, they didn't show any respect for hierarchy. They smiled and said 'hi' like they were at a keg party. Whenever Alessandra asked, 'What's going on?' they never talked about work. It was always some story about their feelings or something they saw on Facebook.

When she was an assistant, Alessandra had never felt insulted. She made sure to look people in the eye and tell them what she was working on or ask intelligent questions – even if she knew the answers. She couldn't begin to count the stupid answers some of her bosses had given to her questions. But she always smiled and thanked them anyway. Some of them were morons, but they felt she respected them and she got promoted.

These kids don't care. They think the latest celebrity gossip is worth an hour of discussion. And the newspaper? Supposedly they get their news from the Internet, but Alessandra didn't see how that was happening.

She also would have been at her desk ten minutes before the head of the department every day, no matter what. And her boss would have had no problem giving anyone hell if they weren't in before him. These kids have no idea how easy they have it. And the way they dress. It made her wish for the days of mandatory skirt suits with nylons and closed toe shoes.

The elevator doors opened and Alessandra realized she had pissed herself off. She stopped in the lobby and tried to remember what that damn serenity coach had said. She closed her eyes and took a deep cleansing breath through her nose and out her mouth. 'Think positive thoughts. Take the negative thoughts and push them away.' This was such bullshit. If those sessions weren't mandatory, she'd tell that woman what to do with her breathing. Alessandra's eyes flew open at the sound of a voice in the office. Had someone seen her? Walking to the pit, she stopped in amazement, staring at a bookshelf and a chair in the hallway.

As she moved forward, she saw Melissa in Crystal's office which looked like a living room with paintings on the wall and knick-knacks everywhere. A cashmere shawl was draped over her chair.

"Interesting," Alessandra said.

"Thanks. I worked really hard on it." Crystal said, which meant Melissa hung things on the wall and moved furniture while Crystal drank her latte. Melissa looked like a drowned rat from all the exertion.

"Picasso's one of my favorites." Alessandra walked around the office.

"My dad has a few originals in his house, so it makes me feel like I'm at home," Crystal said.

Sheila showed up next, looking at the scene.

"Wow. You really cleaned up the place." Sheila hadn't expected anyone but Alessandra to be in yet.

"Well, it was more than a cleaning." Crystal shook her head at Alessandra. "It was a bit Feng Shui and decorating."

"And moving furniture," Melissa piped up feeling a little more confident with Sheila in the room.

"Melissa, here's your latte and croissant. You can go now." Crystal gave Melissa the tray and quickly turned to Alessandra. "Let me show you some of the items I've collected in my travels."

Neither Alessandra nor Crystal seemed to care if Sheila was present, so she turned to leave, bumping into Baxter as he came in the door.

"Whoa! Is this the same office?" Baxter barely looked at Sheila.

"It took a lot of work, Uncle Bax — sorry, Baxter." Crystal smiled sweetly and rolled her eyes.

"Now, this is an office!" he boomed. "I can't believe you did all this in one day. With this kind of initiative, you'll do great here. Won't she, Alessandra?"

"Absolutely. It's great to see someone take initiative." Alessandra said.

"Well, you set the bar high, Crystal. Let's see if anyone else can impress me this much." Baxter smiled at his protégé. "Alessandra, a word in your office."

Baxter and Alessandra walked by Sheila without a word. As they walked by Melissa's cubicle, Baxter said, "Did you see the great job Crystal did with her office? You can learn a lot from her!"

Melissa's mouth fell open revealing some of her croissant, so she quickly shut it. She looked at Crystal, who beamed with satisfaction. All Crystal had done was decorate a room and she was getting compliments from Baxter and Alessandra. Melissa took another bite out of her croissant, staring at the back of Crystal's head, which showed another fancy up-do. Crystal hadn't even done the hard work. Not only that, she didn't give Melissa one word of acknowledgement.

She went to Sheila's office. "Does this seem right to you?"

"No, but Baxter's her 'Uncle', so just let it go." Sheila said.

"All she did was decorate a room by bringing boxes of her stuff and Baxter's telling me that I can learn a lot from her?" Melissa said.

"That's why it's good to work for family," Sheila said. "Now go back to your desk, Baxter's still on the floor."

Melissa returned to her desk and got out her bowl for cereal. So what if she'd just eaten a croissant? As she went to the kitchen to get milk, Alessandra called her into her office.

"Call the maintenance department and tell them they need to remove that furniture from the hallway. It can't stay there." She looked at her watch. "Don't call them until ten. I want everyone to see Crystal's office." Alessandra said. After Melissa left, Alessandra turned to look at her couch. Whatever way this situation played out, she was going to benefit.

11

"**S**he's going to be pissed. How late are we now?" Jenn clutched the wheel.

"Ten minutes." Sheila checked her phone again, but there were no return texts from Alessandra.

This wasn't going to be an easy ride to New Jersey. First it took forever to get the rental car and now they learned the President was in town causing complete gridlock all over the city. The fact that it was freezing definitely didn't help.

The group was heading to New Jersey to visit their biggest client. The meeting was a bi-annual event that usually secured a massive budget every year. But the preparations for the upcoming meeting this afternoon hadn't really gone as planned so everyone was uptight.

After Crystal redecorated her office, maintenance came and changed it back to standard issue, causing Crystal to burst into tears and Baxter to return to their floor once again to argue with Rick.

"This is ridiculous, Rick. The place looks a hundred times better. Surely you can make one exception on my behalf," Baxter said.

"It's never one exception, Baxter, and you know it. Everyone here will start doing it. Plus the furniture has to stay here. It's assigned to this room." Rick instructed his men to move the bookshelf back where it belonged. "But if you want to talk to someone on twenty-five, be my guest."

The domino effect was amazing. Per Baxter's order, Melissa had to take care of Crystal and was given Baxter's American Express card to do so. So Melissa spent the afternoon at a three hour lunch, then shopping to make Crystal feel better, leaving the rest of them to fend for themselves.

Sheila dialed Alessandra's phone again. No answer.

"Maybe I should get out and walk to meet her. I'll probably make it quicker than driving."

"You really want to face her alone?" Jenn turned on the radio. "She should have come with us to get the car in the first place, and then we could have headed downtown."

Another fifteen minutes later, they pulled up at the corner of 59th and Broadway to see Alessandra and Crystal waiting.

"What's she doing here?" Jenn asked.

"Lord only knows." Sheila prepared to move since Alessandra always took the front seat but the rear door flew open.

"Don't bother moving. What the hell took so long? We are freezing! Why the fuck didn't you call?" Alessandra fumed as she got into the car.

"We did call, you didn't pick up your phone," Sheila said.

"Did you hear my phone ring?" Alessandra turned to Crystal.

"No," Crystal answered curtly, glaring at Sheila.

Sheila dialed the number again. "It goes straight to voicemail."

"Do you even have your phone?" Jenn threw over her shoulder.

"Of course I have it!" Alessandra reached into her bag and grabbed the phone for Jenn to see.

"Is it on?" After having two kids, Jenn had patience and a way of pointing out the obvious that could cut anyone down to size. And she was especially good at doing it to Alessandra.

"God dammit!" Alessandra pushed a button. Everyone was silent until Crystal broke the ice.

"So, what are we doing today?" Crystal asked Alessandra. Sheila and Jenn looked at each other quickly.

Alessandra glared at the girl then turned back to texting. "That's a good question, ladies. Please do tell me what we are 'doing' today."

The rest of the ride was awful. Alessandra tore apart everything Sheila and Jenn said. Thirty minutes before getting to the building, Alessandra asked to see their presentation.

"The computer's in the trunk." Sheila replied.

"Well, pull over and get it." Alessandra was still glued to her phone.

"We're on the highway, Alessandra. I'm not getting out in the breakdown lane. It's dangerous," Jenn said.

"Neither of you brought a revised presentation to me yesterday, so I want to see it. Now," Alessandra stated quietly.

As Jenn opened her mouth, Crystal blurted, "I'll get out. My friends and I stop all the time on the L.I.E. when I'm going to the Hamptons. It's so not a big deal."

"It is a big deal, because I'm not sitting in the breakdown lane." Jenn pulled off the next exit. "I'll get the computer, Crystal. You'll have to be a hero some other time."

*****

"Are you kidding me? That's what you've got?" Alessandra stared at the computer as Jenn got back on the highway.

"It's exactly what we discussed." Jenn threw back.

"No, it's not. These graphics are old. Where's the new stuff?"

"What new stuff?" Sheila asked.

"Oh, for Christ's sake. The new stuff I gave to Melissa two days ago. She should have done it yesterday," Alessandra said.

"Melissa was with Crystal yesterday and you were gone," Sheila said. "No one told us about changes."

Alessandra shoved the computer through the two front seats. Sheila caught it just before it hit the gear shift. "I have to do everything myself around here." She took her own computer out of her bag, ignoring them for the rest of the ride.

*****

At the meeting, Alessandra took over completely, showing a charm and grace that belied her mood. By the end of the meeting, she had the clients agreeing to programs that didn't exist and committing to an additional million dollars for the year. Within an hour, they were back in the car.

"How did you come up with all of that so quickly?" Crystal gushed.

"When you've been doing this as long as I have, you learn a thing or two," Alessandra said as she slipped into the passenger's seat. "I don't know how this got so fucked up, but I swear, I'm considering not giving any commission to you two for this extra million.

"And you," Alessandra turned in her seat to face Sheila. "You contributed nothing! What the hell happened?"

"You changed everything on the way here and didn't tell me what you were going to say. There wasn't exactly a run through." Sheila answered.

This sent Alessandra into orbit.

"First I have to stand on the street for twenty minutes because you two were late, then I have to fix the presentation

57

and save the meeting. What next? Do I need to teach you how to wipe your ass? You know what, Crystal? Maybe these two aren't such great examples of what a sales person needs to be. I've never been so mortified in my life."

"Really? Then why weren't you around to go over this yesterday afternoon? We looked for you. Even Stacey didn't know where you went. Where were you?" Jenn said.

Alessandra glared at Jenn, her jaw twitching in rage. Jenn pulled over.

"I'm starving. I'm getting lunch before we head back." She opened the door.

"Are you joking? I'm not in the mood to spend more time in this dump of a town." Alessandra looked around. "Or in this car. Couldn't you have picked something that wasn't hollow?"

"Next time I'll ask for a Mercedes," Jenn said, getting out and slamming the door with Alessandra following close behind.

"Based on this sales call, the only time you'll ever drive a Mercedes will be when you rent anyway. Here, this place will do." She stopped in front of a clean looking deli. "We're eating in ten minutes. In and out. I'm not kidding."

Alessandra breezed into the little deli and walked straight to the counter. "I'll have a lettuce and tomato sandwich with olive oil, salt, pepper and Swiss Cheese on a pita roll. No butter. Bring it to my table."

The woman behind the counter looked wearily at the three remaining New Yorkers. Sheila smiled, ordered something simple and sat across from Alessandra, who was typing furiously on her BlackBerry.

Their sandwiches came and the four ate in awkward silence while Alessandra either ranted about the meeting or returned calls. When she finished, she stood and announced, "I'm going to the bathroom. When I'm done, we're leaving."

"I have to go, too." Jenn said.

"Well, use the men's room. Because I mean it when I say we are out of here when I'm done. I'll meet you at the car," she spat.

*****

Sitting in the car, Jenn looked at her watch. "What the hell is taking her so long? All three of us went and she's still in there."

"Maybe she got a call," Crystal offered haughtily.

"Or maybe her BlackBerry fell in the toilet and she's screaming at gravity," Jenn threw out. Sheila laughed.

"You know, she's really unhappy with you two. I was in the back with her for the entire ride and she looked pissed," Crystal said.

"She always looks pissed." Jenn turned on the radio to stop the conversation.

"Maybe at you, but she was smiling at me," Crystal spoke louder.

Sheila turned to look at the girl. "You've been here three days, Crystal. Give it time."

Suddenly the door opened and Alessandra jumped in. "Okay, team. Let's go." She pulled a lipstick out of her bag and flipped down the visor.

"Oh, I love this song!" She said, turning up the volume while smiling at herself in the visor mirror. Jenn looked in the rearview mirror to catch Sheila's attention. They stared silently at each other for a moment, then drove all the way to New York with a much happier version of their boss.

12

"That was delicious." Sheila sat on the couch after inhaling her dinner.

"I'm glad you enjoyed it and I am also glad you brought more cupcakes. I never think to buy them for myself." Ruth opened the box and sniffed the sugary aroma.

Ruth, was also glad to cook for someone else again. After forty years of marriage and raising her son, the need to nurture someone was still there.

"So you really think I should stay close to Crystal?" Sheila had already told Ruth about her week. After the ride to New Jersey, Crystal hadn't really done much in terms of sales but she certainly had the office buzzing by giving Melissa ridiculous tasks while Stacey and Mark had to pick-up the slack.

"Definitely. She clearly has support from high above. But something is strange. In this economy, I would think they would hire someone who can bring in revenue. Not someone wet behind the ears. My radar says stay on her good side, but do it from a distance. Starting tomorrow," Ruth said.

"Well, tomorrow I'm at an offsite conference so I get another day's reprieve but I will trust your radar instead of mine. It's obviously broken," Sheila said.

"Still no word from Joe?" Ruth asked.

It had been twelve days since Joe left. She knew that counting days was pathetic but she couldn't help it. Every night she was so depressed, she just turned on the TV and ordered dinner from Sam's Noodles. She couldn't even drink anymore. Her stomach was killing her. Instead of a glass of wine, she gulped Pepto Bismal straight from the bottle. Joe still hadn't called even though the last message she left was pretty direct.

"Hi, Joe." Sheila had said. "I know you are dating Taylor and I don't want to talk about that. I need to discuss the money that you took. Half that money was mine and it's unfair for you to take it. I'm meeting with Barbara next week so please call me back. Thanks."

She had tried to sound confident on the phone yet cringed when her voice faltered. She knew it was a cheap shot to mention Barbara, her financial planner. Sheila started going to Barbara right after she bought her apartment. When she and Joe moved in together, Barbara was the one who advised Sheila against pooling all their money.

"Without some sort of contract, you'd be a fool to give him your money. You have more than him," Barbara said. "He can run off with it anytime, my dear. Just use a joint account for living expenses and keep your savings separate."

Sheila did take Barbara's advice at first, which hadn't made Joe happy. In fact, none of Barbara's advice made Joe happy. She was against Sheila using HELOC money to pay for Joe's graduate school and she was doubly against Sheila supporting him while he was in school.

"Are you crazy? He's not going to pay anything toward living expenses? Doesn't he have money saved?" she practically yelled at Sheila.

"Yes, he has money saved and he's going to use it for things like our vacations and stuff." Sheila thought it sounded reasonable.

"Of course he is. He's going to get a free ride and vacations." Barbara shook her head. "You should have a contract so if you break up then he has to repay the money. That HELOC is in your name. You're the one on the hook for it."

But the thought of breaking up had never crossed Sheila's mind. Although her relationship with Joe was different from most, she thought it was great. They were building their life and would get married when it was right, not because everyone said she should after a few years.

When she told Joe what Barbara had said, he was adamant that Sheila get a new financial planner.

"Why can't you just use someone else?" he asked. "She's just an angry woman who hates men. She treats me like I'm using you."

When Joe earned his MBA and was recruited by Goldman Sachs, they opened a joint account at Joe's firm. Then Joe began out earning Sheila, yet he didn't contribute anything extra to the budget. It should have been another red flag, but Sheila didn't tell Barbara about it. She just kept sending a small amount to Barbara each month figuring that Joe was in finance so he knew what he was doing. Sitting across from Ruth now, Sheila realized he certainly did know what he was doing all along.

"No. He still hasn't returned my calls. Maybe he thinks it's too dangerous because I mentioned the money he owes me," Sheila said.

"Well, there is something to be said for knowing danger when you see it. Unfortunately, a person has to see it a few times before they recognize it. Now, where did we leave the story last week?"

*****

Ruth and Sara giggled with delight in Aunt Marta's parlor. They had just seen their first picture show and it was wonderful. They re-enacted each scene dramatically until Dieter came with a frog and chased them out of the house.

"Dieter! Go away!" yelled Ruth running down the front steps. Looking behind her to make sure the frog was not close, she slammed into what felt like a wall. Stumbling sideways, she reached out as a pair of strong hands caught her. It was the same man that had visited the picnic last weekend, wearing the same gray uniform. Up close, Ruth saw that the bird on his belt buckle was an eagle with a symbol that looked ancient. She looked into his blue eyes and he seemed friendly as he smiled at her.

"Hello." He spoke English again. "You've had such an exciting afternoon. Did you enjoy the matinee?" His teeth were perfect, reminding Ruth of the screen stars she had just seen. "You are Ruth? Yes?"

"My father doesn't allow me to talk to strangers, sir." Remembering Uncle Norman's words, Ruth spoke in German.

"You understand English very well but you don't speak it? Well, it's your father with whom I wish to speak anyway. And here he is." The man looked past Ruth with a grin.

"Why are you here again?" Franz demanded, pulling Ruth behind him. "There is nothing to discuss!"

"Oh, but I think there is. In fact, Ruth and I were discussing the matinee. Weren't we?" He smiled at Ruth, but this time it didn't seem so nice.

"Get in the house." Her father pushed her roughly. "Now!"

She and Dieter ran into the house and looked out the window as Uncle Peter went outside. Franz was speaking loudly to the man, who seemed amused. Uncle Peter put his hand on Franz's shoulder but he shrugged it off. Another soldier stepped out of the car and approached the group.

"Never!" was the last word Franz yelled before storming back into the house. He went straight through the parlor into the library. Uncle Peter spoke a few words with the men and then slowly walked back to the house as the men drove away. Eliza directed him into the library.

"How can you sit there and talk to them?" Franz spoke angrily at Peter.

"You don't understand. He is a Captain. The more you fight, the more they harass you. Until this is settled, they are in control," Peter reasoned. "It's not forever. It's just an unpleasant situation to get through." After a few moments of quiet, Peter spoke again. "If you offered to help, they will leave you be. You don't even have to give them all the information, just enough to keep them away."

"I can't, Peter. They are ruining our country. The country I dream about at night. The country I want to return to one day. This is too dangerous. I think we need to leave for America. I'm going to speak with Eliza now."

Uncle Peter came into the parlor and motioned for Eliza.

"Come now, children, there's fresh pie in the kitchen. Let's have some and then you can go outside and play." Aunt Marta shooed them into the back of the house, knowing the conversation between Franz and Eliza was something the children should never hear.

The next morning, the family was packed for the country to visit Mama's cousin, Ethel. When it was time to leave, Franz sat the children on the sofa in the front room.

"As you know, Papa has had to deal with some unpleasant realities since we've been in Germany. In order to clear this mess, I am staying with Uncle Peter and Aunt Marta while you visit Cousin Ethel." The children called out their disappointment but Franz held up his hand, silencing them all. "I wish there were some other option, but I must ensure the rest of our vacation is peaceful and we are safe."

"Safe, Father?" Ruth asked quietly, feeling a knot grow in the pit of her stomach.

He looked at her evenly. "There are changes happening right now which affect the entire country, Ruth. I need to be sure we stay safe as the country settles back into normalcy. Can you be a brave girl while I do that?"

Sara started to cry, but Ruth fought back the tears. "Yes, Papa. I will be brave."

"So will I, Papa." Dieter offered.

"Me, too!" added Greta.

Franz smiled at his children. "Very well. We'll be together before you know it." and the children ran to hug him.

A few hours later, Franz said goodbye to each child as they piled into the car. All the children were settling in, with Uncle Peter at the wheel, while Mama and Papa stepped away for a quiet moment. They were usually a stoic couple in front of the children, so it was a surprise when Papa hugged her tightly and whispered in her ear. Mama looked at him tenderly and touched his face, fighting back tears. Amidst all the chaos, Ruth caught the scene and stared. Although the ride was pleasant with songs and laughter, Ruth was filled with apprehension.

13

When Sheila stepped off the elevator Tuesday morning, she was shocked to see Melissa at her desk and Alessandra's office dark. "Why are you here so early?"

"I have to talk to you." Melissa followed her into her office, shutting the door behind them.

"I have a problem with Crystal and I need your help," Melissa blurted out anxiously. "Not only were you out of the office yesterday, Susan took a personal day to handle some wedding stuff and Crystal thought I didn't have anything to do so she piled on a ton of stuff."

"Whoa. Melissa, calm down. I haven't even had my coffee yet. It can't be that bad." Sheila tried to hang her jacket on the door but Melissa was in the way, twisting her hands. "Sit down and tell me what happened."

Melissa slumped into a chair and took a deep breath.

*****

"Melissa, come into my office so I can give you some things to do?" Crystal yelled from her chair.

"I'm finishing my cereal. I'll be there in a few." Every morning Melissa ate a bowl of cereal at her desk. She was the only one of her friends that had to be in an office before 9 a.m., so she took that time to eat a good breakfast and get herself ready for the day.

"Excuse me?" Crystal now stood at Melissa's cubicle.

"I'm finishing my —," Melissa stopped when she saw Crystal's look. "Do I have something on my face?"

"Are you joking? I have a proposal due and you want to eat breakfast?" Crystal said.

"Um. Yeah. I always do. No one ever minds."

"Your workday starts when I say so. It's almost nine o'clock. I need you now." When she walked back into her office, Melissa stood to follow.

"What are you doing?" Stacey whispered. "Sit down!"

Melissa hated confrontation and the thought that anyone didn't like her so she shrugged at Stacey and went into Crystal's office.

But after thirty minutes of hearing Crystal talk about her weekend and her new outfits, Melissa became anxious as her stomach growled and her phone rang at her desk.

"Melissa, are you going to answer your phone?" Stacey was in the door looking at Crystal. "That is part of her job, you know, and two sales reps are out." She stormed off.

"She's right, Crystal. I've got to make sure my phone is answered. I can't really stay in here much longer," Melissa said.

"Jesus, Melissa. Haven't you ever heard of 'managing up'? I'm your boss and whoever is calling can leave a message." Crystal shook her head.

"Ah, sorry." Melissa had never heard of 'managing up' or anyone telling her it was okay to let the phone go to voice mail, but she sat and listened because, well, it was Crystal.

"I've got tons of stuff to do today. Plus, my first proposal has to be sent this week and I hate the way marketing puts things together. There are a lot of changes."

"Um. This is the proposal template we all use. I'm not sure Marketing can make a new one without Alessandra's approval."

"Alessandra approved it. After Sheila's fiasco in New Jersey, she said she hates the presentation so take this to marketing and don't let them tell you 'no'." Crystal rolled her chair to her computer.

Melissa went back to her desk and tried not to cry. She looked at her bowl of cereal, which was soggy and realized she was starving. Pulling a candy bar out of her desk, she ripped it open and took a big bite. So what if it was only 10:00 a.m.

Mark sent an IM. 'Meet me in copy room. NOW.' Stacey was in there waiting too.

"What the hell was that? Why were you in there so long?" Mark asked.

"She's out of her mind. I'm going to get killed by the marketing team," Melissa said.

"I knew she was going to be a pain the minute I saw her. I'm so glad I don't have to work for her," Stacey preened.

Mark made a face at Stacey. "Don't rub it in. What are you going to do?" he asked Melissa.

"Go to the marketing department." And she left the room with the edited proposal.

Since the marketing team received none of the commissions for winning business, they were generally a bitter bunch. So when Melissa walked into their area, she wasn't met with a whole lot of enthusiasm.

"Are you friggin' kidding me?" the marketing manager said when Melissa gave her the papers.

"Alessandra approved it." Melissa said.

"We'll see about that." She immediately picked up the phone. "Hey, Alessandra. It's Pam. I'm looking at the changes you want for a proposal. Ain't happening." She kept typing while Alessandra sounded off into the phone. "I don't know. One of your assistants is here with a bunch of changes. I don't know which one gave it to her and I don't care. This one says you approved it. Yeah, I'll send her to you."

She hung up the phone and smiled dryly at Melissa. "Alessandra never approved these changes. She'd like to see you now."

*****

"Who the hell told you I would approve this?" Alessandra was venomous, looking at the proposal.

"Crystal." Melissa barely got out.

"Crystal!" Alessandra screamed.

"Hey, Alessandra!" Crystal bounced into the room. "What's up?"

"Melissa tells me that you said I approved these changes. Why would she say that?" Alessandra tossed the document across the desk and Crystal picked it up, glancing through it as if seeing it for the first time.

"I don't know. Melissa and I had a long conversation this morning but she had an attitude because she wanted to finish her breakfast. She didn't seem to be listening when I went through the changes. She told me she'd handle it."

"You were giving a sales person an attitude because you wanted to finish your breakfast?" Alessandra scoffed at Melissa.

"I told her I needed to eat, like I always do, but she kept me in her office for an hour. Even Stacey came in because my phone was ringing." Melissa could barely get the words out.

"Let's get something straight. You do what Crystal says. I don't care if you're starving." Then she looked at Crystal "Why aren't you working with Sheila on this?"

"I can't find her." Crystal said with a shrug.

"Sheila's at the Advertising Conference." Melissa turned to look at Crystal who knew full well where Sheila was.

Alessandra stared at them both. Melissa was clearly terrified of the entire situation and Crystal was cool as can be. If there was one thing Alessandra didn't like, it was a person who showed fear.

"Melissa, it's up to you to make sure Crystal is trained. You can't expect her to know everything and letting her get into trouble with the marketing team is shitty. Both of you go and figure out this mess."

"Maybe I should work on it with Scott? He's always helpful," Crystal offered.

"Perfect. And Melissa, since you've obviously forgotten the rules, you can sit with them while they handle this, even if it takes all afternoon." Which it did. Melissa left the office at 6:30 p.m., missing dinner with her friends.

*****

"Let me make sure I have this right." Sheila tried to regroup. "Crystal told you that Alessandra approved the changes, then when Alessandra freaked, she denied it."

"Yes. And then I had to sit in Scott's office for another hour, watching her fall all over him. Then I spent the rest of the afternoon having her change things over and over. Stacey and Mark had to cover everything for me and Crystal didn't even care. Everyone's mad at me." Melissa looked panicked.

"Melissa, just go to your desk and eat your cereal. I'm sure it isn't that bad," Sheila said as Alessandra walked by. "Good morning, Alessandra."

Alessandra didn't look like she was having a good morning. Her eyes were bloodshot and her clothes were wrinkled. "I want you in my office now." She walked away without acknowledging Melissa.

"So, I heard yesterday was interesting." Sheila sat at Alessandra's desk.

"Don't be cute. Your assistant doesn't seem to know her shit. She got Crystal on marketing's bad side." Alessandra said.

"Alessandra, Melissa did what Crystal told her to do. Crystal's obviously lying."

Alessandra leaned forward in her chair. "Didn't I tell you that Crystal is a family friend of Baxter's? Didn't I tell you that everyone has to be nice to her?"

"Nice is one thing, getting screwed is another. And I wasn't even here, Alessandra. I can't be responsible for her every action."

"Yes, you can. In fact, now you are now fully in charge of training Crystal." She opened and slammed a desk drawer, looking for something.

"Why me? Why can't Scott do it? She loves him. He'll have her trained in no time."

"Because you're better than him. See, that's the beauty of being good at what you do, you get more responsibility." She finally found her bottle of Pepto Bismal and took a swig.

"Well, Crystal doesn't think she needs training." Sheila sat back in the chair.

"Well, let's tell her. Crystal!" Alessandra screamed. Crystal flew into her office with another designer outfit and complicated hairdo.

"Hi, Alessandra! Hi, Sheila!" She settled into the chair like she was getting ready for a chat with friends, Sheila noticed. There wasn't one ounce of guilt or concern that this might be a bad conversation based on what happened yesterday.

"Crystal, you know that Sheila is the most senior sales person as well as being in charge of managing the Support Staff. After what happened yesterday, it's become clear that some of the staff hasn't been properly trained," Alessandra said.

"I agree." Crystal nodded to Alessandra.

"As a result, I think it would be great for Sheila to manage you as you acclimate to our team and work with you one-on-one until you are up to speed. That way she will make sure that you get all the support you need. Especially from Melissa." Alessandra looked at Sheila.

"Well," Sheila started. "Melissa's always been an asset to the team and until yesterday no one has had an issue with her."

"Well, I'm just shocked by that." Crystal continued looking at Alessandra. "She certainly threw me under the bus and I know Baxter expects more from the people he hires."

Before Sheila could respond, Alessandra held up a hand. "You're right and the issue will be resolved. Sheila is the right person to do it. She's the one you go to with ideas. She's the one who will handle Melissa for you. And most importantly, she'll show you the ropes. I'm sure you're both as enthusiastic as I am about this. Now go."

As Alessandra opened her file, Crystal walked out without another word but Sheila stayed.

"You heard what I said, right?" Alessandra kept reading.

"Yes." Sheila's head was spinning. "But Melissa —"

"Screw Melissa." Alessandra slapped the papers on her desk. "Your job is to keep Crystal happy. End of story. If I were you, I'd start doing that now."

Sheila seethed as she walked to Crystal's office. "Why don't you and I have lunch this afternoon? We'll create a list of things we need to work on," Sheila stood in the door.

"I have lunch plans. I'll get back to you." Crystal said, leaving Sheila standing in the middle of the pit with all three assistants looking at her.

Sheila walked closer to Crystal. "Maybe you didn't understand Alessandra. You are reporting to me now."

"No, I report to Alessandra and you are here to help me," Crystal said.

"Crystal, I need to make sure you are trained so you can shine here or Alessandra will start having doubts. You wouldn't want that. So we'll leave here at noon. My treat." Sheila smiled charmingly and walked through the pit with all eyes on her. Behind her, she heard Crystal slam her office door.

There was a flutter of typing, and then Stacey and Melissa laughed. More typing, then Mark let out a guffaw. Sick of the whole group of them, Sheila got up and went for coffee.

*****

Later that morning, Sheila looked up to see Baxter standing at her door.

"Sheila, you're here. Would you have ten minutes to spare for me?"

"Of course," Sheila said.

"Good. I wouldn't want to interrupt our star sales person." He shut the door and sat in the chair closest to Sheila. "I heard a lot of talk about a situation yesterday and I had to check with you to see what you think about it." He leaned back in the chair and crossed his legs elegantly.

"I assume you're talking about the situation with Crystal and Melissa?" She turned to give Baxter her full attention. "How can I help you?"

"Well, as you may know, Crystal's father and I are very good friends. And although it might appear that Crystal has everything, she's had to work just as hard as you or I to get where she is today." He stopped to pull an imaginary piece of lint off his trousers. "So imagine how upset I was to hear one of our assistants had let Crystal go down a path that led to her getting into trouble with our marketing team."

Sheila wasn't quite sure how to respond so she simply nodded.

"You see, Crystal has a lot of contacts based on the fact that she's gone to the finest schools and her father is a very successful businessman. She can do great things for us. Plus, she grew up with the Internet and cell phones." He smiled. "You should see what she can do on her iPhone. All the Apps and ringtones. Things I can't possibly do. Do you have an iPhone, Sheila?"

"No, I have a BlackBerry." Sheila suddenly felt defensive thinking about how she couldn't even change her ringtone.

"You see, Sheila, I need you to keep an eye out for Crystal and I need to make sure that Melissa points her in the right direction. I can't have any more days like yesterday. Crystal was so upset it would have broken your heart."

Sheila simply smiled.

"And here's the other thing. I heard you defended Melissa to Alessandra and I appreciate that kind of loyalty. But I suggest if Melissa can't hack it, then Melissa will have to go."

"But Melissa's been here for almost two years and we've never had a problem until yesterday." Sheila knew she sounded frantic but Melissa was a good assistant and a nice person. "I have to say, Baxter, there are two sides to every story."

"There's only one side to this story, Sheila." He stared intently at her, all trace of his smile gone. "Look, Melissa isn't really motivated or positioned to move ahead. You say Melissa's been here for almost two years, but she's no closer to a sales position. She doesn't have the contacts she needs and she doesn't have the background."

"What do you mean?" Sheila said.

"Melissa's from a regular family. She went to a state college. Crystal was bred for a better life. She's gone to prep school, had a debut, and travelled to Europe every summer. What you need to do now is make sure your loyalty is to someone who can bring you up. Like Crystal. People like Melissa are a dime a dozen. If we have to find another assistant, we'll do it.

"Now, regarding this lunch you want to have with Crystal today. To show I respect you, I told her she will go and that it will be fun. I suggest you use this time to get to know Crystal and learn how she can help you. Make her happy."

Baxter got up and put his hand on the door knob. "I also expect this conversation will stay private between you and me. If Alessandra finds out about it, there will be repercussions. Now that you're single, you only have yourself to rely on. Every decision counts." He opened the door and walked away without another word.

Sheila sat stunned. Was he threatening her? Baxter had been the one to hire Sheila five years ago. He knew she went to a state college, too, but she had been successful so maybe he was willing to overlook it. Or did it have something to do with Joe? Joe came from a privileged background. Baxter had met Joe at holiday parties and found they knew the same people. Maybe now that Joe was gone, Sheila didn't seem as valuable.

Sheila shook away the thoughts. That's insane. In over five years at *Goodliving.com*, Sheila had always exceeded her quota and worked hard. That's why she was still here. Baxter's just looking out for his friend's daughter. She really wished she could call Joe for advice. He would know how to read the situation.

Her cell phone rang. It was her bank again. A few months before Joe left, he calculated that merging the HELOC and mortgage would lower their monthly payments. Since both Sheila and Joe had perfect credit scores, the bank was more than pleased to help. But ever since Joe left, the bank had been calling Sheila non-stop. Joe must have called them to say he wouldn't be part of the refinance and they needed a new application. Well, Sheila couldn't deal with it now. The refinance could wait another month. Sheila hit ignore as she had every time they called.

"Ready to go?" Crystal stood in the door, smiling sweetly.

Sheila grabbed her bag, wishing that she had time to take a gulp of her own Pepto Bismal.

14

"**A**re you kidding?" Jenn asked.

"No. I don't want any surprises. You have to get out first and see if he's around," Sheila said. Jenn rolled her eyes and got out of the cab.

Morgan's engagement party was happening at Glasshouses, one of the most sought after places in the city, on one of the most sought after nights for a party, Sunday. In fact, it was where Joe and Sheila had discussed getting married.

"When we're ready to settle down." Joe had said with his Irish grin.

Don't think about it, Sheila told herself, but she couldn't help feeling like Morgan was having her dream wedding. It had been a month since Joe broke up with her and tonight would be the first time they'd see or talk to each other. It had to be perfect especially since Joe would be the Best Man to Sheila's Maid of Honor.

"Coast's clear," Jenn announced.

"How do I look?" Sheila asked for the third time that night.

"You look like a million bucks," Jenn answered immediately, not bothering to look again.

When they got off the elevator, Sheila was relieved to see the room was crowded with at least two hundred people. Her entire strategy boiled down to a single method: don't look more than three feet in any direction, which is highly effective when avoiding the former love of your life. She figured if she only looked in her immediate space, she wouldn't unexpectedly see Joe, or Taylor, for that matter.

Jenn and Sheila were now at the front of the receiving line where Morgan and Dylan were greeting their guests.

"You look amazing!" Morgan stared at Sheila. Sheila had spent the afternoon at a spa getting the works to make sure Joe saw her looking fantastic.

"Wow! Sexy lady!" Dylan looked Sheila up and down appreciatively. "Too bad Joe's not here to see this." Morgan glared at him while Sheila froze momentarily.

"There's lots of eligible guys here, Sweetie," Morgan said in a low voice. "Just have fun and thanks for coming."

"Of course. Congratulations, you two." Sheila said before walking straight to the bar.

He didn't come. How could this be? Was he that afraid to see her? Was she that horrible a person? Sheila's eyes filled with tears so she turned quickly for the ladies room, bumping into what seemed to be a wall.

"Whoa. Are you okay?" The wall was talking to her, concerned.

"Yes, um. I just stubbed my toe," she lied while staring into his amazing blue eyes.

He looked at her feet, adorned with brand new Jimmy Choo heels.

"Those are some shoes!" He smiled. "I can see how your toes would get hurt, exposed like that. I think they need special protection." He smiled showing perfect, white teeth.

Sheila smiled back, finding herself with nothing to say. He smiled some more.

"Tristan?" A woman came up beside him. "Hi," she smiled at Sheila. "Mind if I borrow him for a minute? You've got to hear what Tom is saying over here."

"I'll catch up with you to check on that toe." He winked as the woman led him away to join a group of people.

Jenn caught up to Sheila. "Are you okay? I was worried after I heard that Joe isn't here."

"Yes. I was actually trying to flirt with someone. Who I think is straight and interested," Sheila said. "The night's looking up. Let's get a drink."

After a few drinks, Sheila was able to relax. Except for the shoes, she felt very little pain. The compliments were great. She now understood why people would dress like this. Everyone noticed her shoes. She looked around for Tristan, who still had that woman by his side. For the next two hours, Sheila talked and laughed with the bridesmaids while discussing wedding showers and bachelorette themes.

Joe not being at the party was actually a blessing, she realized. It was obvious that Morgan had told most people about their breakup, so there were less awkward moments than Sheila anticipated. Plus, she caught Tristan looking in her direction once or twice.

She pulled Dylan aside to get more information.

"That's Tristan Phelan, a friend of mine from college. The woman is his ex-girlfriend. They do business occasionally. He's a great guy," Dylan said.

Suddenly it was time for the toast, which Dylan made beautifully. He thanked Morgan for agreeing to be his bride, telling everyone he was the lucky one. And he put the spotlight on Sheila, thanking her for setting them up and agreeing to be Maid of Honor. Sheila smiled shyly at the crowd as they applauded. Then he thanked his friend, Charlie, for agreeing to be Best Man. Sheila stopped smiling. Charlie? Joe was supposed to be the Best Man. She stared at Dylan as he finished the toast and everyone raised their drinks.

"How is your toe?" Tristan interrupted her thoughts.

"Oh, better, thanks. And how about you? Are your shoes causing pain?" Sheila said, her head still reeling from the toast.

"Yes, these damn shoes pinch my toes and give me blisters. I never should have bought them." He smiled again. "So, you're the one responsible for all this?"

"Yes." Sheila cleared her head. "I introduced them."

"Hey, Tristan." A tall, blond man interrupted. "We've been looking for you, and we've got to run. The limo's downstairs." He walked away without so much as a glance at Sheila.

"Dammit. I'm really sorry. We have a business meeting in Boston tomorrow and we're taking the last shuttle," Tristan said. "I'll have to drive to Boston by myself if I don't go now." He turned to see his friend get in the elevator. "I'll get your number from Morgan and I'll call you. I couldn't forget those shoes. Sorry." Tristan smiled and ran to catch his friend.

Sheila once again stood in silence. What the hell was that? He checked her out all night, and then when they finally get to talk, he has to run for business on a Sunday night? And not only was Joe absent, he wasn't going to be the Best Man. Sheila sped for the bathroom and locked herself in one of the stalls. She stood desperately trying to calm herself. She stared at the coat hook numbly until she heard two women approach the mirrors.

"Wasn't Dylan's toast beautiful?"

"Yes, he really is a catch. Too bad I've already dated most of his friends." She laughed. "Except Joe. Thank God."

"Can you believe what he did to Sheila?"

"No. Can you believe he pulled out of being the Best Man because his new girlfriend didn't like it? She thought it would be too awkward since they're living together. Plus, Sheila's been calling him constantly, so she was afraid of a scene. That's why he's not here. He left Dylan high and dry."

"I'd die if I were Sheila. Poor thing. She did look great tonight though."

"Yeah, but it still doesn't change the fact that Joe's sleeping with a twenty-six year-old."

"I know, can you imagine? One minute your boyfriend lives with you, the next he's living with someone ten years younger. She doesn't even know, by the way. He didn't have the balls to tell her."

"Poor Sheila." They left.

Living together? Joe was living with Taylor? And everyone knows? Sheila suddenly felt like she was in a costume. This wasn't an outfit she would have worn if she and Joe were still together. She only wore it to impress him.

Sheila stepped out of the stall. Staring into the mirror, she realized that her haircut did look great. Her skin glowed. The outfit was impeccable. But those women were right. She wasn't twenty-six. She'd never be twenty-six again and all the exercise in the world wouldn't change that. All totaled she had spent over five hundred dollars to look good for Joe. Five hundred dollars that she couldn't afford.

She went directly to the elevators and stood in the corner so no one would see her. When the doors opened, she hurried inside, banging the 'Door Close' button.

"Sheila!" Jenn called.

But Sheila kept pushing the button as tears started rolling down her cheeks. Finally the door closed and she was alone. When the elevator opened in the lobby, she hurried to the street and jumped into the first cab she could get.

*****

Sheila called in sick the next morning. For the first time in her life, she loafed around on a workday. She sat in her pajamas and cried. The only call she took was from Jenn.

"Sorry for leaving like that. But I have to ask a question and you need to tell me the truth." Sheila's voice was hoarse. "Did you know that Joe was living with her?"

"I found out at the party, Sheila. You were having fun and flirting with that guy. I swear I didn't know before that." Jenn's heart broke to hear Sheila cry. "Listen. You should take a few days off. You really need it. Maybe you should plan a vacation."

"I can't afford it."

"Make it simple. A few days at a spa or someplace really fun with another single friend. What about Nicole?"

"She's divorced and hates all men."

"What ever happened to Kristen? I think she's still single."

"I haven't talked to her since she went into AA."

"Well, listen. Take a few days and just veg. Go to the movies or rent some, but only funny ones. Promise me you're not going to sit and watch 'The Way We Were' over and over again."

Sheila hit the mute button on her remote and looked at Robert Redford's gorgeous face. "No, I won't," she lied.

"All right. I won't bother you unless something crazy happens here."

They hung up and Sheila went back to watching Barbara Streisand fall in love with Robert Redford. "Don't do it," Sheila said to the TV and eventually she fell asleep on the couch.

That phone! I'm going to kill Mark. For some reason only some of the calls rang with 'Single Ladies' and Sheila couldn't figure out how to change it.

"Hello?" Sheila was groggy.

"Sheila, its Alessandra. Do you plan to be in the office tomorrow?"

"I'm not sure." Sheila hesitated.

"It's a 'yes' or 'no' question." Alessandra sighed into the phone. "There's medication you can take for this, you know."

"Yes. I'll be in." Sheila slumped into the couch.

"Right. See you then." She hung up.

I'm such a wimp Sheila thought. How did I get here? Tears slid down her face as she realized, once again, that there was no

81

hope at reconciling with Joe. She had put so much hope into last night, like a fool. Joe hadn't called once since the night he left. Yet Sheila had hoped that when they saw each other, he would realize he had made a mistake. It was hopeless. She was hopeless and she had no clue what to do next.

Sheila looked at the television again. Jenn was right; she needed to get out of the house. She needed a new perspective. So she splashed water on her face and put on some clothes. Padding across the hall, she knocked on Ruth's door and was welcomed in for tea.

15

Cousin Ethel's house was a large, rambling farmhouse at the base of the Hartz Mountains with a barn full of animals on acres of fields. Ethel and her husband, Jacob, had raised their six children here. Now only their youngest, seventeen-year-old Johan, still lived at home, so Ethel was thrilled to have the house full with children again. Ethel was Eliza's favorite cousin and it was easy to see why. She was always smiling and ready with a joke, and her cheery mood brightened anyone's day. Her husband, Jacob, was equally as jovial and made the Königs feel at home immediately.

There had been no celebrations in the two days since they arrived, which was strange to the children. They had been surrounded by visiting relatives for weeks. It never occurred to them that no one knew where they were. The children were on their own during the hot, sunny days, hiking in the woods or splashing in the stream. The evenings were cool and often called for a sweater, even in July.

At night, the farmhouse creaked and groaned, often keeping Ruth awake. It didn't bother her, though. She used the time to daydream since no one could interrupt her thoughts and she had a lot to think about. Papa had traveled for business before, leaving the family for a week or two at a time. It always put things off kilter. This time, it was different because she didn't really know why Papa stayed behind. As the oldest, she felt that she should have been told, but Mother wouldn't say.

"Go play with the others," was Eliza's usual reply whenever Ruth asked questions.

Even Dieter behaved better. He idolized Johan, following him from chore to chore each day. That left Sara, Tomas, Greta and little Annabelle to watch, which kept Ruth busy.

Each night, Ruth stared at the moon miles beyond the mountains and thought about her life. It was wonderful on the farm, so different from their life in New York. Ruth felt she could live here forever and wondered what it would be like to not live with her family in New York. And if she wanted to live on a farm, what kind of husband should she have? Papa was the perfect man, but would Papa know what to do on a farm, she wondered? He wore a suit to work to the university. Ruth couldn't imagine Papa milking cows or knowing how to plant a field, then instantly felt bad. Of course he would. Papa was the smartest man on earth and she missed him terribly. She looked at the moon, hoping maybe Papa was looking at it right now, too, and somehow they were connected.

As she fell asleep she wondered what her father was doing without them.

*****

When Hitler's Army invaded Austria a few years back, the University where Franz worked in the U.S.A. severed ties with the University of Berlin but they wanted to keep Franz. Franz was prepared to refuse the offer until he received a surprising call from his former Supervisor in Berlin. "I heard you have been offered a large sum of money to stay in America. You must be proud to be so well regarded." "Thank you, but I intend to honor our agreement." Franz replied. "Well, I'd like to make a new agreement. I would like you to stay in America until the project is finished. Then you can come home and you can share the information with your homeland. You are more valuable to us in America."

So, of course, Franz stayed in New York.

Although the two universities no longer communicated, Franz occasionally corresponded with his former partner in the laboratory, Robert Schäfer. Now that Franz needed help, he headed to the city to talk with his friend.

It had broken Franz's heart to send his family away, but he had to keep the soldiers from them. The way the Captain had looked at Ruth put a knife in his heart. And the others, they were still young enough to drop their guard and say anything. Although he knew this was a risk, Franz fervently hoped that Robert could be trusted and provide some help for Franz to get his family safely back to America.

"Franz!" Robert stared in shock. "What a surprise."

"Thank you. Sorry that I am unannounced, but I just happened to be in the city today doing some shopping and thought of you. May I come in?" Franz walked into Robert's office, putting his shopping bags on Robert's desk. "I hoped that we could have lunch."

"I'm afraid I am on my way to a lunch meeting. In fact, I was just leaving. Why don't you walk out with me?" Robert grabbed his hat with the door still open. Stepping into the hall, Robert nervously looked to the right and then rapidly motioned for Franz to come. Franz stepped through the door without a sound.

Robert pointed to a door on the left, then ushered Franz down a stairwell and through an exit into the courtyard, which they crossed at a quick pace.

"We're being watched, Franz. The offices are bugged and your name is on the list. They will be down here very soon," Robert said. "You have been very valuable to the University, doing good work in America. Now that America doesn't give them any information, they want you. Need you, in fact," Robert said.

"I know. They approached me twice. I've told them no. Now I'm beginning to fear for my family's safety," Franz said.

Robert stopped abruptly. "You should. They are not playing games. Many of our colleagues have turned informant and some of our faculty are on 'leave,' but no one's heard from them."

"Robert, I need to get my family back to America," Franz said.

"It will be hard to get out." Robert started walking again. "Right now, as we speak, there's a man on the corner bench who has been watching us. I will most likely be questioned about our conversation. To get to America, your best bet is to leave from England. Chamberlain's been putting up a good front. They won't be taken over anytime soon." Robert walked through the main gate of the University and stuck out his hand. Franz's heart fell as he realized his friend would not be able to help.

As they shook hands, Robert said, "You walk to the north, I'll go south. We'll meet at our old lunch spot where I know we can have a private conversation. I have friends who can help."

As Franz watched Robert stop to crush his cigarette on the ground, he realized he left his bag in Robert's office. He considered leaving it, but it contained a scarf that Eliza had seen in a magazine. Eliza never asked for things so the longing on her face was all Franz needed to see. He also bought a doll for Ruth that she had seen the day of the picture show. His little girl was growing up and this might be the last doll she ever wanted. No, he had to go back.

Franz moved swiftly through the courtyard, not surprised to see the man from the bench was gone. He re-entered the building and scaled the stairs two at a time. Reaching the second floor, he came upon Robert's office in seconds. As he reached for the doorknob, a shadow moved behind the frosted glass door and the knob turned. He jumped back quickly as muffled voices came from within the office. Unsure where to go, he ducked back into the stairwell, closing the door softly. Robert had set him up. Franz paced the small landing, heartbroken over his bad judgment. Robert had set a trap at the restaurant and gone back to his office to call the authorities. Steadying himself against the unforgiving concrete wall, Franz knew he had no option left but to go to the American Embassy on Tiergartenstraße. It was less than a mile from the University but first he had to find a way out of the building. He headed down the stairs when he heard voices approach from the lower floor.

Franz changed direction, running up the stairs as fast as possible. He rounded the next landing as the stairwell door flew opened.

"They were here?" a man's voice demanded.

"Yes. They exited the building from the courtyard door," came a second voice. "Then they walked to the east entrance and parted ways. Schäfer went south, König north. I came here immediately to see if there was anything of interest in the office."

"You should have followed König! My men handle the interior and you know it."

"I sent soldiers to follow each of them. Neither man had a package so I went to get the bag that König brought."

"What was in it?"

"A doll and a scarf."

"Idiot!"

The two men hurried down the stairs as Franz stood frozen, willing himself not to make a sound. When the exterior door shut with a click, he slid along the wall to peek through the window on the landing. A young man, no more than eighteen, was talking to the man who had spied on Franz from the bench. The boy pointed in the direction that Franz had walked and shrugged his shoulders. He shook his head 'No' in answer to a question and looked at the ground ashamed. He must have been sent out to follow Franz, but Franz lost him by going back into the building. He smiled slightly at that good turn of events, but the victory was short lived as a soldier stepped into view and slapped the boy across the face. As he turned in a rage to the others, Franz fell back in shock. It was the Captain.

*****

When Franz finally made it to the street, he walked quickly in the direction of the Embassy. Not only was he in danger, he had put his friend in jeopardy. After walking for a while and being sure that he wasn't being followed, Franz stopped at a payphone and called Robert's office.

"Robert Schäfer." He answered.

"Can you talk?" Franz said.

"I'm sorry I missed our appointment, I was unavoidably detained. If you talk to my assistant, she can reschedule our meeting." Robert paused but before Franz spoke, he continued "No, I'm afraid I cannot meet after work. I have someone waiting for me at home. Good bye." And he hung up.

Franz clutched the receiver to his ear, instantly understanding. The soldiers were waiting at the house. He put down the phone and walked as fast as he could without drawing attention to himself. Franz's thoughts swirled. What if Peter or Marta were forced to say where Eliza and the children were staying? What if the soldiers went to Ethel's farm?

Franz plowed into the heart of the city. Turning left onto the street which housed the American Embassy, he hid his face by looking at the ground, only to be pushed backward by someone's shoulder. He shifted his weight to catch himself against a stone wall, ready to fight his attacker. Pulling back his fist, he looked into the eyes of an elderly man who stared in shock but did not flinch. Staring at Franz, the man reached his hand out, not to protect himself, but his wife of forty-seven years.

She grabbed his arm, not taking her eyes off Franz, who was too stunned to move. Relief poured through him that they were not soldiers, and then shame weakened him completely. Slumping back against the wall, he covered his face with his hands. He had never raised his hands in anger. Now he had almost assaulted an elderly couple. The couple watched Franz fearfully. Still, they did not speak nor did they move. Franz needed to get the embassy, quickly.

"I. I." Franz stuttered. "I'm so sorry. Please excuse me, Sir. Madam." Franz stood unsteadily. "I'm not feeling well. I must go."

The woman let out a small groan, pulling her husband closer to her. He hugged her tight.

"I meant no harm," Franz began, and then realized she was looking at something beyond his shoulder. Turning around, Franz was face to face with two young soldiers.

"What is going on here?" the thinner soldier asked Franz.

"I don't feel well. I accidentally bumped into this elderly couple. I apologize." Franz said.

"You apologize?" The heavier soldier narrowed his eyes. "Why are you apologizing to these Jews?"

Franz looked at the hate in the man's eyes and turned to the couple. Jews? Franz looked at the couple in confusion.

"Do you have your identity cards?" the other soldier demanded.

The old man pulled his card out of his pocket, handing it to the thin soldier. As the lady opened her purse, the groceries shifted, spilling items all over the sidewalk.

"You clumsy fool." The heavy set soldier walked to her, grabbing her bag to find the card. "You are to have this ready at all times. Not hidden in your purse." He flung the purse to the ground and examined the card.

Franz's conscience tore at him while the soldiers interrogated the couple, harassing them with insults until the poor lady cried. The weight of responsibility hit Franz hard. If he had been looking ahead, this encounter wouldn't be happening and he would be in the embassy.

"Why is an old man like you trying to carry groceries? You are weak! And not because you are old." The soldier waved the identity card under the man's nose.

Franz looked away, trying to gain perspective. He needed to think fast for the right answers and get to the embassy. He focused his gaze on the shop windows across the boulevard, only to have his blind faith in the goodness of life shattered. Christian Youth posters were in every window. Nazi SS propaganda hung on all the building walls. People walked on the street with their heads down while the soldiers strode purposefully along each road. And they were everywhere.

"Why didn't you make them move? Are you a sympathizer with these pigs?" The heavier soldier stepped toward Franz.

As Franz looked into the soldier's glare, he began to feel the smallness of his life in relation to this machine that had taken over his country. The hatred toward Jews didn't stop with them, it encompassed anyone who did not support the movement, and for the first time, Franz feared for his life.

"Young sir. I told you I do not feel well. My head was down; I didn't notice the couple as Jews. Now I must get to a doctor. I'm sure you have bigger issues than an unwell man." Though he wanted to turn and walk away, something told him to wait for permission, so he continued to hold the soldier's gaze and waited patiently.

The thin soldier spoke. "Jews! This man is sick and you are interfering with his right to pass. You know you must give Germans the right of way on the sidewalk," he turned to Franz. "You must be sick if you didn't smell the scent of these Jews. Go to your doctor." He raised his arm in salute.

Franz froze in his spot. Was it such a big deal to salute back so he could get in the door of the embassy? It was twenty yards away. That salute was only a movement that meant nothing to him, yet his arm didn't budge.

"Only a sympathizer or a resistor would not salute. You said you are not a sympathizer," The heavier soldier stepped within inches of Franz's nose. "Are you lying?"

Before Franz could answer, an explosion of glass pierced the air. The elderly man had dropped his bag of groceries, sending a spray of milk and glass across everyone's feet. "You oaf!" yelled the thin soldier. "You have dirtied my uniform." The heavy-set soldier now looked at his own boots. "Pick it up! You filthy Jews!"

The man bent to the ground, picking up the rest of his food as the soldiers stood above him, berating him for his clumsiness. He was shoved to the side by a boot, landing on a piece of glass. Sitting on his haunches to examine the cut, he glanced quickly at Franz's eyes for only a second. In that instant, Franz saw it. The man was trying to give him a way out.

As Franz made a small step in the direction of the embassy, he saw two more soldiers coming down the street toward the melee. Catching his expression, the elderly woman turned to see. Everything had unfolded so quickly, her mind was in a state, but she knew this man was a good person and she knew he was in trouble. Risking a kick herself, she motioned for him to go back the way he came then she dropped her bag of food and started to wail. As the soldiers focused their tirade on her, Franz slowly walked backward to the corner, disappeared from view and ran.

16

"**P**apa's here!" yelled Sara, running to greet Uncle Peter's car in the driveway. Eliza rushed to the door with Annabelle in her arms, relief flooding through her body. Her smile faded, however, when Peter got out of the car alone and looked at her grimly. It was only Eliza's faith that Franz would rejoin the family that kept her strong. Now, seeing the look on Peter's face, her breathing became weak. Passing the baby to Ethel, she fainted.

*****

"Eliza. Wake up." Ethel held a cool cloth to her forehead. "Eliza, can you hear me?"

Eliza opened her eyes. "Where is Franz? Ethel, did they take him? I need to talk to Peter!"

"Peter had to leave immediately. He couldn't risk being caught." Ethel paused. "Yesterday morning, Franz went to the University to see a friend but he never came home." She continued to stroke her cousin's forehead. "We don't know where he is."

Eliza let the information sink in. She had known Franz since she was fourteen years old. He couldn't be gone. It just wasn't possible. "Do the children know?"

"No." Ethel was concerned for her dear cousin.

"I must talk to them. Please gather them in the parlor." Eliza went to the mirror to smooth her hair and pinch her cheeks. She looked in the mirror. At twenty-eight years old, she wasn't a beautiful woman but she was pleasing and healthy. Her family was her joy, always putting a smile on her lips. But now she suddenly looked old and serious. Drawing up her shoulders, she went to see her children.

*****

Ruth lay in bed that night listening to the crying of her younger sisters. It couldn't be. Papa was gone but everything was the same. The animals still needed to be fed, she even felt hungry. It seemed to her that the world should have stopped at the news.

Though Mama did tell them to pray that Papa returns, Ruth didn't see the point. That Captain carried a gun and the look in his eyes was so cold. As she listened to her sister's sobs, she turned her head to look at the moon. Did Papa see it the other night or was he already gone by then? Would he ever see it again? Sitting on the bed, Ruth pushed her face to the window. Please, God. Please give me a sign so I know. But what sign does God give in this situation?

Her mouth trembled as pain started to rise in her stomach. She pushed it down remembering the last words she had said to her father. I will be brave, she thought, no matter what. She lay down, pulling the covers over her head, trying to shut out the sniffles and sighs of her siblings.

17

One Monday morning a few weeks later, the conference room phone rang in the middle of the sales meeting.

"Let it ring," Alessandra directed when Melissa stood to answer. "Keep going," she said to Scott, who had been describing his last big deal but the phone kept ringing, ruining Scott's presentation.

"Who the fuck calls a conference room?" Alessandra finally exploded. "Melissa, answer the phone and tell whoever it is to stop calling." She nodded to Scott.

Scott tried to get his bearings only to be interrupted, once again, by Melissa.

"Ah, Alessandra, it's for you." She held out the receiver, looking petrified.

"Take a message." Alessandra shook her head in disgust.

"It's your sister Vicky. She said it's an emergency."

Melissa quickly went back to her seat when Alessandra ripped the phone from her hand. Her sister used to interrupt her at work all the time for stupid things like her wedding plans or her kids walking for the first time. Alessandra had finally gotten her to understand that she wasn't to call during working hours. Alessandra never even gave her family her cell number. She just didn't have time for this shit.

"Vicky, this had better be important, I'm in a meeting." Alessandra turned to the wall. "When? Where? I'll be there."

"The meeting is over. Get back to work. We'll finish this tomorrow at 8:30. Stacey, follow me." Alessandra grabbed her things and left the room while everyone sat stunned.

By the time everyone reached the office area, Alessandra was gone and Stacey sat at her desk not saying a word.

*****

The next morning, they reassembled in the conference room to finish the meeting. Alessandra was there, impatiently waiting for everyone to sit down.

"Hurry up! I have things to do. Scott, finish your story. Everyone, take notes. I expect each of you to get five appointments to discuss a deal like this by the end of the week."

While Scott finished describing his great win, Baxter walked by the room and stopped.

"Alessandra?" Baxter looked at her strangely.

"I have to finish some things. Then I'll go." She turned back to the room.

"I think you and I should speak for a moment. Excuse us." He smiled politely to the room as they stepped outside.

"What do you think it is?" Sheila whispered.

"Maybe Alessandra blew a deal," Jenn offered.

"Oh, please. He would have told us to make her look bad," Susan replied, working on her phone.

"Baxter wouldn't be so low," Crystal said. "You obviously don't know what's going on."

Susan raised her eyes at Crystal. "And you do?"

"I can't say." She picked-up her iPhone and began typing.

"Sure you can. You're part of our team. We tell each other everything. Right Sheila?" Susan leaned forward in her seat.

"Absolutely," Sheila said.

Crystal smiled and put her phone on the table. "Okay but you have to swear you won't tell—"

"Crystal, I wouldn't say anything if I were you." Stacey glared at her.

"You're not me." She leaned in to tell the team.

"Crystal, you're making a big mistake," Stacey said.

"Jesus, Stacey, back off," Crystal said.

"It's none of anyone's business what happened with Alessandra. Maybe you should spend some time telling us why Baxter is here today. He's never on this floor." Stacey looked at Crystal.

"You're just jealous because you're not the only one who knows so just sit there quietly so I can talk to the other Sales Reps," Crystal said.

The room sat in silence.

Stacey had once been Baxter's assistant. She started as a temp but soon integrated herself into Baxter's good graces with her ability to get things done quickly, raunchy sense of humor, and discretion. She covered for him when he was out for one of his three hours lunches or when he needed the keys to the company co-op. She loved being part of his inside circle and she always played her part. As a result, Baxter paid her well and made her job easy, taking her side whenever anyone got in her way, even after she was transferred to Alessandra.

But no matter what Stacey had done for Baxter, or what secrets she kept, Crystal was his new protégé and had more power than anyone else had ever had on the sales team.

As Stacey started to speak, the door opened and Baxter walked in shutting the door behind him.

"Hi, everyone. I'm sure you're all very curious about what's happening, but not to worry. You see, Alessandra's father passed away suddenly and being a dedicated teammate, she wanted to finish some things before leaving to attend his funeral. But I want each of you to know that my employees' well-being comes first. At a time like this, Alessandra should be with her family. She'll return in a week or two. Until then, I'm here for all of you." Then he turned and left.

"Guess it's not a secret anymore." Crystal shot a look at Stacey as she quickly walked out the door to find Baxter.

"But it was a secret," Stacey said to the rest of the group. "So how did Crystal find out before any of you?"

18

Exhaustion took over as Ruth fell asleep, dreaming of her father. He was laughing at the head of their dining room table in New York. It was a celebration, but there was no sound as Franz spoke to the family. Eliza laughed, as did the other children, but Ruth couldn't hear, so she silently observed the party. Holding his wineglass in the air, Franz made a speech as everyone raised a glass, even the children with their milk as they used to at home. They all took a drink and went back to their conversations, except Franz, who began to cough, which Ruth heard.

It began as a few gasps that quickly grew into an uncontrollable spasm. Yet no one noticed. Ruth called for her mother but found she had no voice. Not only was she deaf to the conversation, she could not speak as the coughing grew louder in her ears. Ruth attempted to help her father, the sound of his cough echoing in her head, but her legs would not support her. Panic set in as Franz put his hand to his throat, gasping for air. The coughing grew more violent with each moment until it was all Ruth could hear. She woke gasping for air.

Looking around the room, she saw that everyone was asleep. There wasn't a sound. Had she really gone deaf, she wondered? Usually at least one of her little sisters snored or made some sound. Then she heard the cough from her dream outside the window. Looking to the ground, she expected to see Uncle Jacob standing outside the house with his pipe. But he wasn't there. Again, she heard the coughing, louder this time. Could she still be dreaming, she wondered? She stared into the distance, looking out into the forest at the mountain base and her heart froze.

A man was walking toward the farmhouse.

The soldier! He had found them. Papa was gone and now the soldier was coming for them. She threw herself from the bed and ran to Eliza's room.

"Mama!" Ruth opened the door and jumped on the bed. "He found us! I saw him coming out of the forest. He's come to take us!" The girl shook uncontrollably, sobbing into her Mother's breast.

Ethel and Jacob ran into the room. "What's happened?" Jacob demanded.

"Ruth saw a man coming out of the woods. Coming toward the house," Eliza said.

"Stay here," he directed the women. "Do not speak."

All three huddled together on the bed as they strained to hear Jacob's footsteps.

He crossed the kitchen and opened the back door slowly. After a few seconds, it closed with a thump and heavy footsteps sounded quickly across the downstairs floor. Jacob had gone in bare feet. The man was in the house.

Eliza silently turned to Ruth and motioned for her to get under the bed. She put her fingers over Ruth's lips and whispered "Do not say a word and don't come out until I tell you. Stay there all night if you have to." The footsteps rounded the stairs, getting closer.

Aunt Ethel went behind the bedroom door holding a heavy candlestick while Eliza hurried to the far side of the room waiting for whatever would come. The footsteps stopped directly by Eliza's door. The knob turned, slowly releasing the door into the room. Ethel prayed for strength to protect her home and forgiveness from God.

From under the bed, Ruth could see Aunt Ethel's bare feet. As the door swung into view, the heavy candlestick fell to the floor as Aunt Ethel let out a groan. Her Mother's cry came next and a pair of black boots moved swiftly across the bedroom. Ruth panicked in the small space under the bed while her Mother sobbed.

Squeezing her eyes tight, she covered her ears and curled into a ball. She bit her lips together to stifle her cries. Adrenaline buzzed in her ears as she sunk into oblivion until a hand grabbed her. Pulling away in terror, Ruth kicked at the hand. Scrambling from under the bed, Ruth opened her mouth to scream when she saw her mother being held by the soldier.

Aunt Ethel grabbed her from behind, covering her mouth. Ruth struggled to help her mother as Aunt Ethel pulled her away. They wrestled against each other in the small room.

"Help her!" Ruth yelled.

"It's your father." Ethel held her tight.

Ruth stopped fighting and looked. It was Papa! He was here! Her parents held each other tightly as Eliza sobbed into Franz's chest. Ruth stepped toward them but Aunt Ethel held her back, forcing her into the hallway.

"Let me go," Ruth sobbed. "I want to see Father!"

"Your mother needs to see him first." Holding Ruth tightly in her arms, Aunt Ethel consoled her. Ethel held her until she exhausted herself with sobs of relief, and then tucked her into bed.

Ruth looked out the window at the bright full moon. Her prayers had worked. Now everything would be fine and they could go home. The last thought that passed through her mind before she fell into total oblivion was, 'Thank You, God'.

19

The next morning, the children crowded around Franz yelling and hugging him. When he finally settled them on the couch, he made an announcement with Eliza at his side.

"Children, your Mother and I have made plans for us to visit friends in England." He held up his hand to silence their objections. "We know you love it here but tonight we must leave, so go pack your things. When you are finished, you can play but you must stay in the house."

"In the house? We can't even go in the field?" Dieter asked.

"No, Dieter. You must stay in the house. Now go pack your things," Franz said.

"Yes, Father." They each murmured and went to pack. Ruth hoped their friends in England lived on a farm. As she packed, she daydreamed of living with a husband and family on a farm. Coming downstairs to play, she came upon Sara eating pie.

"Sara, are you packed?" she asked her sister.

"I'll do it later." The girl answered rather grumpily. Ruth often had to help Sara because she was the slowpoke of the family. With Mama busy with the younger children, Ruth felt it was her duty to chide her sister.

"You will do it now, as Papa said." Ruth took her plate.

"Give it back, Ruth! It's mine and I'm hungry!" Sara grabbed for the plate. The ensuing argument brought Eliza down the stairs to scold both girls.

"We can't hear ourselves think!" Eliza said just as Johan ran into the house, knocking into Ruth and sending the plate of pie to the floor.

"Good heavens, what is going on here?" Franz came out of the living room, stopping suddenly when he saw the look on Johan's face. The boy was white with purple lips and trembling in fear. He had run so fast, he could barely speak.

"Johan? What is it?" Franz sat the boy on a chair.

"They're coming! They're coming here! Now!" His eyes grew wider as the words began to pour out. "I was delivering milk with my father to the country store and Mister Krieger had just gotten a phone call from another store that SS officers were trying to find an American and they were heading his way. They are stopping at all the houses along the way to see if anyone had seen you. Father made me run through the woods to tell you and he continued his routes so no one would get suspicious."

"How close are they?" Franz stepped closer to the boy.

Johan looked at his Uncle with dread. "Probably two hours away. There's more. They showed a drawing of you. They asked if he had heard of the Königs."

Eliza and Franz looked at each other with dread, and then sprang into action.

"Ruth, get the children downstairs immediately. Grab only their clothes. Gather back in the kitchen in ten minutes," Eliza said. "Sara, you help. Now!" she ordered when the girl didn't budge.

Ruth grabbed Sara, who had begun to cry.

"What's wrong with you two?" Dieter asked as he finished packing.

"We need to pack Greta's and Annabelle's things quickly," Ruth demanded, pulling a small suitcase from under Annabelle's crib.

"We're not leaving until tonight. I'm going downstairs." He turned to Sara "Is she being bossy again?"

Ruth went over and grabbed her brother's shoulders. "They're coming! The soldiers are looking for us and they're not far. We have to go now! Help me pack the girls' clothes and then we'll get Tomas.'"

She turned to gather Annabelle's clothes while Dieter stood immobilized by the news. He snapped to when Ruth grabbed Greta's suitcase from under her bed and threw it to him.

"Pack!" she said and he started throwing clothes and shoes into the bag as fast as possible.

Johan came into the room to break down the cots for storage in the attic.

"We're not done," wailed Sara.

"We have to hide the beds so they don't know you were here," said Johan. "Move!"

Within ten minutes the children were in the parlor while Eliza and Ethel packed food in a burlap bag. A car engine roared down the driveway. Ethel looked out the window waving in relief when she saw it was Jacob. He drove to the back and came in through the kitchen.

"You have to go now. The soldiers are maybe an hour behind me so I cannot drive you to the train. They are searching homes. If I drive you, I won't be back when they arrive here. I cannot leave Ethel to face them alone," Jacob said. "There is only one way you can go."

Ten minutes later, Johan was leading the family through a path into the woods as they carried a tent, sleeping bags, blankets and food. The younger children were carried by the older children to make good time while Annabelle stayed in her Mother's arms.

"Here is the hardest part." Jacob had said when they reached a clearing on the trail. He pointed to a hill on the right. "There is no clear path up this hill which means you won't run into anyone. When you reach the next clearing, do not follow the trail. It will lead you back to town. Instead look closely and you'll see an opening to the left. It leads to a clearing where we often camp. There's a lake close by and a meadow. It will be perfect for tonight."

He hugged Eliza and shook Franz's hand. "I'll come for you tomorrow." Jacob said goodbye to the children with a brave smile then turned back to get ready for the Nazis arrival. The Königs were left to hike through the woods in silence, each of them wondering if they were on the right path.

20

It had been kind of pleasant while Alessandra had been on bereavement leave. Yes, she had texted and emailed, even once during the funeral which caused a fight with her sister.

"I'm sitting in a limo, for Christ's sake. What am I supposed to do? Look out the window?" she had said while typing frantically on her BlackBerry.

The tension in the office was definitely lower, except when Crystal was around. The girl just didn't know how to behave in an office. After getting Melissa in trouble, she decided to befriend Mark, who now gossiped with her to the point that he basically didn't get any work done. Since Alessandra was gone, Crystal somehow thought she didn't need to come in every day either, which was fine with Sheila until Crystal missed a deadline for a proposal. Then Crystal created total chaos to complete a five day project in two hours and, of course, Sheila had to make sure it got done.

Now Alessandra was back but she was leaving in two days for a two-week business trip which meant terse emails at all hours of the night, but at least Sheila wouldn't hear her grating voice. Luckily, Crystal would also be gone on a three-week tour of Machu Pichu that she had planned for the past year and talked about ad nauseam since joining the team.

For an entire three weeks, Sheila could pretend that Crystal didn't exist and fix some of the problems she had created like getting Mark back on track. Sheila smiled as she stepped into the elevator to get lunch.

"Hold the elevator!" Susan called, crossing the lobby in three easy steps. "Thanks. I'm going to be late for my nail appointment because Crystal is truly out of her mind." Susan pulled a lipstick from her Gucci bag.

"Well, she'll be on vacation soon enough." Sheila smiled, relaxing against the wall.

"Maybe not," Susan scoffed.

"What do you mean?" Sheila glanced suspiciously at Susan. "What happened?"

"She came into my office to tell me that Mark couldn't work on my stuff until she leaves for vacation. Mark's not even her assistant. He's mine and he just stares at her like a freaking puppy. Can you believe the balls on her?" Susan said.

"Yes. I deal with her every day," Sheila said. "But why did you say she might not be going on vacation?"

"I told her if she was so busy with work, she should cancel her vacation. Then she started asking me if Alessandra ever asked anyone to cancel a vacation and if I thought Alessandra was mad that she was going on vacation, and if she should act like she didn't want to go because she is so busy." Susan rolled her eyes. "So I told her if she's so concerned, go ask Alessandra if she wants her to stay. I told her Alessandra will love the gesture."

"You did what?" Sheila's eyes bugged out of her head.

"I told her to go ask Alessandra if she should cancel her vacation. Little brown noser will do it, too. It'll be great because you know Alessandra will make her do it." Susan smiled victoriously just as the elevator door opened on the first floor.

"No!" Sheila hit the door close button over and over. "This can't be happening. You're coming upstairs with me to tell her it was a joke. I need her out of the office."

"Sheila, I'm already late." Susan began to walk out of the elevator but Sheila blocked her way.

"Don't you see? Crystal will go to Alessandra and tell her she wants to cancel her vacation and you know that Alessandra will tell her to do it, which means we won't get rid of her for the next three weeks! This means I can't prove to Alessandra that she is just getting in the way! I won't be able to retrain Mark and you'll never get anything done again." The doors closed.

Susan shrugged. "Sorry, but you know she's a family friend of Baxter's. She's not going anywhere." When the doors opened on the fifteenth floor, Sheila left the elevator as fast as possible. Susan sighed and followed behind her.

Sheila had to intercept Crystal before she went to Alessandra's office, she just had to. She turned the corner to the pit. Looking past Melissa, she could see Crystal's office – empty.

Sheila walked down the hall to look into Alessandra's office and saw Crystal sitting in front of Alessandra's desk. She quickly turned back toward the elevators and bumped into Susan.

"Ouch!" Susan said.

"Sheila! Get in here. We need to discuss something. Is Susan with you?"

"Yes," Sheila replied with no enthusiasm, glaring at Susan, who simply shrugged.

Crystal smiled demurely at the women as they walked around the side of Alessandra's desk. For a brief second, Sheila considered keeping her mouth shut and letting Crystal get a severe dose of reality, but then she'd lose her chance for peace and quiet. She had to think fast.

Alessandra was throwing things in her bag and turning off her computer. Before any major travel, Alessandra got her hair done and had her legs, eyebrows and lips waxed, and now she was running late for her appointment. She told everyone it was because she needed to represent the company in the best light. Behind her back, everyone gossiped it was because she got drunk and couldn't get out of bed in enough time to actually shave her legs, and the highlights helped mask her hangovers. Or, as Stacey graciously added, "She just wants to make sure she's in good shape to get laid." Whatever it was, Sheila just wanted Alessandra to go and would do anything to undo the chain of events Susan had put into place.

"Crystal's just told me that she feels badly for going on vacation and leaving us to handle her workload, especially since Melissa can't keep up. Apparently, she had a conversation with you," Alessandra looked at Susan, "and you suggested that she offer to stay because Mark's too busy to help her."

Susan's eyes narrowed, so Sheila jumped in swiftly.

"Crystal's just overwhelmed getting ready for her vacation. I'm sure she's being extra sensitive because she wants to do such a good job for all of us."

Crystal smiled innocently, imagining how Alessandra would tell everyone how dedicated she was.

Alessandra squinted at Sheila. "Really?" She cocked her head. Something was up. Sheila had been complaining about Crystal pretty much since she arrived and Crystal had been backstabbing Sheila since day one. She leaned back in her seat, crossing her arms and legs at the same time. She resembled a lion with her thick mane of hair and her 'fuck you' look aimed at all of them. They were like tiny animals she wanted to bat around before devouring them.

"Susan?" She raised her eyebrows and smiled but really, she bared her teeth.

"Yes?" Susan stared right at her.

"Did you really suggest that Crystal cancel her vacation if her workload is too much?" She leaned forward and put her arms on the desk.

"Well, she was freaking out because she has so much to do before she leaves. I thought she should consider staying, since she's so dedicated." Susan didn't dare look at Sheila. "Ah. Well, it's a great suggestion," Alessandra said. "This is why you're so successful. I can see now why Crystal would follow your lead." Then she turned to Crystal. "Congratulations on stepping up to the big leagues. You're a true team player to stay here and work." Alessandra put her bag on the desk and stood.

Crystal's eyebrows lowered as she moved forward in her chair. Did Alessandra actually take her up on her offer? She panicked.

"Ah, Alessandra." Crystal stuttered, her face red. "I —"

"What?" Alessandra was grabbing her coat from the corner rack. She was now officially late for her appointment but more than that, she was bored with this game.

"It's just that I paid for the plane tickets and the hotel rooms —" Crystal blurted out.

"Expense them. I'm going to my appointment and then I'm gone. You'll hear from me on my BlackBerry, if you're unlucky," she screamed as she bolted down the hall leaving the three women in the office and taking all the air with her.

Crystal turned to stare at the empty door, slowly comprehending that Alessandra had taken her up on her offer. She was actually going to miss her vacation. The vacation she had planned with her friends for the past year. The trip of a lifetime, and now it was gone. With Baxter also on vacation, there was no way to reverse this. Crystal got out of the chair and grabbed her things from her office. Everyone stared as she stomped to the elevator, crying into her phone.

Sheila stood with her lips pursed, staring into space as she realized she wasn't getting rid of Crystal for the three weeks. She sighed and dropped her head to one side. Susan was staring at Sheila, fully realizing how much of a problem this was causing her.

"Let's go get a latte. I'll cancel my appointment." Susan said.

"Yes," Sheila sighed. "Let's."

Susan turned her toward the door, worried that Sheila was going to slip into a coma or something.

"What's going on?" Melissa looked slightly panicked.

"Crystal gave up her vacation to stay here and work," Susan said. No emotion, no sarcasm, just the facts.

"You mean she's not going away?" Melissa's voice raised an octave.

Sheila looked at Melissa realizing that she wasn't the only one looking forward to Crystal's vacation.

"Yes, dear, that's what it means. Now, what would you like from Starbucks? Susan's buying."

21

"So Crystal didn't go away?" Ruth asked, taking a bite of her sandwich.

"No. And she's been insufferable. I don't even think she's making any sales calls. How am I supposed to train someone who not only thinks she knows everything, she doesn't seem to care?" Sheila sat back.

"Maybe you're not supposed to. Maybe you're supposed to let her fail."

"If she fails, I'll fail. And I can't fail at anything else right now." Sheila looked intently at her sandwich. "I just can't."

"At what else did you fail?" Ruth asked.

Sheila looked at Ruth quizzically. "My relationship. Joe left me for a twenty-six year-old."

"Ah, that. Well, I hardly see that as a failure. I think it's almost a blessing." Ruth ate her macaroni salad.

"Blessing? I thought you were on my side." Sheila had expected some sympathy from Ruth.

Ruth laughed. "I am, my dear, which is why I said it. I'm not sure if you've realized, but Joe is a very immature man and experience would indicate that he blamed you for all his shortcomings. Now that he's with someone else, eventually he'll blame her. Then he'll either grow up or move onto someone else. Either way, it stops him from trifling in your life."

"How do you mean?" Sheila was definitely confused.

"Well, first of all, if he's living with her, he can't just call you when he's looking for sex." Ruth said.

Sheila just about fell off her chair at Ruth's bluntness.

"Oh, don't be such a prude. I may be an old lady, but I was once a young woman," Ruth said. "You did live together, after all. Now he can't just call you when he has needs. Secondly, he can't just call you when he's frustrated with his life and pull you into it. You can move on, free and clear."

"But it also stops me from being able to call him," Sheila said. "I mean, I was with him for seven years. Don't I have the right to call him?"

"Oh, Sheila." Ruth couldn't hide the disappointment in her voice. "You're not calling him, are you?"

Sheila just stared at her sandwich.

"Sheila, a man has to be the one to chase a woman. If he isn't chasing you, he's not interested. How can your generation be so educated and still not know that?"

"Things have changed," Sheila said defensively. "There's no stigma in calling a man anymore."

"Well, there may be no stigma, but there's also very little happiness, from what I can see." Ruth shook her head. "A man must feel like he won a prize. If he doesn't, he won't feel like a man."

"You don't know what it's like, Ruth. You were married forever. You've never been left wondering what you did wrong."

"Oh, I know a lot more than you think." Ruth stared past Sheila at her credenza. She still hadn't put away the photos and knick knacks. Why she had let her son convince her to bring them downstairs, she didn't know. Every day they whispered to her, reminding her of things she had long forgotten. Things she found painful to remember. Coupled with the visits from Sheila, it seemed her head was in a different place most of the time. Snapping out of her thoughts, she saw Sheila staring at her, concerned. Poor thing thinks I've lost my marbles. Ruth smiled.

Ruth hadn't intended on telling her life story to Sheila. In fact, there were parts of her story she had never shared with anyone, not even her son, Nicholas. Everyone from Ruth's generation had a bad story from the war or the depression. So why talk about it? Problems didn't make one unique. Plus, people got together to be happy and forget about those things.

Yet Sheila was so fascinated by her stories that Ruth felt it was her duty to share, to help Sheila realize her problems weren't that bad, something Sheila wasn't ready to hear yet. So she would continue to tell her story, enjoying Sheila's company and, hopefully, teaching Sheila that life could be glorious, even after losing someone you love deeply.

22

Franz, Eliza and their brood hiked into the woods for two hours until they found the clearing. They settled in for the night, eating the food that Ethel had packed. But Jacob had not come back the next day. The soldiers stormed into his home shortly after he returned from the woods and searched every inch determined to find the Königs. In fact, the soldiers asked so many questions of poor Ethel that Jacob forbid her to get out of bed, lest she crack under the pressure, sending them all to prison. When the search led to nothing, the soldiers stayed in the area for a week returning daily to harass the family.

In the meantime, the smaller children, led by Ruth, were quickly given the task of finding berries and kindling for firewood every day while Dieter hunted rabbits and squirrels.

Franz chopped wood for a fire. Eliza organized the camp and kept things as fun as possible.

A few days after the soldiers left, Jacob and Johan delivered another tent, a few pots and pans, forks, knives, and spoons plus food, explaining that the family would have to wait before returning to town.

"It is just too dangerous," Jacob said. "I'll bring more supplies as often as I can, but you should try to be as self-sufficient as possible."

*****

Clothing hung on a line strung between two trees while Ruth sorted through dried berries and Eliza prepared dinner. During the summer the family had grown fruit and vegetables in a garden with seeds from Jacob.

"Woo Hooo! Woo Hooo!" The soft sound filtered through the air. Everyone stopped moving and looked to Franz.

"Woo Hooo! Woo Hooo!" he called through cupped hands. A few minutes later, Uncle Jacob and Johan appeared with two bags full of food and a home cooked meal in a big pot from Ethel. Eliza and Ruth rushed to grab the bags. It had been days since the family had finished the bread Jacob brought last time.

The children eagerly grabbed one of Franz's handmade bowls and a spoon from the kitchen pile and stood quietly in a line while Eliza uncovered the pot to serve her family. The smell of the chicken with rice almost made her faint, she was so hungry, but she gave each child a decent ladleful, then Franz, then herself. Thankfully, there was enough for everyone. Ruth took her bowl and carried nine month old Annabelle to a spot where she could prop the baby against a tree to feed her. Franz said grace as Annabelle anxiously waited to be fed.

Everyone else sat on logs that had been moved together to create a dining area in the campsite. Jacob leaned against a large tree while Johan sat on the ground with the children.

"Tell us what's happening, Jacob," Franz said from his log.

"The Gestapo is expelling foreigners by the thousands, mostly Jews. They are being sent to their homelands," Jacob said. "Does that mean we can go home?" Greta asked with a lopsided smile. She had turned seven and was now showing a big gap in her front teeth.

"Not yet, I'm afraid. As a matter of fact, Franz, I was hoping to have a word with you." Jacob motioned away from the family. "We can talk here." Father smiled. The days of privacy were over for the family. "Even if we walk away for a private conversation, everyone will demand to be told. And I've nowhere to hide."

"True." Jacob smiled slightly. "There are refugee camps at the border of Poland. The country won't accept them. In our own towns, the Hitler Youth are gaining power; many are turning on their own parents. They are trying to force Johan to join. There may be a law passed demanding it. Either way, it's getting more difficult for everyone to stay safe. The soldiers still look in our house at random times. I'm afraid we will all be caught if I continue visiting as often."

Father looked over at Eliza, who continued eating her food.

"We can try to meet partway once a month or so, but it has to be at midnight or later. When the snow comes, our tracks will be easy to trace."

"We'll still be here in the winter?" Sara looked at the adults in horror.

"Be still, Sara, and eat your lunch," was all Eliza could manage for her daughter.

So far, the fall of 1938 was mild. A small blessing they all appreciated. But nine-month-old Annabelle had been extremely fussy. More teeth were coming in and she cried quite a bit. Eliza often had to walk with her at night in the tent that Franz, Eliza and the three younger children shared while the three older children slept in a second tent.

"So, we will stay here and take care of ourselves while we strategize how to get to England." Franz look to Eliza, who could no longer eat.

23

Ruth stirred in her sleep trying to ignore her full bladder. In the damp, cold January night, going outside the tent was not appealing. Turning on her side to relieve the pressure, the blankets shifted allowing the cold air to seep into her clothes waking her a bit more. Curling herself in a ball, she chided herself for not going to the bathroom right before bed. At least she could have warmed herself by the fire before crawling between the three blankets she used as her bed.

In the winter of 1939, snow had fallen and the temperature in the mountains was so low that it was too cold to clean their clothing because the fire outside could hardly dry them. Ruth had been wearing the same dress since Christmas. Now the worn collar on her coat scratched against her jaw and the chafing of the fabric under her armpits reignited the burning sensation as she tried to stay warm under the blankets. She had made new outfits for her growing siblings out of the clothing they owned but as the oldest, she didn't have hand-me-downs. Instead of creating new outfits, she became quite good at loosening seams and using strips of extra material to add an inch here and there. She quite liked sewing the clothes for her family. Not only was she good at it, it made them happy for days to wear clothes that fit.

It was no use, the pain in her belly coupled with the cold were no match. Ruth sighed as she pushed herself to sit and looked for the best path to the door. All eight of her family now slept in one tent as a defense again the cold. With all of them huddled together, the tent was warmer but that was a relative term given the circumstances.

"Are you okay, Ruth?" a whisper came from behind. She turned and caught the outline of her mother sitting on a blanket with Annabelle in her arms.

"I have to go to the bathroom," she said. "Can you come with me?"

"No. Annabelle just fell asleep. If I put her down she'll wake up. You'll have to go alone."

Ruth stared at the shadow of Annabelle. The baby cried so hard at night that the sound didn't register anymore. She imagined the poor thing was just as upset about the cold as the rest of them. Ruth wished she could cry and be cuddled. Instead she prepared to go out in the cold by wrapping one of her blankets around her shoulders.

Stepping outside, Ruth moved quickly behind the tent into the still woods. She hated being alone in the darkness. Nothing moved. Even the icy air seemed to hang on her, seeping into her bones.

She much preferred the noise from her family than silence. It scared her. She finally arrived upon the shallow ditch that served as the family's latrine. Careful not to let her clothes and horse hair blanket hit the ground, she readied herself. As relief spread through her body, the sound of snapping twigs echoed throughout the dark silence jolting her to attention and stopping her from what she had come to do. Listening intently, she shut her eyes as if that would help her ears perform better. The animals were gone for the winter so what could it be? After a few seconds, Ruth opened her eyes and tried to finish but it was no use. Shivering, she quickly rearranged her clothes to start back inside when she heard the distinct sound of footsteps snapping the twigs once again. Staring into the darkness, a cold sweat beaded on her upper lip as she felt her legs shake uncontrollably. After what felt like minutes, she slid along the side of the tent, seeing nothing. As she quickly scrambled around the tent to the flap, a strange male voice gently called, "Hello?"

The panic hit Ruth so hard, she couldn't get air into her lungs to scream. Nor could she force her legs to move. She simply stared in the direction of the voice, praying for courage to do something.

"Hello? Franz König?" the voice called again.

Be strong, Ruth scolded herself, but her breath still wouldn't come. Terror wrapped the young girl so completely she could only shake and pray that someone inside the tent would sense her need. She tried to call for her Papa but nothing came out. Leaning against the tent, she shook her head as shallow breaths made her faint. Another snap of the twigs brought her back. Staring into the night, she blinked slowly recognizing the outline of a man emerging from the shadows. Only then did the paralysis give way, allowing her to turn toward the tent. Fumbling for the snaps at the door, Ruth jerked frantically at the cloth wall, banging on it as fear left her cold and sweating. The fabric finally released allowing Ruth to fall into the tent only to be greeted by the click of a rifle.

"Get back!" Franz yelled, pulling Ruth behind him as he stepped outside.

The shadowy figure waved his hands in the air.

"Please, sir. I was sent by Jacob. I am with my mother and sister. We are running from the Gestapo."

"Please, Mr. König," came a woman's voice. "My husband is a doctor who was taken by the SS last night. Jacob sent us here. Please help us."

"Show yourselves, slowly," Franz commanded.

Ruth stared over Franz's shoulder as the group entered the clearing, revealing that there were, in fact, three people. The woman was petite, dressed in a fur coat and heels that looked painful in this setting. With her left arm, she hugged a girl slightly smaller than Ruth, who was wearing a wool coat with a fur hat and muff. On her right stood a young man, tall and beautiful. His features clearly Roman with black hair falling around his eyes in curls. His long wool coat hung from wide shoulders. A white silk scarf draped around his neck.

"I am Vincenzo Scalese. This is my mother, Senita, and my sister, Virginia. My father was taken last night, after the opera. We had to leave the city quickly. Our cousin is Jacob's neighbor and he remembered meeting you. He asked Jacob for help. Please, sir. May we stay? Jacob gave me a note to give you." Vincenzo reached into his pocket and retrieved an envelope.

"Ruth, go back inside," Franz ordered.

In the darkness, Ruth tried to hear her father's conversation but Annabelle suddenly wailed. Even Eliza could not comfort her, no matter how she tried.

"Franz?" Eliza called. "I need help."

Franz re-entered the tent with Senita close behind.

"Do not worry," Franz said to Eliza. "This is Senita Scalese. Jacob sent her and her family. Her husband was taken by the Gestapo last night. He worked as a doctor at the university."

"The baby is unwell?" Senita asked.

"Teething," Eliza replied.

"I have my husband's medical bag." Senita stepped forward, opening the snaps on the well-worn leather bag to grab a vial. "May I?" She held out the vial to show Eliza the Oil of Cloves.

Eliza turned the baby so Senita could put the liquid on Annabelle's gums and the crying stopped almost immediately.

"Thank you." Eliza smiled with relief at the silence.

"If there's anything you need, please ask. I'll do the cooking tomorrow so you can take care of your little one," Senita said. "Thank you so much for your kindness. I'll let you sleep now."

Senita walked to the second tent where her son and daughter sat stiffly on the floor, Vincenzo's arm around his little sister. Tears streamed down Virginia's face. She had been so excited about last night. Having just turned eleven, Virginia was finally old enough to join the family at the opera. For years, she had watched as Vincenzo dressed up to go with their parents. Being sixteen, Vincenzo had been included in many things that Virginia was not yet able to do. The night had been beautiful. Virginia sat on her father's lap in a private box, watching the singers while her father's breath tickled her ear as she leaned against his shoulder.

She had felt so grown up in her fancy shoes and new clothes. As if she was on a date with her father. When the soldiers approached him in the theatre lobby, Virginia didn't think anything bad would happen. She had heard rumors of terrible things they did, but to her young heart, even they had to see this was a special night. When he told Vincenzo to take her and her mother to the car while he talked to some friends, he hugged Virginia close and kissed his wife, then whispered something in Vincenzo's ear.

Virginia didn't think it strange when Vincenzo started the car and drove in front of the crowded theatre as he had begun driving this past summer and took any chance to practice. When they drove past the theatre, she grew concerned.

"You forgot to get Papa, Vincenzo," she said.

"Don't worry, sweetheart. Vincenzo knows what he's doing," her mother answered.

"But he'll be waiting in front!" she said.

"Virginia, my love, everything will be fine," Vincenzo told her.

But it wasn't. As they drove to their street, black sedans were in front of the apartment building where they lived. As Vincenzo turned left well before the scene, Virginia pressed against the window to see what was happening, only to have her world crumble as she saw her father being pushed into the backseat of a black sedan by two soldiers. She had started to cry as Vincenzo sped into the night bringing them to the country and finally this awful tent.

Senita went to her children, hugging them to her. "Don't worry, darlings. They will let us stay."

"How do you know?" came a voice too small for an eleven-year-old girl.

"Because Mrs. König is a mother. She's not going to hurt anyone's child."

*****

True to Senita's word, the Königs had let the family stay, which turned into a blessing for all as Annabelle developed a fever that could only be controlled by medicine from Dr. Scalese's kit. In addition, Senita had prepared the meals and organized chores so Eliza was able to devote more time to Annabelle, keeping the baby comfortable inside the tent without interruption.

As winter turned to spring, Vincenzo was also a tremendous help to Franz, doing some of the tasks his young son couldn't handle, such as properly chopping and stacking logs for firewood. Vincenzo didn't seem to mind getting dirty, which surprised Ruth, based on her first impression of him. His cousins had given them a bag of clothes the night they escaped that were better suited for the forest. Somehow, the rough farmer's clothes only made Vincenzo's good looks stand out more.

"If you stack the wood like this," he showed the children, "it will dry faster and produce less smoke when it burns." He took a small log from Ruth. "I'll handle the rest. Your back must hurt."

"Thank you. Your hands are worse for wear since you arrived." Ruth struggled for small talk.

"Yes, I guess they are." Vincenzo looked at his hands. "I hadn't really noticed. I'm just happy we're safe."

124

"True. I can't believe we've been here for six months already. Have many things changed in Germany?" Ruth asked.

"Well, there are more soldiers and people are more afraid. But people are also pulling together. There's a kindness. As proven here." Vincenzo smiled.

"Were you in school?" Ruth felt her face turn red.

"Yes. I was at the International School in Berlin. My father was training surgeons when the SS decided his services could be used for research."

"Research? What kind?" Ruth asked.

Vincenzo stopped stacking the logs to look at the young girl. Ruth was pretty, with strong features and thick, wavy hair and innocence that was unexpected, considering her circumstances. Yet he knew from the way her father spoke in front of the children that she had been sheltered long before she had gone into hiding. Of course, she had also grown up in America, where they knew very little of what was happening in Europe.

"Let's just say the Führer wants to know many things about the human body and will do anything to get the information." He changed the subject. "The most exciting things are the movies."

"I saw a movie once! It was wonderful. What did you see?" Ruth's eyes sparkled with interest.

"I've seen many. What kind of story do you like?" Vincenzo smiled at her guilelessness.

"Anything but war and hardship." Ruth answered.

"Okay, so not *Gone With The Wind*." He smiled again. "I will tell you about *The Wizard of Oz*."

As Vincenzo told the story to Ruth, the other children came over to listen. He patiently recalled as many details as possible about the movie for the children, with commentary from Virginia, whom he had taken to the theatre. While they all helped with dinner, Virginia taught them the words to *Somewhere Over The Rainbow*, which seemed the most beautiful song in the world, as it was the first new one they had heard since leaving the farm.

While the group ate dinner, Ruth daydreamed about seeing a movie in Technicolor and what the Emerald Forest would look like on a movie screen. Certainly not like this forest. Ruth looked at the trees, barren and covered with snow, wishing that wicked people could simply be melted with water and there were such a thing as red shoes that could take her home safely.

Her reverie was broken by her mother's yell.

"Franz! Senita! Come quickly!"

*****

"40.5 Celsius." Senita looked at the thermometer. "This is the last of the medicine. If we send Jacob to get more, he'll be exposed as knowing my husband. This drug is still in the research phase. She needs a hospital." Senita took a cold cloth and held it to the child's head, causing more screams.

"Franz, you must go now. Jacob and Ethel have to take Annabelle to a hospital." Eliza sobbed.

"I'll go when the sun has set." Franz was pained as his youngest daughter screamed in agony.

"If we wait, she'll be worse," Eliza pleaded.

"We cannot risk being found. We must wait." The two parents stared at each other.

"Everyone go back outside. Leave Eliza to care for the baby in peace," Senita said as she prepared to give Annabelle the last dose of medicine.

But Ruth stayed in the tent with her mother, praying for her sister. She fetched a bucket of cold water and rinsed bits of cloth to replace the ones that almost sizzled upon contact with Annabelle's forehead. After twenty minutes of rocking her baby, Eliza had finally comforted her to sleep.

Sighing deeply, Eliza shut her own eyes. There had been only a few moments of peace for the poor child in the past few days. Eliza prayed, *Please, Lord, help us get Annabelle to the hospital before her pain starts again.* Tears crept down Eliza's face as she silently begged for mercy for her baby.

"I can hold her, Mama. I'll sit right here and you sleep," Ruth said.

Eliza just rocked silently, providing no answer.

"Eliza, you need rest," Senita said gently. "Let us help."

But Eliza could not take their help. Her baby was sick in this awful place when she needed a hospital. The good Lord had sent Senita with medicine but it was not enough. No, Eliza could not let go of her child. She was too afraid of what the Lord was really planning.

"Mama?" Ruth said.

Eliza opened her eyes to stare at her first born. Ruth was Annabelle's favorite. Maybe it would be all right for Ruth to hold her for just a little while. As Eliza moved to accept the help, Annabelle spewed green bile. The poor baby wretched uncontrollably covering her Mother.

"Ruth, get every rag you can find." Senita instructed, moving Ruth out the door.

Eliza held the baby as the sticky ooze soaked into her dress. Again and again, the vile liquid spewed from the baby's mouth until she lay limp in Eliza's arms. Eliza sat waiting for another episode but it seemed to pass. Gently singing a lullaby, Eliza laid her daughter on her lap. Too weak to even cry, Annabelle wheezed pitifully while her Mother stared into her face, trying to get Annabelle's glazed eyes to focus. As she sang, her hands gently unbuttoned the wet dress while Senita stood with a blanket ready to cover her. Annabelle moved her head slightly as Eliza sang a little louder to get through to her child. Moving the dress over Annabelle's head, Eliza stopped singing as red, blistering marks were revealed on the baby's torso. Senita dropped to her knees while Eliza sat in shock. Annabelle moved her head slightly rasping for air. As the two women stared at the child, Eliza began singing again. It was all she could do.

Ruth searched the campsite, gathering scraps of cloth as Senita ran past her to the river where Franz was collecting fresh water. Their eyes connected briefly, but Senita said nothing. Ruth rushed into the tent with the cloths. Her Mother leaned over her bent legs, sobbing uncontrollably.

"Mama?" Ruth quickly scanned the tent for Annabelle, trying to listen for her cries. But there were none. She stepped slowly toward her Mother. "Mama? I have the cloths." Standing over her, she touched Eliza's shoulder, suddenly noticing Annabelle's tiny face staring up at her. The child looked peaceful, her eyes open but unseeing. Ruth froze for a brief moment wondering if she was looking at a doll.

Franz burst through the door, running immediately to Eliza's side on the ground.

"No. No. It cannot be," he cried, holding his wife and youngest child.

The air suddenly became heavy and hot. Ruth rubbed at her throat trying to coerce air into her body but she couldn't breathe. What was happening? Why were her parents crying? Why was Annabelle so still? No. Certainly God would not be that cruel. Ruth backed away from the scene, running from the tent past her siblings, who were being herded into the Scalese's tent by Senita. She couldn't be near them; she couldn't bear to tell them. Blindly running into the woods, she kept going. She had to get away. She could not go back. She ran faster. As tears filled her eyes she tripped and stumbled.

Hands caught her before she hit the ground. Being the son of a doctor, Vincenzo had been taught that death was part of life so when Senita whispered the news to him, he knew he was expected to help. But Ruth still believed in fairy tales and had probably never been close to death. Now the poor thing was hidden in a country torn apart by a vicious war where death would soon touch every person in some way. Vincenzo held Ruth tightly as she fought to get loose, sobbing unintelligible moans that eventually turned to shuddering gasps.

Annabelle's face was etched in her mind and she couldn't shake it loose. How can this happen? Her darling baby sister. All Annabelle needed was a doctor. If they had been home, in America, she would have been fine. But now Annabelle was dead and their family was altered forever. Ruth leaned against Vincenzo for support and continued to release tears of grief for Annabelle's lost life.

*****

It had been like a dream when Vincenzo carried Ruth back to the tents, carefully putting her on a blanket while her brothers and sisters looked to her for answers that she couldn't give. It seemed like hours before Papa came to gather the children to say good bye. Being in the woods, there was no time for a wake or funeral. There would be a burial after prayers in the tent, Franz told them through his tears.

As Vincenzo helped Franz dig the grave, Senita and Eliza dressed the baby for her eternal nap, wrapping her in a large blanket that Franz and Eliza had used for a bedspread. Senita had delicately tried to convince Eliza that the blanket would be of more use to the family, but Eliza only cried harder.

"My baby won't even be protected by a casket. It's all I can give her. She needs it more than I," Eliza wept.

When the time came to say goodbye, the group gathered in the tent and prayed, each laying a hand or a kiss on Annabelle's forehead as her mother sat holding her tightly. But when it came time for the burial, Franz did not want the children to see. "Remember your sister this way," he told them before leaving with Vincenzo to bury the child.

Unable to think of her sister alone in the cold, Ruth ran from the tent, insisting that she join them.

"No, Ruth," Franz said. "You need to stay with Mama. She needs you more."

Senita gently guided the sobbing girl back into the tent while the men went forward into the darkness. When they found a clearing, they worked in silence, digging a deep grave then gently shaking dirt over the blanket, gradually covering the small babe.

The men had dug the gravesite close enough to the campground to visit easily, yet far enough not to be a visible reminder of the loss. When they finished, Franz excused himself to his tent to comfort his family while Vincenzo lit a small campfire to make some tea. Although he was exhausted, Vincenzo needed to warm himself and burn off some of the energy from the last few hours.

As he sat staring at the fire, Ruth came from her tent to squat next to him.

"I need you to take me to her. I need to see where she is," Ruth whispered through tears.

"Ruth, I can't." His heart broke for her. "Your father will be very angry. He will take you in due time. Let me make some tea for you."

"No, you don't understand." She held up a small wooden doll that Vincenzo recognized as Annabelle's favorite toy. "She can't sleep without this. I need to bring it to her, then I'll come right back. Please."

"Ruth." Vincenzo thought carefully. "Annabelle is in a place where there are so many dolls that she can have whatever she chooses. I think she would want you to have the doll, to remember her and keep her near you."

"No." Ruth shook her head, pleading with Vincenzo as tears streamed down her cheeks. "She needs this doll. Uncle Jacob made it for her last Christmas. She loves it. I beg you; I cannot rest unless she has it."

Vincenzo knew Franz would be angry if he brought Ruth to the gravesite. It is one thing to see someone ready for burial; it is another to see the fresh ground covering their resting place. But as Vincenzo looked into Ruth's eyes, he felt an overwhelming urge to protect her from all of this. If doing this would ease some of her pain, he was willing.

"You can never tell your father or mother. I will never forgive myself if I cause them more harm." he said.

"I won't," Ruth whispered. "I promise."

Vincenzo grabbed a shovel and led Ruth by the hand through the trees to a small opening where a mound of dirt was covered by a stone. The moon shone brightly through the leafless trees, shining a light on the spot. Vincenzo stood Ruth next to a tree a few yards away and for the second time that day, he dug up the grave.

"I cannot dig any deeper, Ruth." He went to her side. "Why don't you give me the doll and I will leave it with Annabelle."

"No. I can do it," Ruth said. She walked the few steps to the shallow grave, knelt and placed the doll delicately in the center of the hole. "I love you, baby girl. Sleep tight," was all she said. Then she started pushing the dirt into the hole with her hands, crying again as the pain tore at her heart. Vincenzo came from behind her and knelt down, pushing the dirt with his hands also. When they were finished, he wrapped her in his arms, rocking her as she wept.

When they returned to the tent, the fire was a pile of burning embers but the kettle of water was still lukewarm. He took Ruth's hands and washed them with the water so she wouldn't be caught.

"Thank you. I will never tell our secret," she said.

"Neither will I."

24

Sheila had finally taken the bills out of her desk drawer, arranging the envelopes by return address. Electric, cable, mortgage, insurance, credit cards, HELOC, Sheila dealt the envelopes like playing cards until there were nine piles on the desk. As she padded across the floor to refill her wine, her stomach began to hurt. Sheila worried how she was going to afford everything on one salary.

Sheila sipped her wine as she stared at the piles of bills she had ignored since Joe left. She knew Joe had set up automatic bill pay, so at least the bills were getting paid, but Sheila had no idea what the actual amounts were. True, Joe had given her spreadsheets and explained their finances every three months or so, but Sheila didn't really pay attention. Who knew he wouldn't be around to keep doing this?

It wasn't like she didn't know how to pay bills. Sheila had paid her own bills before Joe moved in. Now it seemed like a big mystery she had to unravel.

Staring at the table from the safety of her kitchenette, Sheila noticed something. The piles for the utilities had three or four envelopes each, but the mortgage and HELOC piles were much larger. There must be a problem with the refinance, since Sheila hadn't called the bank since Joe left.

Grabbing her wine bottle by the neck, Sheila walked back to her desk eyeing the envelopes suspiciously. There were fourteen letters from the bank in a matter of two months. Sheila hadn't listened to any of the messages from the bank, she realized with another jab of pain in her belly. Scrolling through the missed calls on her phone, she found the bank's number and hit the call button, praying that she was being paranoid and everything was fine.

After navigating the phone system for a few minutes and telling the system that she wanted 'customer service' more than once, Sheila was finally connected with a human being and listened in frustration as the woman read a disclaimer that was required by law. After a full seven minutes of being on the phone, the two women finally got to business.

"I'm calling to check the status of my refinance. My boyfriend and I were combining the mortgage and HELOC to lower our payments," Sheila said, biting her lip and hoping that the application was approved.

"Miss Davenport, refinance is handled in a different department. I'm in collections. We have been calling you because the person listed as first contact informed us two months ago that he should no longer be our contact," the lady said rudely. "And I highly doubt your refinancing is still being processed."

"Okay. Well, that's my ex-boyfriend, who did move out since we applied for the refinance, but it's my co-op anyway. I didn't lie on the application," Sheila said nervously. "I can handle the payments on my own. Why is the refinance in collections? Do I have to fill out another application?"

133

"Miss Davenport, did your ex-boyfriend pay your bills, by any chance?" the lady asked, a little nicer this time.

"Yes, why?" Sheila's head swam. Did it matter who actually paid the bills?

"Miss Davenport, I'm sorry to tell you this but there's no chance for a refinance." The lady spoke kindly now. "Your mortgage hasn't been paid for four months. In fact, if the account isn't brought up to date in thirty days, we may begin foreclosure proceedings."

"But he had everything on automatic bill pay." Sheila sank into her chair, her head spinning as she tried to process the information.

"The last payment was in December. To bring your account up to date, you need to pay sixteen-thousand, four-hundred, and ninety-eight dollars and twenty-seven cent to cover payments, late fees and penalties within thirty days just to save your mortgage."

"And then I can reapply for the refinance?" Sheila asked.

"I'm sorry, sweetie." The lady was now full of sympathy, which rarely happened on these calls. "The missed payments have been reported to the credit agencies. You'll never qualify for a refinance now. Plus, the HELOC is being called in already."

"Meaning?" Sheila clutched the phone to her ear.

"Meaning you have to pay the entire sixty-one thousand dollars within ninety days. Can I make a suggestion, honey?"

"Sure." Sheila said.

"You should check all your other accounts immediately. If your ex-boyfriend's this low, he probably stopped paying everything else, too."

25

Baxter stood at the head of the conference table while a relatively young man sat to his right. Sheila tried to mask her concern because the man was Paul Lynch, well known for being basically useless in his current position at the company. However, Paul's father had been an executive at the company for decades so he wasn't going anywhere. At one time, he had been a whiz kid in the magazine world and been named on *AdAge*'s "30 Under 30" list. But now, at forty-three, he'd been in the same office for seven years. Career suicide by today's standards.

"Hello, team." Baxter said. "Let me start by saying, change is good." He showed his megawatt smile to the team.

"Many of you know Paul Lynch, the head of our Business Development Division for the Magazine Group. Not only have I had the pleasure of working with Paul for the past seven years, his father was my first boss over thirty years ago, and a real ballbuster." Baxter turned to Paul as the two of them laughed. "I've known Paul longer than some of you have been alive." He looked around the room for emphasis.

"So it is with great pleasure that I announce Paul's new appointment as VP, General Manager of New Media." Baxter smiled and clapped, followed enthusiastically by Crystal, which pulled everyone out of their shock. "Paul will be responsible for our Profit and Loss for the division and making sure we are well poised for the future. Paul will report to me with a dotted line to Alessandra, who wishes she were here now to share her support about the announcement, but our inroads into the Asian market are a huge part of our future success, so she will be away for an extra week. I'll finish by saying that anyone who works for Paul is more successful for it. Paul, would you like to say a few words?"

Paul cleared his throat and stood. Next to Baxter's six foot frame, Paul was dwarfed at five and a half feet.

"I'm so excited to be leading this team into the next phase. In this tough economy, we need every edge and I plan to get as close to that edge as possible to win new business and keep this division in the black. Together, I know we'll score the touchdowns we need to crush our competition and win the big trophy." He smiled excitedly at the group while searching for a friendly face which he found, of course, in Crystal.

*****

"Oh, he's awful," Jenn said with a mouthful of sandwich. "This is going to be the worst!"

"Any guy who has to use sports metaphors in this day and age is an idiot," Susan claimed. "I know his wife, who's also an idiot, by the way. When did your friend work with him?"

"Five years ago. He was just pathetic. Tabitha had been successful at every job she had, but when she left Paul's department, she told HR that she'd rather see his head on a silver platter than work for him another day," Jenn said.

"Well, you better watch it." Susan pointed at Jenn. "He doesn't like working moms. When his wife had her second kid, he made her stop working."

"That's right!" Jenn's eyes opened wide. "When he had his first kid, he went to his boss and demanded a huge raise, plus, he took accounts away from some of the single reps and took their commissions! You better watch it, too." Jenn pointed at Sheila.

"Great. Maybe Alessandra will run him out." Sheila added more mayo to her sandwich.

"What are you doing? Stop that." Susan grabbed the knife. "Do you want to be miserable and fat?"

"It just doesn't make sense that Baxter's announcing this while Alessandra's not here. Do you think he's trying to get rid of her?" Sheila took Jenn's knife and put more mayo on the sandwich.

"I think he's trying to get rid of all of us." Susan ate her salad. "Think about it. Why is Crystal able to do the things she does? Now Paul's here. God, I hate his wife."

"You said that already." Sheila put even more mayo on her sandwich, hoping to improve her mood.

"I tell you one thing. I'm glad I'm getting married and getting out of here in a few months because it's going to get ugly in there." Susan daintily ate her salad while Sheila and Jenn stared at each other in joint misery.

26

"Who told you to meddle in this?" Alessandra asked.

"No one. I've known Gary Maygar for years. It was no big deal. He felt bad," Sheila said.

"It is a big deal. Crystal went to Baxter and said Melissa screwed up her account. She also said you didn't prepare her properly. He wants to know why Melissa still isn't following orders and why you're not helping Crystal. I can either cover for her or you, not both." Alessandra seethed.

"All I did was help Melissa out of a bad situation," Sheila said.

"Bad situation? She got fucking flowers and was invited to lunch," Alessandra said scornfully. "Please tell me why you needed to get involved in that?"

Sheila stopped to think carefully before she answered. It had all started innocently enough, but like everything involving Crystal, it was now a mess. The reason she got involved seemed pretty stupid now, but when Melissa started crying at her desk the other day, no one could ignore it.

*****

"Why are you crying over flowers?" Stacey asked Melissa.

"Because they're not from my boyfriend and he's really mad." Melissa sniffled at her desk while Sheila, Mark and Stacy looked from Melissa to the gorgeous flowers still on her desk.

"Why did you tell him?" Mark asked.

"I didn't think he'd get mad at me. Now he thinks I like someone else." Melissa wiped her eyes.

"How did you meet this guy?" Mark asked.

"Crystal brought me to her meeting at Scant Advertising. He asked me to sit next to him at the meeting while I was handing out the presentations," Melissa said.

"And you had no idea he was Gary Maygar, the CEO? He's all over *AdAge*, for crying out loud," Mark said. "What did he say to you?"

"Nothing." Melissa was too embarrassed to repeat it.

"Has anyone told you that you are beautiful?" was the first question Gary had asked her, leaving Melissa to blush and smile shyly. "Your profile is amazing. We could use you in commercials. Have you ever done any acting?"

"No." She shook her head and blushed some more. She tried to concentrate on Crystal's presentation, but Gary touched her arm gently.

"Did you put this presentation together or did she?" Looking directly at her, his sharp green eyes left Melissa speechless for a moment.

"Um. I did. Crystal's new on our team and I've been doing this for almost two years." She smiled. Crystal caught her eye and gave her a subtle glare that quickly wiped the smile from

Melissa's face, reminding her that she was there to be quiet and take notes.

After Crystal muddled through the presentation, during which most of the attendees checked BlackBerries and iPhones, she asked for questions. Gary leaned forward in his chair.

"What clients have you worked with that are similar to ours?" He stared intently at Crystal.

"Excellent question, Gary. Our company has worked —" Crystal smiled widely.

"No. I don't want to know about the company, I want to know who you have worked with." He continued to stare.

"Oh, right. Well, I've worked with the same people who have worked on these accounts."

"But you've never worked with these accounts?"

"Not exactly…" Crystal tried to keep her smile bright

He turned from Crystal to Melissa. "Have you worked on any of these accounts?" The entire room looked at her.

"Yes." Melissa said nervously. "Yes, I've worked on most of them."

Gary turned to Crystal. "Which of our clients are you looking to work with?" All heads turned.

"All of them." Crystal smiled and tossed her hair. Then she shot Gary the sexiest look she could but it fell flat.

"That makes no sense. Do you even know our client roster?" He continued staring while the entire team watched in amusement.

"Well, I —" Crystal stammered.

"Yes, she does." And Melissa named them all. Melissa couldn't bear to see Crystal being shamed. True, she was a pain but maybe by helping her, Crystal would be nicer.

"Everyone, let's thank our guests and get back to work." Gary turned to Melissa. "How would you like to go to lunch and talk about some of my accounts? You're too smart for this job. Plus, you're cute." He smiled slowly.

"Well, I've got a boyfriend," she said.

"Then it's just lunch to discuss your career. He doesn't have to know. I'll call you next week."

Melissa sat in a daze. She didn't go on meetings very often. Most of her days consisted of going to the office and going home to her boyfriend. Even though she would never cheat, she was flattered that someone so successful and good looking wanted to call her. She smiled and turned to Crystal to share her enthusiasm but quickly froze. The face staring back at her was filled with absolute fury.

Apparently, Crystal went straight to Baxter as soon as she returned to the office, which is how Sheila found herself in Alessandra's office once again.

"I gave Crystal plenty of opportunities to go through that presentation," Sheila said. "She keeps blowing me off."

"I don't know what's more pathetic; that you can't manage Crystal or that you feel bad for your assistant." Alessandra rubbed her hands over her face.

"Why is it bad that I want to help Melissa? Her boyfriend is mad because she was going to lunch with a guy who sent her flowers. I called Gary and he's going to lunch with me. Really, Alessandra, I think this is getting blown out of proportion —" Sheila said.

"It's bad because I told her to keep Gary interested until we close the deal," Alessandra said. "This is a bad economy and the CEO of one of the best agencies has a crush on our assistant. I don't care how her boyfriend feels about it. I'm using that to my fucking advantage and if you were smart, you would have too, instead of blowing everything.

"So now you're a hero to an assistant and I have a mess to fix. I'm beginning to think maybe you aren't cut out to move up in this company, Sheila. I suggest that the next time you want to fix something, think twice. Now go."

Sheila was speechless. As she walked by Melissa's empty desk, the scent from a bouquet of flowers enveloped her. Although they were two days old, the flowers were still vibrantly fresh and absolutely gorgeous. Anyone would have been thrilled to get an obviously expensive arrangement like this, Sheila thought as she stroked one of the pink rose petals. Unfortunately, the flowers also somehow turned into a problem, as everything involving Melissa and Crystal did. Sheila stepped closer, inhaling the fragrance once more, and then dumped the entire thing in the garbage.

27

Sheila was putting away the groceries she had bought for her night of babysitting, glad she wasn't going to spend another Saturday night alone. Her oldest friend and ex-roommate, Courtney, had called a few days ago in a panic when her baby sitter cancelled. She and her husband, Tom, had plans in the city and Sheila jumped at the chance for something to do. She had just enough time to shower and make sure the place was kid proof when she heard a knock on the door.

"Surprise!" Courtney stood at Sheila's door with a bottle of champagne and a huge smile.

"Where are the kids?" Sheila looked down the hall expecting to see four year-old Sebastian and his two year-old sister, Elizabeth.

"Home," Courtney replied, pushing by Sheila. "I lied about needing you to babysit because I knew you'd say 'no' to a night out with me. Where's the glasses?"

"A night out?" Sheila's stomach fell. "I'm all prepared for babysitting. Look." She pointed at her coffee table covered in Disney DVDs and unopened Play-Doh.

"Don't care. It's for your own good. You've got to go out more," Courtney said. "You are single. Why are you in on a Saturday night?"

"Because I'm babysitting your kids."

"Well, you should have been too busy." Courtney shook her head and handed Sheila a glass of champagne. "Now drink this and I'll pick your outfit while you shower. Just like old times!"

"You're way too perky for a Saturday night in New York. Where are we going, a Broadway show?" Sheila said.

"No, we're going for drinks at the Four Seasons and Cielo," Courtney called from Sheila's bedroom.

"Cielo? We'll never get in there!" Sheila said.

"Yes, we will. You are so lame. When has anyone ever turned us away?" Courtney said.

"Courtney, no offense, but that was at least ten years ago. When we were in our mid-twenties!"

"And now we're thirty-six with money and, I must say, I'm in the best shape of my life." Courtney walked into the living room. "Look at this ass. I didn't have this ass at twenty-seven."

It was true, Courtney's ass had been the recipient of hundreds of Pilates classes a year and did look great in her three-hundred dollar designer jeans. Sheila grew depressed, realizing that her own ass had been sitting in ergonomically engineered office furniture during that time and, therefore, looked nothing like Courtney's. Maybe Courtney was right. Maybe she was getting lame.

"OK. I'll get ready. What did you pick for me to wear?"

*****

Sitting at the bar in the Four Seasons, Courtney practically moaned over her Cosmopolitan.

"I forgot how delicious these are. Why didn't you get one?" Courtney asked Sheila.

"Because no one drinks them anymore and they're deadly. You better not have more than two if you want to make it home tonight," Sheila warned as she sipped her white wine.

"That's ridiculous. It's a night out. Plus, I'm staying over." Courtney sipped again. "Perfection. Now, let's see who you can flirt with."

Sheila ordered appetizers, ignoring that last comment.

"Seems like a lot of older guys here." Courtney clearly wasn't pleased with the selection.

"We'll, its 7:30. All the younger guys are napping so they can go out at eleven. But don't worry, I ordered Chicken Satay to keep us awake," Sheila said.

"Seriously, Sheila. You have to stop making jokes about this. I know you think it's too early to move on, but remember, I met Tom only a month after William and I broke-up. You need to trust me," Courtney said.

"You and William dated for seven months."

"Yes, but at the time, seven months was a larger percentage of our lives. And I was in love with William. Don't you remember how I was devastated?"

"Where do you come up with this stuff? Seven months doesn't equal seven years unless the person is four years old," Sheila said.

"Well, you can't wait too long, sweetie, or you know what will happen." Courtney threw her a knowing look.

"No. Tell me."

"You won't be able to get anyone because you'll dry up."

Sheila moaned and rolled her eyes at Courtney. "Are you still reading *Cosmopolitan?*"

"Yes. They have great sex tips, so don't laugh. Remember how Helen couldn't get a date for, like, three years?"

Sheila choked on her drink. "Helen didn't get a date for three years because she was gay and didn't want to come out. In fact, she was getting more sex than any of us with her boss, Jill, who was married. Now she lives in Vermont with her partner, Susan, and they have a son."

"You're kidding. I just thought she was giving off bad vibes or something." Courtney motioned for more drinks. "Well, OK. So she's not a good example. But you know what I mean. Look at Nikki. After she and Carl broke up, she's been insane and she looks pretty bad, too."

"Carl left her with three kids under the age of five and she had to go back to work full time. Plus, his new wife doesn't want his kids in the house. When is she supposed to find time to date?" Sheila said.

"I have three kids and go out plenty."

"And an au pair," Sheila interjected. "And no job."

"Raising my kids is a full time job. Do you have any idea how much I volunteer at their school?" Courtney said defensively.

"Yes, but if Tom left and took most of your money, your life would be completely different," Sheila said.

Courtney stared at the bottles behind the bar, weighing that comment.

"Look, you've got a great life." Sheila tried to diffuse the situation. "You just need to go easy on the rest of us who don't have it so great right now."

"Thank you." Courtney smiled at the compliment. "I just want you to have a great life, too, so let's get out of here and go to Cielo." She took her purse from the bar and swung her long legs off the stool practically kicking a handsome man approaching her.

"Sorry." Courtney said with a shrug.

"No worries. I don't mind getting kicked by legs as gorgeous as yours." He leaned in with a smile. "I see you're on your way out, but I couldn't miss the opportunity to at least give you my card. If you're interested in getting together, contact me." He squeezed her arm and walked to the men's room.

*****

"See? Plenty of men around." Courtney waved his business card at Sheila as they tried to hail a taxi. "You could be going out with Ashley if you had taken the time to smile and maybe do a few of those hair flips you make fun of. Ashley Madison. That's a nice name."

"His name isn't Ashley Madison, Courtney. Ashley Madison is a dating site," Sheila said.

"Ah, online dating. You should try it. Here, you call Ashley. Tell him I'm married and say you really liked him."

"Well, he's not going to be interested in me," Sheila said.

"Sheila, you need to stop putting yourself down. You are a fabulous single woman who has a lot to offer." Courtney said as a yellow taxi stopped for the women and they got in.

"Well, that's the thing." Sheila tried to figure out how to tell this next piece of news to her friend who clearly wasn't listening. "He's not looking for someone single. You see, Ashley Madison is a site for married people who are looking for affairs."

Courtney stared at Sheila blankly while this information registered.

"What do you mean dating service for married people?" Courtney said.

"Their tagline is, *Life is Short. Have an Affair*, so that should tell you all you need to know," Sheila said.

"You mean this is a SERVICE for married people who want to cheat?"

"It's actually a website," Sheila said.

"And I've just been propositioned by a married guy who is actively looking for someone to cheat with?" Courtney said.

"Yep. He's just one guy. There will be others. Get out there and keep meeting them, you'll find the right one," Sheila joked.

"It's not funny," Courtney pouted. "I mean, I'm married and this thing is out there, making it easy for husbands to cheat. Before their only option was having an affair with their

147

secretaries and since Tom is forty-five, I know that's not going to happen. I'm sorry. I didn't mean that."

Sheila stared out the taxi window, trying to push away the hurt, but it wasn't just the hurt about Joe. The entire night had been awkward. Since Courtney had had her third child, their phone conversations were brief and farther apart, but Sheila had never seen how different their lives really were until now. Courtney would look to Sheila for reassurance about her latest fight with Tom or some mother at school and Sheila could gossip about her coworkers or Joe, knowing her words couldn't come back to haunt her.

They were a lifeline to a time when things had been simple. When they were young, single and new to Manhattan. It was comforting and safe to know each was there – a touchstone. In reality, they didn't have much in common anymore. Since Sheila's life was now reliant on her friends and her job, the thought made her stomach turn.

They sat in silence for the rest of the ride. As they pulled in front of Cielo, the line snaked around the corner.

"Come on. Forget what just happened. Let's go dance." Courtney smiled weakly, and then walked to the doorman.

Without looking up from his clipboard, he asked "Are you on the list?"

Courtney threw him her signature smile and said, "Yes."

"Name?"

"It's right there." As Courtney pointed to the list, a rolled twenty dollar bill landed on the clipboard. She winked at Sheila and waited for the rope to move.

The doorman casually noted the bill, and then wiped it off the clipboard on the ground. "You're not on the list; you've got to wait in line."

Courtney's smile froze as some people at the front of the line snickered.

"Excuse me." She touched his arm. He finally lifted his head to give her an incredulous look as a gigantic bouncer stepped forward.

"Let me explain. My friend and I are celebrating and we'd really like to celebrate here. There must be room for two attractive women in there," Courtney continued smiling.

"There is a lot of room for attractive women in there. But here's the thing, I have a certain kind of clientele here and they expect to see 'attractive women' like them." The doorman pointed to the line where at least a hundred people waited to get into the club, every one of them prettier than the next. Then he looked Courtney over from head to toe and went back to his clipboard.

"Come on. We look like them. We're great for your clientele," Courtney cajoled and flipped her hair circa 2000.

"Listen." His sigh clearly communicated his boredom with this conversation. "You're what? Forty?"

"I'm only thirty-six!" Courtney's eyes widened in horror.

"Uh-huh. From the suburbs, right? Thought you'd come here and hang out? Pretend its 1999 again? And I'm supposed to be so flattered that I'll just let you in? Sweetheart, do yourself a favor, go somewhere else. Or better yet, go home, where you belong." He turned slightly, pressing the earpiece closer to his ear and gave a signal to the bouncer, who let six people into the club.

"Courtney, come on. We'll go someplace else." Sheila reached for Courtney's arm but Courtney pulled away, still looking at the doorman, her smile now gone.

"My husband comes here all the time. He's got a VIP card."

"Well, you don't. But they do, so you better move." The doorman pointed past Courtney's shoulder and she turned to see three women approaching the VIP rope. They were absolutely stunning. Every one of them must have been six feet tall and dressed to perfection with just the right amount of skin showing to look sexy and classy at the same time. Their bodies were perfectly sculpted, tanned and young. As they walked toward the club, the bouncer unclipped the velvet rope allowing each girl to pass without breaking her stride. They continued through the door into the club, never once acknowledging Courtney, who

149

had almost been trampled as if she were on safari in Africa and came across a group of giraffes.

"Renaldo, please take care of this lady." The doorman went inside the building without another look in her direction.

Renaldo bent and picked the rolled twenty dollar bill off the ground, held it out to Courtney and said, "Lady, you need to go." Courtney turned on her heels and left without the money.

"Are you okay?" Sheila asked after walking an entire block in silence.

"Of course. Screw them. It's their loss." Courtney shrugged. "We'll find someplace better."

"Courtney, please. Let's just go to a movie or get something else to eat. I'm starving," Sheila said.

But Courtney was already looking at her phone.

"No. We are not two old ladies that can be turned away. We will stay out until 4 a.m. and dance and be young again."

Watching Courtney swipe at her phone in a minor rage, Sheila realized that Courtney wasn't here to rescue Sheila or help her at all. This night was about her.

During their entire friendship, Courtney had been at least one step ahead of Sheila and therefore, always able to give advice and direction on the road Sheila's life should take. She had told Sheila not to wait too long for Joe to give her that ring but clearly, Sheila had gone a different way. It gave Courtney another notch on the expert belt that Joe never proposed. But now Sheila was single and Courtney thought she would fix everything, show her how it's done. Instead, Courtney's plan wasn't working. She been propositioned by a married man and humiliated by a doorman at a club her husband went to all the time. Not only was Courtney realizing that she wasn't an expert on life, the night was ruining her illusion that if she were suddenly single, she'd be fine.

"Courtney, what's going on?" Sheila said.

"You need fun and I'm going to get it for you."

"I need fun or you need fun?"

"What's that supposed to mean?" Courtney scoffed, poking at her phone.

"Is this really for me or is it about you? Because going to that club and talking to any one of those people would have been torture. I don't need any more meaningless conversation. I have them all day at work."

"I think you're being a little ungrateful, Sheila. I'm just trying to help you," Courtney said, finally looking up from her phone.

"But all your help isn't helping. In fact, you keep telling me to do all the things that were fun in our twenties which aren't fun now," Sheila said.

"That's ridiculous!" Courtney's drew herself up. "These are things plenty of people our age do. I just went dancing with a group of friends last month!"

"At a fundraiser in the suburbs, not in New York."

"We still had fun. Believe it or not, people have fun outside of New York City." Courtney had started to shout.

"It's not the same as getting into Cielo!" Sheila said.

"Well, Tom goes there all the time!"

"But you don't," Sheila said in a tone she usually didn't use with Courtney.

"Tom takes me into New York all the time. And we go with our "boring suburban" friends who love it!" Courtney pushed her hair behind her ears, a sign that she was upset and usually Sheila's clue to stop, but she couldn't this time. No, if Sheila was ever going to feel good about their friendship again, she had to push back.

"But he doesn't take you to Cielo. Is that why you're so determined to go there? Because I know this has nothing to do with me." Sheila said.

"I can't believe you're saying this. I try to be nice and take time away from my family —"

"But I didn't ask you to!" Sheila finally flipped. "YOU showed up at my door with this plan. I thought I was babysitting. You didn't even ask what I wanted to do. You TOLD me what we were doing. And I went along with it thinking you must know what you're doing, but you don't! Not this time."

Sheryn MacMunn

"Well, I'm so sorry I tried to get you out of your apartment to find a boyfriend. I get it. There's no one out there for you. I guess I'll just hang out with friends who appreciate a good time and you can sit alone." Courtney turned and walked away but Sheila ran to follow right beside her.

"I never said there was no one for me. I said there's no one for me in Cielo or a bar. I'm thirty-six for Christ sake, not twenty-four! I think I know what I need and I'm not going to find a boyfriend in there. Anyone that goes to that club is only looking to get laid."

Courtney's face fell, sending Sheila's heart to her toes. They stopped walking and stared at each other. The secret was out. After what seemed like an eternity, Sheila spoke first.

"What's going on, Court?"

"I don't know," Courtney said softly. "Ever since Joe cheated on you, I've been watching Tom for signs that he might do it, too. They work in the same industry and Tom's assistant adores him. He's out three nights a week for business and always tells me it was dinner or some game at Madison Square Garden. But I'm not stupid, I know they go to strip clubs, they always did. But when we were younger, it didn't matter. I thought it was cool and I was cool for accepting it. He shared his raunchy stories and I felt like I was part of that world. Now he keeps things from me. I just find the receipts and when we go out with other couples, the guys talk business while I talk diapers and PTA meetings." Courtney looked at Sheila hopelessly. "I don't have a career. Tom pays all the bills. All my friends are moms in the same situation and we all get together at school and look our best and not one of us mentions that our husbands were out until 3am or didn't come home at all. We just work out, look good and take care of the kids. It makes me want to scream. So I tell myself, if Tom ever does leave I'll find someone else. Now I came to show you how to do that and show myself that I've still got it. That I'm not just Tom's wife and a mom with no options. But I don't have it. If I were in your position, my life would be over." Tears slid down Courtney's cheeks.

152

"First of all, you love your life, so of course you'd go crazy thinking it might end." Sheila put her arm around Courtney's shoulders. "Second, you don't even know if Tom's cheating. And Tom's not Joe, he married you. I never even got a proposal."

"It's just so unsettling. Everything's upside down," Courtney said.

"I don't know how different a marriage is from living together, but if I had to do it again, I would have trusted my gut more. I never thought Joe was cheating, but there were times when I didn't feel he was really committed to me. But I let it slide. I thought, when we get married that problem will be fixed." Sheila laughed at her naiveté. "I would have said the difficult things because ultimately, whatever the situation, it will come into the open. At least I would have found out sooner."

The two women stared in different directions, exhausted from everything that had been said. The truth was out there and now they had dealt with it. Most importantly, they were still there, leaning on each other, just like old times.

*****

Thirty minutes later, they were sitting on Sheila's couch in pajamas with their hair in ponytails.

Courtney grabbed a pint of New York Super Fudge Chunk and said, "Let's watch the first season of *Sex And The City*."

It was just like old times.

28

While the war swept through Europe in the summer of 1942, the two families grew their gardens to prepare for the next winter knowing that it was pointless to dream about being rescued now. Germany had occupied most of Europe and had now officially declared war on the United States. It was rumored that General Eisenhower was in Europe getting ready for the fight.

Eliza and Senita had taken a cooperative approach to raising the children. The chores were divided with Ruth in charge of the girls and Vincenzo looking over the boys. After chores were finished, the ladies taught the children lessons, mostly literature, though some math was included. But concentrating in the fresh summer air was difficult, so they were often allowed to play or try to catch fish in the river.

Being sixteen, Ruth felt too old to play games, preferring instead to keep busy with more chores. Now that she was bigger and stronger, she was in charge of the garden and doing the laundry in the river, which allowed her to keep moving so she wouldn't think – or remember. It still didn't seem real that Annabelle was gone, even two years later. When Annabelle died, Ruth felt the pain acutely. In many ways, she felt that Annabelle was almost her own baby. She had been home when Mama delivered Annabelle in the bedroom and was the first to hold her, even before Papa. Annabelle had been the first baby that Ruth had changed and bathed. When Franz finally took the family to the grave that spring, they made a small monument of stones. Even at the time, Ruth hadn't told anyone how she felt. No, that would have been selfish as she knew everyone else suffered, too. Instead she took care of her mother who was unable to get out of bed for weeks. It wasn't until Eliza overhead Greta telling Senita "I'm glad you are here. Now I still have a Mama," that Eliza found the strength to get out of her bed.

But Ruth didn't have other children to fill the void. In fact, she felt quite apart from her siblings when they began to play games again and behave, well, like children. Not wanting to burden her mother or father, she kept her pain to herself, reading the few books they had over and over again. It was Vincenzo who tried to reach her in those early days. Although his father could still be alive, he understood the hole in Ruth's heart and the unfairness of it all when a family is torn apart. He missed his father every day yet never said a word. It broke his heart to see her youthful innocence destroyed. He had seen it in his sister the night of the Opera; it angered him then as it did now.

So Vincenzo made a point to read the books that Ruth read and talk to her about them. Her point of view was often astute, making the conversations interesting. He also helped with her chores when the laundry was too heavy or she had been in the garden too long. She was really quite an interesting girl, he thought more than once.

When food was scarce, Vincenzo often gave Ruth some of his even though he went hungry. After Annabelle died, Ethel became consumed with guilt and brought hot food herself until

Eliza told her it was too dangerous. So Jacob brought a few chickens and materials for a coop to give the family eggs on a regular basis, fishing rods, and a small shotgun to hunt rabbit and other small game.

Ruth, for her part, was forever indebted to Vincenzo because he never told their secret. In fact, he carved a little doll like Annabelle's and gave it to Ruth so she would be connected with her sister forever. The doll stayed in Ruth's pocket at all times as a talisman.

"You look tired," Vincenzo said as Ruth worked the garden.

"I am." Ruth stretched her back. "But it's okay."

"You know, the summer weather won't be around for long, and we'll go back to huddling around a fire for warmth. Why don't you take a break and have a swim in the river? I notice you haven't done much swimming this summer," Vincenzo said.

Ruth blushed. It was true. Swimming with the family wasn't something she enjoyed anymore. Her body had changed over the winter, leaving her embarrassed to remove her clothes and swim with the others. Her mother offered to make her a swimsuit out of old clothes but that just made the difference in her body more pronounced, so she hadn't had a swim yet this year.

"Why don't we go to the river? If you don't want to swim, we'll at least put our feet in the water and have some fun. I will finish the gardening later," Vincenzo said.

"No, I need to finish or we'll be behind when autumn comes." Ruth kept working.

"Ruth." Vincenzo came and touched her arm. "The garden will be fine while you take a small break." He looked at her, concerned. "Please, let's do something fun."

Ruth looked into Vincenzo's eyes, fully intending to say 'no,' but somehow answered 'yes' and off they went.

Ruth immediately felt cooler as she waded into the river, the water swirling around her knees. Oh, she did miss the feeling of just jumping into the water uninhibited, but this would do. Vincenzo kicked some water at her and they laughed, splashing each other in the hot sun.

"Why don't we go for a swim?" Vincenzo suggested, but Ruth demurred.

"I don't have anything to dry myself," she said.

"We'll lie in the sun." Vincenzo took off his shirt and threw it onto the land.

Ruth turned away at the sight of his naked chest. Feeling her face turn red, she looked across the water. Just last year, she had played with everyone in the water without a care, but now she froze. Her stomach felt warm and tingled, a sensation she had experienced a few times when Vincenzo was around. He splashed at her, but she couldn't look his way.

"Ruth?" Vincenzo said.

"I think I'll go back. You can stay and swim," Ruth said and started for the shore.

Afraid that he had hurt her feelings somehow, Vincenzo ran to get his shirt and caught up with Ruth. Touching her shoulder, he stopped her and stepped forward to look into her eyes. "Is something wrong? You seem upset," he said.

"No. I'm not upset," Ruth said. "I just don't want to swim right now. But you should."

"I don't want to swim without you. We can do something else." Vincenzo continued looking at her face for clues. "I just thought you would enjoy swimming like we did last year."

Ruth didn't know what to say because she didn't understand it herself. She didn't have her monthly bill, which had started a few months ago, so she could have gone in the water. She was just uncomfortable in her body. It seemed gangly and awkward and she did not want Vincenzo to see her that way. Ruth looked back into Vincenzo's eyes and saw that she had hurt his feelings. Unable to help herself, she started to cry.

Vincenzo watched Ruth with total confusion. All he wanted was for her to have some fun instead of worrying about the garden or how much food the family would have for winter. All he ever wanted was for her to smile and now she was in tears, unable to look at him. Vincenzo put his arms around Ruth and held her close.

His hug felt good. Ruth forgot that Vincenzo had always had her best interest in mind. Through the years they had lived in hiding, he had never been anything but kind. So Ruth took a deep breath and told him why she didn't want to swim and many of the other feelings she had which she feared made her a bad person. Other than not knowing how to deal with the changes in her body, Ruth really found being around her siblings tedious and her parents didn't seem to really see her. It was only with Vincenzo that she felt camaraderie and now she was afraid she ruined it.

After listening to her patiently, Vincenzo wiped the tears from her face with his shirt, smiled and said, "You are not so strange. You are growing up, that is all. Remember, I was sixteen when I arrived here. It is not bad to want to be with someone close in age to you. I feel the same way about being with you."

Their eyes connected, blocking all sights and sounds around them. The tingling in Ruth's stomach spread to her arms and legs as she looked in Vincenzo's eyes. Gently taking Ruth's face in his hands, he drew her close so she could feel his warm breath on her skin, Vincenzo said "Ruth, you are so beautiful, let me take care of you."

All thoughts flew away as Vincenzo lightly pressed his lips to her. It was the first kiss for both. That sweet moment when young lips touch, making the head spin and ears buzz, causing one to lose their breath in anticipation of all that can lie ahead.

"I will always take care of you, Ruth," Vincenzo whispered. "And I think you are beautiful."

For a few moments more, the two young lovers kissed innocent short kisses, afraid to break the spell. Then they hugged each other tight and silently turned back to the camp, holding hands until they got so close that someone might see. Neither felt like they were doing something wrong, but being young, they wanted to keep this a secret. Even if they did want to share it with their families, it would have been impossible. Being so secluded from society and raised in hiding, Ruth and Vincenzo didn't have the language to convey that they were truly in love.

*****

Ruth had been so distracted when getting ready for dinner that she forgot to give everyone the tiny bits of old cloth they used as napkins, a detail her mother noticed. When Ruth finally received her plate of food, instead of eating it as quickly as possible, she played with it, daydreaming.

"Ruth, are you okay?" Eliza asked feeling Ruth's forehead for fever.

"Mama, I'm fine." Ruth ducked away, embarrassed at being treated like a child while sitting next to Vincenzo.

Eliza stepped back to the fire, stunned. That was the first time one of her children had pulled away from her. As any mother, Eliza felt relief when her children passed certain stages, but she really didn't like this sign that she was unneeded.

"It's hard when they grow up." Senita smiled sympathetically at Eliza, handing her a bowl of food. "But the adults they become bring a whole new joy."

"Yes." Eliza was happy to have someone who understood. Senita would have gone through this with Vincenzo. Looking back at Ruth, she suddenly saw a young woman instead of her responsible oldest daughter with pigtails. Working hard to survive every day, Eliza had treated the changes in her daughter's body as something to handle. Finding dressing for periods, new clothes to fit her growing breasts and hips were just another thing to get through. There were no joyous milestones such as school dances or graduations to measure her life so Eliza had somehow missed that her little girl had, in fact, grown up.

Staring at her daughter in this new light, she relaxed to see Ruth's dour expression had all but disappeared. It was as if Eliza had just been given a gift and she would honor it by treating her daughter like an adult, talking to her about life and love, marriage and family. It was time for her to learn. As Eliza gazed with love and appreciation, she noticed Ruth's beautiful smile as she laughed at Vincenzo's words and tossed her hair over her shoulders. When Vincenzo casually put his hand on Ruth's knee, however, Eliza dropped her bowl.

*****

"But, Franz, this is not unreasonable," Eliza said gently as she hugged a sobbing Ruth. Over the past few weeks, Ruth and Vincenzo had spent the same amount of time together, but were conspicuously different, gaining the notice of Franz who was not happy.

"I understand, Eliza, but this situation is not suited for courtship," Franz said.

"Why not?" Ruth said.

"Well, to start, you are too young," Franz said.

"That's not true. Mama had me when she was sixteen." Ruth lifted her head from Eliza's shoulder.

"That was different. There is a lot you don't know about life yet. When the war is over, you will see that," Franz said.

"And when will that be, Papa? Can you tell me? Because I remember we were only supposed to be here for a night or two and that was four years ago." Ruth shuddered for breath while Eliza rubbed her shoulder.

"Ruth," Eliza tried to comfort her daughter. "I know how you feel. I was sixteen once, too. But I met your father as part of a community. We were chaperoned. This life isn't real."

"Isn't real?" Ruth said. "Yes, it is! It most certainly is real and it's the only life I have. This war could last forever. It's not my fault I don't live in a community, Mama." She started crying in earnest again.

"One day we will be free and you will go back to America while Vincenzo goes to Italy. What then?" Franz said.

"Vincenzo will come to America and live with me in New York. We already promised each other." Ruth cried again.

"Has he asked you to marry him?" Eliza gasped.

"No, but he will. He's going to talk to Papa," Ruth said.

Eliza put up her hands to calm her husband. Thankfully the three had gone to the river to talk privately, so no one was around to hear this. Franz was livid. All Eliza's warnings about young girls in love were forgotten when he realized that Ruth had no intention of obeying him. It was turning into a mess, with Franz and Ruth being similar in their stubbornness. He stared at his daughter not knowing what to say. She stared back, however, looking as though she had plenty to say. As Ruth opened her mouth, Franz raised a pointed finger ready to battle when a voice yelled 'Halt!'

Franz and Ruth stared at each other for a moment in confusion. It sounded like it came from the campsite. They looked around expecting to see Vincenzo. Had he followed them? Eliza moved forward, taking Franz's arm. They waited in silence but no one came. Franz turned back to his daughter, had she told Vincenzo to join them? Had she gone behind his back? This was going to stop. He pointed his finger at her again when a blast of panicked, shrill screams came from the camp.

All three ran through the woods to the camp while more screams and cries filled the air. Franz arrived to the tents first, but he stopped in his tracks. Nazi soldiers surrounded his children and the Scaleses, all huddled together in tears. Waiting patiently in the center of it all was The Captain who had chased them all those years ago.

"Professor König. You are surprisingly resilient. We thought you'd be hiding in another country and here you are, in our own backyard. How lovely." The Captain stared at Franz before turning to look at the frightened group huddled before him. "You've gone to great lengths to keep your family together. They must mean a great deal to you."

"You must be an orphan, Captain, to not know the power of family. Maybe that is why you chose to join the Nazis. Is there no one to love you?" Franz walked forward and stood between his children and the soldier. "I would do anything to protect my family and keep us together."

"Well, Professor, you shall have your wish." He signaled to the soldiers, who locked their guns on the Königs.

"March!" called the Captain.

The family looked to Franz in stunned silence. "Let's go. Stay together."

As the soldiers led them from the campground that had been home for the past four years, Ruth stopped to make sure her younger brothers and sisters went ahead.

"Keep moving!" a soldier shoved Ruth from behind. In a few quick steps, Vincenzo was there to catch her as she stumbled down the path. He moved her swiftly from the soldier's reach and held her tight as the group continued walking.

Her anxiety grew with each step. There was no conversation and no indication where they were going. Ruth clung to Vincenzo's hand as they walked in total silence. Ruth had not been away from the camp since they arrived, therefore, she had no idea where she was going. Was it the way to Uncle Johan and Aunt Ethel's? Had the soldiers been to the farm and harassed them into giving information about her family?

She was absorbed in these thoughts until she heard the sound of running motors. They couldn't be near town so soon, could they? She peered through the trees. Instead of a village road, she saw a landing with four wagons and more soldiers pointing guns at the group.

"All of you, climb in. The Königs first," The Captain yelled.

Franz walked to the nearest wagon and held his hand to Eliza to climb on first, then assisted each child as they settled into the back. Ruth was the last to climb on, assisted by her father and Vincenzo. As she settled onto the hard metal truck bed, Franz held his hand out to Senita. The Captain gave another signal prompting two soldiers to pull her and Virginia from the group while another pushed Vincenzo to the ground.

"You are not going with them. Your husband has given us our information. I have a different destination for you and yours," the Captain said.

Senita looked in terror while a soldier pointed his rifle into Vincenzo's chest as he lay in the dirt.

"Mr. König, if you love your family, I suggest you get in the wagon," the Captain said.

Franz climbed aboard quickly.

"No!" Ruth stood as another soldier shut the tailgate.

"Aah. What is this? We have two young lovers? I noticed the two of you walking together." The Captain sauntered to Vincenzo. "Let him up."

Vincenzo sprung from the ground. "Ruth, sit down," Vincenzo pleaded as she stared back.

"This is so sweet." The Captain turned to smile at Ruth. "Are you helping each other during this horrible time? Turning your love of the resistance into something more?" He turned back to Vincenzo and whispered. "You should know your father may not approve. He has seen the way and was helpful to us. You should be proud."

"My father hated you," Vincenzo replied while his sister stifled a cry at the mention of her Papa.

The Captain smiled slightly. "That was before he knew he could save your life. Now you have fallen in love with a German from one of the most respected intellectual families in the area. Though her father isn't as cooperative as yours." He put his face close to Vincenzo's, staring at the boy with malice so deep, Senita began crying. Vincenzo didn't flinch.

"Are you in love with her? Have you promised her you will always be true?" the Captain mocked. "I guess since your father was so cooperative, I should let you stay together. Then you can tell your story of love for years to come."

The Captain turned with a smile and a wave at Ruth, who sat expectantly, waiting for her young lover. He then patted Vincenzo on the shoulder and laughed.

"But since they will be on the losing side of this war, I will do what is best for you."

Motioning two soldiers forward, he said quietly, "Don't let him move." Then the Captain turned back to Ruth, shrugged his shoulders and waved his hand in the air. The wagon began rolling away.

Ruth fell as the wagon lurched, landing on the hard metal bed. What was happening? Why wasn't Vincenzo coming? The Captain had smiled at her, and then shrugged. Had he given Vincenzo a choice? Did he decide to stay?

"Stop!" Ruth screamed. "Stop!" The wagon kept rolling, turning onto a path, but she did not notice. She could only stare at Vincenzo. Desperate to stay with her love, Ruth moved to throw herself over the side of the wagon but her brother wrestled her to the floor.

"Let me go!" she screamed. "Stop! I need to talk to Vincenzo!" She struggled as more hands held her down in the wagon.

"Ruth! Ruth!" She heard Vincenzo's voice.

He was coming for her! He wasn't going to let her go. Ruth stopped struggling, but when she looked over the side of the wagon, Vincenzo wasn't there. In all the turmoil, she hadn't realized the wagon was on solid ground and picking up speed. She turned her head and saw him running down the hill through the woods, almost intercepting the wagon.

"I will find you!" Vincenzo ran as fast as he could with his hand outstretched. "I will find you, Ruth! I promise!"

Ruth reached over the side of the wagon, narrowly missing his fingers.

"I love you, Ruth! After the war, I promise I will come to you!"

He tore his gold chain from his neck and threw it into the wagon as the driver sped up, leaving Vincenzo and his promises getting smaller and smaller until the wagon went around a bend and he was gone.

*****

Sheila had sat in complete silence when Ruth finished. As Ruth had talked, Sheila saw glimpses of the young woman Ruth had been and the very real pain in Ruth's blue eyes as she remembered her lost love for Vincenzo. It was only now that Sheila realized two hours had passed and she still had not finished her dinner.

"I don't know what to say." Sheila finally spoke. "Did you ever find him? I mean, I know you married Bill, but what happened to Vincenzo?"

"I do not know," Ruth answered simply, exhausted from the memories.

"What do you mean?" Sheila asked.

"That was the last I ever saw of Vincenzo Scalese."

"He didn't find you?"

"No." Ruth shifted, realizing her left leg was asleep and her hip was aching.

"Did you ever go to Italy to look for him?"

"No. He said he would find me. I waited. Then I moved on." Ruth said.

"But how could you bear not knowing what happened? I mean, after a year or so, I would have written or tried to go to Italy," Sheila said.

"Why?" Ruth shook her head. "It's one thing to know a fact, Sheila, but the problem is a person then needs to act on it. Let's say I found out that Vincenzo was alive and I turned up in Italy. What could I do? Force him to tell me why he didn't want me or force him to marry me? Either way, I lose. Even if he did marry me, he would never have been happy because he would have felt trapped. Ultimately, I wouldn't have been happy either, because I would have forever wondered if he truly loved me or married me out of guilt. And if I found out he was dead after a few years of waiting, then I would have just mourned the loss all over again."

"It kills me that Joe wouldn't give me an explanation. Would it have killed him to have one phone call and explain what happened?" Sheila said.

"Apparently so or he would have done it," Ruth said. "You already have your explanation, Sheila. He left and not in a polite way. A relationship is not something you win like a trophy. It breathes and grows and it can be difficult at times, even the best ones. A man's silence is sometimes all a woman needs to find the truth. It is better to move on and concentrate on your own life." The aching in Ruth's leg throbbed. "I'm sorry, Sheila, but I'm actually quite tired. Do you think you could help an old lady off the couch?" Ruth smiled. "We'll have to continue this conversation another day."

*****

After Sheila left, Ruth sat on the edge of her bed. She stared into space as the image of Vincenzo running after the wagon played like a movie in front of her. A pain rose in her chest, causing sobs to escape as she remembered the agony of that sixteen year-old girl.

Ruth held her hands to her mouth. She had forgotten this pain of lost promises and the special anguish that comes when love ends. When Sheila talked about losing Joe, Ruth often compared it to losing Bill, but she now saw that she had been unfair. The loss wasn't the same at all. Bill didn't leave willingly. She and Bill had raised their son, Nicholas, and lived their lives into old age. Ruth sat and held Bill's hand until the end of his life.

But Vincenzo simply disappeared and the uncertainty of never knowing if one had been truly loved is much different.

29

Alessandra woke slowly, sensing that something wasn't right before she opened her eyes. It wasn't only that her head was pounding, that was normal these days, but the pillow under her head was flat and the blanket covering her body made her itch.

Opening her eyes, Alessandra frowned slightly as nothing looked familiar. She glanced to her right, sitting up quickly when she saw the back of a blonde head next to her in the strange bed. Next to that was a guy who couldn't have been older than twenty-nine with a chiseled stomach and cheekbones to die for.

The room was so small that Alessandra couldn't even stand next to the bed. Who puts a king sized bed in a tiny bedroom? Alessandra groaned inwardly.

She felt sick. Not because she drank herself into a blackout last night, but because she couldn't believe she was in such a shitty apartment.

Alessandra managed to shimmy to the end of the bed without waking the couple. Years of practice, she thought with a grin, escaping to the living room where her clothes were literally all over the place. Oh shit! Her new Proenzer Schouler top hung from a lamp. She would have screamed except she had no desire to talk to either of the two people in the other room.

Examining the blouse for burns from the bulb, Alessandra somehow remembered that the lights never were on last night, which was too bad. She definitely would have left if she had seen this place – no matter how good looking the couple or how drunk she was.

Alessandra quickly grabbed her clothes but couldn't find her bra, which she needed. Even she couldn't be that brash in broad daylight, being over forty and all. When she finally found the bra under the couch next to a few dirty socks, Alessandra quietly dressed. She opened the door with her shoes in her hand, planning to put them on in the elevator, and gasped out loud when she saw she was in a walk-up.

Her standards were really falling. Her drinking didn't concern her, it was the fact that she slept with two people who lived in a fourth floor walk-up. She ran down the stairs as fast as she could which, really, was not fast at all. Judging from the type of building, Alessandra figured that she must be in the Lower East Side so she wouldn't be seeing anyone who really mattered. By the time she reached the landing, she felt sick and panicked, wondering what day it was.

Looking at her BlackBerry, a new feeling of fear set in when she saw it was 7:30 a.m. on Thursday. A quick scan of her calendar showed she had a meeting at 8:30. There wasn't even time to go home.

She ran to the street. There wasn't a cab in sight. God, where the fuck was she? She strained to see the nearest street sign but noticed a man looking at her oddly.

"Oh, please," Alessandra called to the man. "You're in sweats and you're judging me? Get a job."

Thankfully, a cab stopped and Alessandra gave the office address. Looking at the street signs, she saw she was actually in the Lower East Side, so she would be at the office in twenty minutes and could wear the extra dress she kept on the back of her door for situations like this. Taking a package of baby wipes from her bag, she wiped herself down in the back of the cab.

Catching the stare from the cab driver in his rearview mirror, she squinted at his name, which she couldn't pronounce.

"I've been up all night taking care of my sick kid. Did you ever think of that?" Alessandra sneered.

The cab driver shook his head, muttering under his breath in his native language the rest of the drive.

Alessandra stepped off the elevator at 7:50 a.m. and went straight to her office. She had just enough time to change and clean up a bit more in the bathroom. For once, Alessandra was happy that her staff was lazy and no one was in.

*****

This printer! Sheila gave it a small kick. She had been at the office since 7:00 a.m. trying to finish the presentation for a huge meeting, which Crystal should have been doing but she was nowhere to be found. Now it was just before 8:00 a.m., so Sheila texted her again. The fact that Crystal hadn't done any work on the presentation was one problem. Now, Sheila faced the impossible task of making sure that Crystal could articulate the information in front of Alessandra at an 8:30 a.m. practice run and they were leaving at 9:00 a.m. Her phone rang and Crystal's name showed on the screen.

"Where are you?" Sheila demanded.

"I'm on my way. The train was delayed, not my fault. I just got off at 59th Street. Do you want anything from Starbucks?" Crystal sang into the phone.

"Are you joking? I've been here for almost an hour, Crystal. You better skip the coffee and get up here. This is your presentation, remember? Alessandra's going to demand perfection."

"I need my Starby's, Sheila. I'll call when I'm at the head of the line in case you change your mind." She hung up.

Sheila kicked the printer once more. This was too much. If Crystal failed, it wasn't her fault and she planned on letting Alessandra know. She went back to her office and launched her browser. If everyone else around here can screw around, she thought, so can I.

When she heard muttering and banging by the cubicles, Sheila prepared to let Crystal have it but quickly ducked back into her office at the sight of Alessandra rifling through Stacey's desk.

Sheila carefully snuck back to her chair, afraid that Alessandra would demand to see the unfinished presentation immediately. Plus, Crystal's absence was a sure sign that Sheila still couldn't handle her. Beyoncé suddenly blasted from Sheila's phone.

"Who's that?" Alessandra called out.

Diving for the phone, Sheila called out, "It's Sheila. Good morning, Alessandra!"

She heard Alessandra's office door slam as she hastily answered the phone. If Mark didn't change this ringtone today, she was going to kill him. Turning her attention to the phone she let Crystal have it.

"You need to get up here now. Alessandra's already here and she's pissed," Sheila said.

"Hello?" came a male voice after a moment of silence.

"Joe?" Sheila froze.

"Ah, yes. Interesting way you're answering the phone these days." he said.

"I thought you were my co-worker. She's running late." Sheila took a breath, trying to pull herself together. "Well, this is a nice surprise. How are you?"

"I'm well, thanks for asking. Since you're busy, I'll get to the point. I've realized that we need to talk. There are some things from our relationship that I'm missing and I need your help. Are you able to talk?" Joe cleared his throat nervously.

"Yes. Sure. Where should we meet?" Sheila cringed at the sound of her voice. She should be ashamed but it was such a relief to hear his voice and hear him say he missed her. They were finally going to discuss things and just maybe there was hope.

"Meet?" Joe sounded confused.

"Yes, we should go someplace private. There are some things I miss too. I'm so glad we'll have a chance to talk," Sheila said.

"Sheila." Joe sounded exasperated. "I meant I want to talk now, on the phone. There's no need for us to meet."

"Oh." Sheila was taken aback at the tone in his voice. It was the tone he used when he dealt with waiters or doormen or anyone that he thought should take his order and move quickly. Come to think of it, Sheila recognized this was a tone that Joe had used with her many times when he was tired of answering her questions. "Sure, I have some time now," she lied.

"When I left, I tried to be as thorough as possible so we wouldn't have to go through any protracted situations. Unfortunately, it turns out that I am missing some *items* and you need to send them to me." Joe stressed the last part.

"I see." Sheila's heart sank.

"I need my tax returns. They're on your computer, which I obviously can't access. I need them by end of week so you need to email them immediately. Tonight would be best," Joe said.

"Hey there! I decided to get you a Caramel Macchiato to sweeten your day and some carbs to sweeten your mood." Sheila turned in a daze to see Crystal standing with a tray of Starbucks coffees and a bag of food.

"Not now," Sheila told her.

"Sheila, I don't want to get forceful here," Joe continued in the same condescending tone. "They are my documents and I have every right to them. Don't be bitter about this. It's unattractive."

"First you tell me to hurry, then you yell at me when I get here. Are you ever happy?" Crystal put the packages on the table.

"I'm not talking to you." Sheila said into the phone.

"Who are you talking to?" both people asked Sheila at the same time.

That was a good question, Sheila realized. Who was she talking to? The person on the phone wasn't the man she thought she knew. Joe was an obnoxious jerk who was trying to intimidate her. Sheila took a moment, trying to think of the last genuinely nice thing that Joe had done for her and came up with nothing. He had never made her dinner or cared for her while she was sick, she slowly realized. He had never given her one of those selfless moments like Ruth had described with Vincenzo. It was always about Joe needing something and somehow making Sheila feel she owed it to him to react.

Then there was Crystal, a spoiled brat, plain and simple. She, too, had Sheila jumping through hoops and Sheila foolishly did it because she wanted to keep her job. If experience had taught her anything, it was that she could lose the very thing she wanted to keep by turning herself inside out to make people happy. Joe had proved that by leaving.

I've been a fool, Sheila realized.

"Hello?" Joe's voice came through the phone.

"Sheila?" Crystal looked annoyed. "You're wasting my time here."

"Sit down and be quiet!" Sheila shouted at Crystal.

"And you." She said into the phone. "Who the hell do you think you are, calling me and making demands? You need something from me, Joe? Everyone needs something from me. Remember, that's what you didn't like about me. So here's the deal. You'll get your tax forms when I'm damn good and ready to send them."

"Well, I see being single has changed you—" Joe said.

"That's right and it's for the better. You ever call with this attitude again, I'll erase those files. And as for revenge, living with that mouse of an assistant is going to give you the revenge you deserve." She hung up the phone.

Sheila then turned her wrath to Crystal, who sat wide-eyed in her chair.

"The next time I tell you to get in the office and you decide to go to Starbucks," Sheila took the bag of food and tray of coffee, "You better apply for a job there."

Sheila dumped everything into her garbage can.

"What's going on here?" Paul entered Sheila's office. "I heard screaming down the hall."

Crystal and Sheila both said nothing. Although Crystal usually had the upper hand when it came to, well, just about everything, she knew that Sheila was crazy right now.

Before Sheila could open her mouth, Alessandra's voice came from down the hall.

"I'll handle this, Paul," she called out. "Ladies, I'm really tired of this problem. I want both of you in the conference room to figure out why—" As she entered the room, Crystal gasped loudly while Paul and Sheila could only stare in horror. Alessandra stopped short, looking at the group.

"What the hell is wrong with all of you?"

30

Crystal and Mark were laughing hysterically.

"Please tell the first part again." Mark was in tears. "I just love the way you tell it!"

"So Sheila was going ape shit all over her ex on the phone, which was kind of impressive, I have to say. I didn't think she had it in her. Then she starts yelling at me, takes the coffee and croissants and dumps them in the trash. So I'm about to go off on her when Paul came in because he heard her screaming all the way down the hall. He was about tell her off when Alessandra came into the room with her neck full of hickies and lipstick all over her face! I mean, it was on her forehead and her cheeks. She was definitely making out with some woman."

"Don't you think you should talk about something else or maybe get some work done?" Stacey had heard Crystal tell this story at least four times already and it sounded worse each time. "I'm not sure you should be laughing because someone's in rehab."

"When does she have to go?" Melissa was agog, having just arrived.

"She's probably there already. Someone from HR escorted her out the back door and the company called an addiction specialist to meet her at her house. It was either that or lose her job." Crystal shrugged.

"So if Paul hadn't told HR, Alessandra could have stayed?" Melissa asked.

"Melissa." Crystal sighed impatiently. "The woman clearly needs help and Paul got it for her. We should all thank him. It's not like he killed her."

"What are you talking about?" Sheila walked into the pit.

"Take a guess." Crystal looked at Sheila sarcastically while Mark quickly turned to his keyboard and started typing.

"Uh, huh. Well, they want to see you in HR," Sheila said.

Crystal followed Sheila to her office.

"Why do they want to talk to me?" Crystal asked nervously.

"Take a guess," Sheila mocked without looking at her.

"Do you think they heard me talking about Alessandra?" Her eyes narrowed as she considered the possibility.

"Crystal, do you honestly think the company has the office bugged?" Sheila dropped into her chair.

"I don't know. Maybe."

Crystal stepped forward again, hovering over Sheila. "What did they say, exactly? You have to tell me everything." Crystal put her hand on her hip, causing a charm bracelet to jingle, irritating Sheila even more.

"I don't have to tell you anything. Just go to HR. Now." Sheila looked up as the charms on Crystal's bracelet tinkled together seductively. She stared at the bracelet, sure she hadn't seen it on Crystal before, but it looked familiar. Was that a charm of the Eifel Tower?

"I bet they want me to keep my mouth shut." She started playing with the charms, irritating Sheila even more.

"Bingo." Sheila had seventy-six emails already.

"So, what did you get for your silence?" Crystal asked.

"Ah, nothing." Sheila looked at Crystal in disbelief. "We don't need our clients knowing that our SVP of Sales is in rehab. It can seriously damage our reputation." As Sheila turned back to her computer, she noticed another one of the charms was of the Arc de Triomphe in Paris.

"Oh, please. This story is great! My friends loved it!" Crystal said.

"You told your friends?" Sheila gasped.

"Of course! Finally, something exciting happened here. Now we don't seem as old and stuffy." Crystal caught Sheila's look. "Oh, don't have a cow. Celebrities go to rehab all the time. It's no big deal."

"It is a big deal, Crystal. Our sales can go way down if clients think we're run by an addict," Sheila said.

"But people like me are making the decisions about ad budgets." Crystal crossed her arms over her chest. "I'm not keeping quiet without getting something in return from HR."

"Well, good luck with that."

When Crystal finally turned to leave, Sheila noticed more of the charms were of Paris landmarks. It was driving her crazy, knowing that she had seen the bracelet somewhere. She Googled 'charm bracelet Paris.'

There on the screen was the bracelet that Crystal was wearing and Sheila knew why it looked familiar. It was the Hermès special edition charm bracelet advertised everywhere and it cost ten thousand dollars. How was it possible that a Junior Sales Rep living in Manhattan could have such an expensive bracelet? Sheila knew what Crystal made, so someone had to be giving her the money. Her father, probably. No wonder she didn't care about selling. She doesn't need the commissions with Daddy around.

When the phone rang, Sheila was still clicking through the Hermès site, reading about each charm and the workmanship that goes into them.

"Well, Crystal agreed not to mention the situation with Alessandra anymore," Deborah Adams, VP Employee Relations in the HR Department, said.

"Good. Did she give you a hard time?" Sheila said.

"She's a tough negotiator, that's for sure." Deborah said

"What do you mean?" Sheila asked.

"Well, we usually keep employee records private but since she reports to you, she wanted me to tell you about the arrangement we made." Deborah said just as Crystal appeared in Sheila's doorway. As she leaned against the door, Crystal's bracelet jingled when she crossed her arms over her chest.

"Arrangement?" Sheila's smile faded as Crystal's grew. Deborah informed Sheila that Crystal was receiving an additional week of vacation and a two thousand dollar American Express Gift Card.

"To deal with the stress," Deborah said dryly.

Sheila looked at Crystal, who cocked her head and shrugged her shoulders with a smirk before turning to leave. As Deborah droned on, Sheila was distracted by the jingle of the charms across the hall.

31

Thursday morning, Jenn rolled into work and stopped by Sheila's office.

"Are you coming with me tonight?" Jenn asked.

"Tonight?" Sheila clicked on her calendar and saw a meeting with Barbara, her financial advisor, at 6:00 p.m. "What's going on tonight?"

"Dinner at Paul's house in Westchester. We got the email on Tuesday. He's having us to his new house to promote team building while Alessandra gets well." Jenn rolled her eyes. "I'm driving."

Sheila searched for the invitation but didn't find it. "That's weird. I don't have anything." she said.

"Well, you're on the list, so you're going. We need to leave here by 5:30," Jenn said. "Hopefully, we won't have to ride with anyone we don't like."

"Can't wait," Sheila said.

Now she had to cancel her meeting with Barbara, which wasn't going to be pretty.

Sheila used to have quarterly meetings with Barbara to go through her finances, but in the past few years, she had been lax. Mostly it was because Barbara disapproved of the way Joe handled the finances. When Sheila showed up without any statements to her last meeting, Barbara didn't bother to hide her anger.

"What are we supposed to discuss if you have no information? Do you even know where he's investing your money?" Barbara folded her arms across her chest. "Does he ever give you an update?

So Sheila had stayed away, though Barbara reached out every quarter. When Sheila emailed that Joe had left and she wanted to meet again, Sheila couldn't bring herself to write about the money he took. She was too embarrassed and afraid of Barbara's reaction. In some way, it was a relief to reschedule her appointment though it was strange that Sheila was just hearing about Paul's dinner party today.

*****

Paul's house was a huge stone and shingle country manor with five bedrooms, six baths, and five thousand square feet. Paul's wife, Lisa, led them all on a tour, beaming with pride as everyone 'oohed' and 'aahed' over the furniture. She looked like a model with her blond hair in a low chignon and her designer dress held tightly against her tiny waist with a Hermès belt that looked just like the one Crystal had worn many times at work.

"They must hand them out at the club," Jenn said.

Dinner was served al fresco on their massive stone patio with four round tables for five. Each place setting had a name tag but as Sheila went from table to table, she didn't see one for herself. Gradually everyone was seated except Sheila, who stood alone. "Is there a reason we're waiting for you, Sheila?" Baxter called from across the patio.

"Yes, I can't find my name," Sheila said. Everyone stopped talking and looked at her. "Does anyone see my name at a place setting?" she asked.

Everyone began looking at their tent cards, making sure they were in the right place, except for the table where Baxter, Paul, Lisa, Crystal, and Scott sat. At their table, Crystal kept talking to Scott, Lisa sipped her full glass of wine and Paul stared at Crystal. Only Baxter noticed Sheila standing alone, becoming more embarrassed by the minute.

"Paul." Baxter interrupted Paul's thoughts. "Could you possibly see why your guest doesn't have a seat?"

"Oh, that's impossible!" Paul said loudly. "Lisa, want to help me, darling?"

"I'm sure something will turn up," Lisa called out and turned back to her drink with a casual smile.

"I'll just use the powder room," Sheila managed to say with a smile. Jenn stood to go with her, but Sheila waved her off. Wanting desperately to be alone, Sheila went through the nearest door into the kitchen. Feeling dizzy, she sat at on a stool in front of the black marble island where the staff was busy preparing the meal. One by one they stopped to look at her with blank stares as she put her elbows on the countertop and hid her face in her hands.

Embarrassed and humiliated, Sheila felt the tears building behind her eyes. As she slid off the stool to find somewhere private to calm herself, she caught site of her name printed neatly in black marker on a tent card at the end of the counter. Picking it up, Sheila turned it around to see *Table 5* written on the back side. Returning to gaze at the counter, she quickly registered a placemat, plate, wine glass, napkin and utensils and realized that she was looking at her missing place setting.

So it wasn't a mistake - Paul had deliberately left her without a seat. Sheila escaped quickly through the kitchen and into a hallway she hadn't seen before, trying to find the front door. She had to leave. Nothing was worth this humiliation. She was almost at the front door when she heard Paul and Baxter's voices behind her. With the tears still in her eyes, Sheila crossed the hallway in two steps and dove into a massive closet.

"This is why you didn't get promoted earlier, Paul. You do stupid things. What the fuck were you thinking?" Baxter spat at Paul as they entered the hall.

"I, I..." Paul stammered.

"I told you, we need everyone on board for at least a couple of months until I'm ready. Got it?" Baxter said.

"She's not in the bathrooms on this floor." Lisa clicked across the floor then gasped. "Do you think she's in our bedrooms? I told everyone not to go upstairs unattended."

"I imagine she's somewhere trying to figure out why there's no seat for her." Baxter said.

"I don't know what happened," Paul said.

"You told me you wrote the wrong email address for the invite so she wouldn't be here." Lisa said, "When she showed up, I forgot about it because Crystal and I were talking about clothes —"

"I could kill you, Paul. I promised your father I wouldn't bug him with your bullshit, but I may just have to call him on this one," Baxter said.

"We'll fix this Baxter. I promise." Paul became frenzied to think that his father would hear of his latest screw up. This was exactly why he didn't have a better position in the company. "Paul, you just don't think things through. You need to grow up," His father told him time and time again. Now he had another debacle on his hands. Instead of waiting like Baxter told him, he just had to show off.

"I'll tell the caterer to put the place setting at the assistant's table. We'll just act like she didn't see it." Lisa said.

"No! God, you two —" Baxter bit his tongue. "Put her next to me and blame the caterers. Now get outside and stop everyone from talking about it while we wait for her."

"But she's in my house. I don't like people unsupervised in my house," Lisa whined.

"You've just humiliated her in front of all her co-workers," Baxter growled. "I wouldn't blame her if she were shredding your sheets."

"But they're Egyptian cotton! Six-hundred thread count!" Lisa whined as she and Paul followed Baxter out of the hallway.

Sheila sat on the closet floor trying to figure out what would be worse, leaving or going back to face them all. If she stayed, how could she face them after hearing what Baxter said? Alessandra was going to be in rehab for one month, so why did he need a few months? Was he going to get rid of Alessandra? There were too many strange things happening, starting with the fact that Sheila was in a closet instead of enjoying dinner. After a few more minutes, she extricated herself from the closet. She wasn't going to let them think they won. After finding a bathroom, she fixed her make-up, took some deep breaths and walked back to the patio.

"There's our superstar!" Paul boomed, putting his arm around Sheila. Lisa smiled and grabbed Sheila's other arm.

"I talked to the caterers about this disaster! I specifically asked for English speaking help, but – you know how it is." Two server's heads snapped up. They clearly understood English quite well. Lisa hugged Sheila's arm until Sheila twisted out of her grasp.

"So, where did you put me?" Sheila looked directly at Paul. Before he could answer, Baxter stood, clinking his knife against his glass.

"Well, it's always interesting when we leave the city, which is why we do it so little!" There were laughs and polite titters from the group. "Sheila, your seat is here, where I had planned all along. It's a snafu that we'll never figure out but I poured you a big glass of wine, so come on over and start drinking."

Baxter raised his glass. "To the best team that I have ever had the privilege of leading. Cheers!" The group yelled their toasts and went back to their conversations while Sheila finally sat down to dinner.

"No need to read anything into this, Sheila." Baxter busied himself with his linen napkin. "It's a simple mistake. Right?"

"Not sure if 'simple' is the word, but it is a mistake." Sheila smiled and lifted her glass.

32

Ruth enjoyed her Sunday dinners with Sheila. It brought a feeling of having family back to her life. Though her son, Nicholas, called three or four times a week from Boston, it was the rituals of family life that Ruth missed and Sunday dinners had always been Ruth's favorite ritual of all.

As dinner cooked each Sunday afternoon, the house filled with aromas that still made Ruth's mouth water. Oh, she missed her mother's cooking and her laugh. Eliza would put out the fine china and her favorite things for dinner so the family could sit at a beautiful table, then store them away so they wouldn't get broken.

Ruth had prepared a stew for Sheila's visit this evening, making her apartment smell like the home she missed so. With a few hours left, Ruth had plenty of time to dust the living room and set the fine china that had once been Eliza's.

Her son would be so angry, Ruth thought, as she caressed each object on her credenza with the dust cloth. Nicholas had hired cleaners to come each week after Ruth was mandated to use a cane by her doctor, but Ruth still enjoyed taking care of her own house, thank you very much. There was something comforting about touching the things in her home. It made the memories come alive. Plus, it wouldn't do to sit at the coffee table with a cover of dust since the cleaners came on Tuesday. If there was one thing Ruth knew about living in New York City, it was that dusting was a full time job.

Moving to the coffee table, Ruth put down the oilseed rag to hold her blue vase in both hands. Running her fingers over the pattern, Ruth gazed from the intricate blue and white design to her hands. Although she knew these were her hands, they looked like the hands of a stranger as Ruth remembered a Sunday long ago when she held this vase with hands that were young and dimpled.

*****

"Ruth." Eliza gently admonished, taking the vase from the eight year-old girl. "You mustn't touch Mama's nice things."

"But it's so pretty, Mama," Ruth said, staring at the brilliant blue. "I can't see it when you put it away."

"I put it so high because if you touch it too much, it will break." Eliza stared at the beautiful vase. "It was a gift from my Mama when I married Papa."

"Why can't I touch it? I won't break it," Ruth said.

"Because it is valuable," Eliza said.

"You mean it cost a lot?" Ruth stared at her Mother, wide eyed.

"No. It is valuable because it is from my Mama." Eliza smiled as she put the vase in the cupboard, imagining her mother buying the vase just for her.

"But it's so beautiful, please don't hide it. I won't touch it. I promise."

185

Ruth's plaintive, innocent plea touched Eliza. Ruth was so like her grandmother in many ways. Eliza knew that her mother would be disappointed to see the vase's beauty wasted in a cupboard but with four small children, the chance of it breaking was too much for Eliza to bear.

"I'll be careful." Ruth hugged her mother tightly.

Eliza smiled at the girl, running her hand over her thick braids.

"It is beautiful and I want it to stay that way." Eliza put her hand under Ruth's chin, lifting her face to her. "So when you are an old lady, you will have it to look at and remember me the way I remember my mother."

"When I have the vase, I will keep it in the open so people can see it and admire it," Ruth said.

Eliza smiled and kissed Ruth on the forehead before returning to the kitchen while the girl stared at the cupboard where the vase was now hidden.

*****

Holding the vase now, Ruth looked at her hands again. It sometimes shocked her to see the liver spots and veins on her skin. She remembered her mother's hands clear as day. Strong, square and graceful. A sudden gust of sadness knocked Ruth's breath away as she realized that her mother's hands had never been this old. Ruth was eighty-six. Eliza hadn't had the privilege to be this age. Ruth shook her head, trying to clear her thoughts. Going down memory lane was becoming more difficult, the older she got. It was sometimes too much, especially since her life had once been full of people all around her all of the time.

As Ruth bent to put the vase back on the coffee table, her right foot moved forward but her left leg couldn't hold her. Falling to the left, Ruth lurched forward and to the right, pushing her body over the coffee table. Reflexively, she threw out her hands to break her fall on the table, instantly regretting her decision as she watched the vase fly through the air. Ruth fell faster than the vase, but both headed for a crash into the table. Ruth caught herself, jarring her right hand on the coffee table. As the vase came down, she reached with her left hand, miraculously swatting the vase mid-air. Ruth watched the vase somersault to the right in a graceful arc. Slowly, it fell. Ruth watched breathlessly as it bounced on the red velvet couch and rested there, safe at last.

Turning herself to sit on the coffee table, Ruth slid close to the couch and grabbed the vase. She hugged it tight, sweat dotting her forehead. It took some time for her to feel confident enough to stand again. Once she did, she grabbed the cane vowing to walk everywhere with it. It was at that moment that Sheila knocked on the door.

*****

"Sara, it's time to get up." Ruth nudged her sister. Silently the two dressed and walked with their mother through the cold air to the Officer's quarters.

"Get to work!" the Report Leader, Irma Ulrich, shouted as they entered the kitchen. Ruth kept her head down as she walked by the woman, taking a large pot to the sink while Eliza began cleaning vegetables for the stew they were making that day.

It had been three years since Ruth and her family were brought to the internment camp. Although they were all technically together, Franz and Dieter lived in the men's barracks while Tomas and Greta had been separated from the family upon arrival to stay in the children's nursery. They attended the school for non-Jewish children to teach them an abiding love for the Reich.

The women were not allowed to fraternize while preparing or serving the food. The tiniest comment could bring the wrath of Irma, which the women had seen too many times. So they worked in silence.

When the family was first separated, Greta used to cry every time she saw her relatives, breaking Eliza's heart. Now if they did see Greta in the yard, she didn't even appear to notice them. Over the years she had turned into a beautiful ten-year-old, attracting the special attention of the guards and receiving treats from the headmistress for her good work at the school. Like Greta, Tomas didn't acknowledge his family either, but his reaction was born from fear. Every day, the teachers and soldiers told them stories of the evil that existed among the prisoners. Although Tomas didn't believe that was true, he became afraid and stayed silent.

Another duty of the kitchen workers was to serve the two-hundred guards while they ate in the main dining room in shifts. It was a large, beautifully appointed room with fine chestnut tables, silver utensils, and linen napkins. When the meal finished, the workers cleaned the kitchen then Irma marched a select few to throw the leftovers in the incinerator. Ruth's mouth watered each day as bowls of food, homemade bread and desserts fell into the roaring flames, but she didn't dare steal any as Irma glared with her stick held firmly in her right hand. Ruth had seen Irma use that stick more than once and had no desire to live with the physical scars it would leave.

But today something was wrong. Most of the guards did not come for lunch and the ones in the dining room whispered in hushed tones, glancing nervously out the windows. Ruth found it difficult to look straight ahead as more and more guards looked out the windows. Their faces, usually passive and cold, showed reserved concern.

Ruth jumped along with the rest of the room when the doors to the dining hall crashed open. Two low ranking guards entered the room with guns drawn, followed by the Chief Overseer.

"Heil, Hitler!" the Chief Officer saluted. "Men, come with me immediately. Report Leader; take these women to the kitchen. I want it spotless."

"Move!" Irma yelled. As Ruth passed through the dining room, picking up plates, she glanced out the window to see prisoners lining up in the yard which was strange for this time of day. The guards had their guns drawn, too. "What are you looking at?" Irma pushed Ruth forward. "I told you to move. Get to the kitchen now."

In the kitchen, Ruth took two bowls of leftovers in her hands. In the past week, meals had dwindled to a small piece of stale bread in the morning with a cup of tepid brown water that was supposed to be coffee. The aroma from the stew with carrots and onions filled her head. If only she could take one bite.

"I see you, you pig! That food is not for you!" Irma thrust her stick inches from Ruth's chin. "Don't get stupid, girl. Take the bowls and go."

Ruth and two other prisoners walked in front of Irma to the incinerator with a few bowls each. Once outside, however, the chaos in the yard drew their attention. Ruth looked over and saw Papa and Dieter in a line along with hundreds of the prisoners. As she walked, a guard grabbed Franz by the arm and brought him to stand with another group which Ruth recognized as prisoners dubbed 'top resistors' because they hid Jews in their attics or something equally offensive to the Reich. As Ruth stared at Papa silently willing him to look at her, her foot hit a stone. Ruth stumbled, spilling the food.

"Idiot!" Irma came at Ruth fast with her stick in the air. Ruth turned, taking the hit on her left thigh. The pain shot through her body like an explosion, almost causing her to fall. As Irma raised her arm for another blow, a group of prisoners marched by, stopping her in midair

"Where are you bringing these pigs?" Irma called to the guards.

"The field. Do you want us to take any?" the guard asked.

"No. I'll deal with them myself." Irma said. Watching the group pass, Irma smiled sadistically at the fear in the prisoner's eyes. Her smile faded as an old man passed who did not look afraid. In fact, he was staring at something. Following his gaze, she realized he was staring at Ruth with a look of concern.

"What are you staring at, old man?" Irma demanded as he passed. Franz looked her in the eyes, saying nothing.

"Do you know that man?" Irma turned to Ruth, still holding her stick.

Ruth knew what Papa would want her to say. He would want her to say "No." He would want her to avoid being hit again, but Ruth could not do it. She could not leave her father alone now, not for this.

"That is my father," Ruth said, glaring at Irma.

"Well then, you must be a filthy traitor, too," she said. "Ladies, back inside! You follow them." Irma pushed Ruth ahead of her to catch up with the group.

The pain in her leg was quickly forgotten as a new pain spread through Ruth's body. It was a numbing pain, a pain that causes a person to lose their breath and shake while the mind goes completely blank. Then smells and sounds rush back into consciousness with a clarity that does one of two things: it makes you weak or gives you strength.

The group was a ragged bunch. Some were worn out from the abuse, malnutrition, and cold. They shuffled along, some bent at the waist, heads hung low. Yet a few men walked tall, shoulders straight and heads held high. Ruth didn't know if it was luck or courage that had let them all survive, but as she stared at her father's head held high, strength came back to her.

Looking Irma straight in the eye, Ruth threw the bowls of food at her feet, spilling the stew over Irma's shoes and legs before turning to follow in her father's footsteps. Enraged by Ruth's act of insolence, Irma grabbed the girl by the arm, dragging her quickly to the field. It would be her personal pleasure to see this through. As for Ruth, she was at peace. There was nothing left to fear of Irma now. Ruth touched her waist, feeling the familiar lump of her secret pocket. Ruth was going to the field. A place from where no one ever returned.

33

Hot air roared with stabbing velocity, scorching Ruth's left ear as she was thrown to the right. The landing was equally violent. Her head smashed against a hard object, leaving her glued to the ground in agony. The painful rumbling in her ears blocked all sound as black smoke swept over her, stinging her eyes into blindness.

In her darkness, the world became peaceful. Ruth lay still, lulled by the sound of gently breaking waves that now soothed her. Maybe it was a dream, she told herself, as a sudden wave of tiredness washed over her. Yes, she felt her pillow under her head. She would stay here and rest. After a few more breaths, she snuggled further into sleep.

A rough yank on her arm interrupted her thoughts as she was forced to sit up. A gale of gray spew exited her body in every direction. Her eyes watered while the coughing spasms tried to clear the soot and sulfur packed into her lungs.

Scrambling on all fours, Ruth coughed and heaved as two hands tried to lift her to her feet, but she collapsed. She wanted to rest but the hands kept grabbing at her. As she turned to bury her face in her pillow, she realized something was wrong. The hands helped her sit as she rubbed the soot from her eyes. Finally able to see, she saw her pillow was actually a fleshy thigh that belonged to Irma who now lay motionless among shards of broken debris from the bridge a few meters ahead. Her eyebrows arched above the dead eyes as though surprised by this outcome. As Ruth stared in shock, she saw the missing flesh from Irma's neck next to the SS pin that Irma so loved hanging loosely from her epaulet.

Ruth reached over and tore the pin off the jacket just as the hand yanked her by the arm, forcing her to run. As she ran forward, she periodically looked back at Irma until she was a small lump, undistinguishable from all the others.

The blast from the bridge had killed almost everyone that had been in line ahead of Ruth. Their bodies lay haphazardly over the field, so utterly lifeless there was no doubt that they were dead. In the camp, some prison houses were in flames and prisoners ran in every direction.

Ruth grabbed at her ears as the sound of gunfire and screams filled her head. The pure pain in the voices enveloped Ruth like a wet sheet, stifling her, weighing her down. She couldn't escape it. Every step she took seemed to bring her closer to the noise. It was then that Ruth realized it was Franz who had her arm and they were running to the camp.

"No!" Ruth screamed. "There!" She pointed to a stream of prisoners fleeing into the woods.

"Your mother and the others are still in the camp. We cannot leave them," Franz yelled, pulling her with him.

The women's barracks had been set on fire, the smoke enveloping the building. Ruth and Franz looked around the yard, praying they would see their family.

In the chaos, it was impossible to see clearly. People ran quickly in all directions. Some fell and stayed on the ground, clearly hurt, but no one was free to help. Panic rose as Ruth scanned the crowd for what felt like hours, not seeing her mother or siblings anywhere.

"She must have gone to the children!" Ruth grabbed Franz and they crossed the yard. Of course, Eliza would go there to get her youngest children.

As they rounded the men's barracks, they stopped short. There was a crowd staring as the nursery burned.

"Papa! Ruth!" Sara and Dieter ran to them.

"Where is your mother?" Franz yelled.

"She went to get Greta and Tomas. There are children inside," Sara cried tearfully.

"You three go to the bridge. Wait there for us." Franz turned to Ruth. "Leave if we are not there in ten minutes. Head south. Get to Jacob's house somehow." Then he ran into the nursery without even saying goodbye.

Ruth grabbed Sara and Dieter by the hand and the three ran to the field where another bomb exploded. As Ruth let go of Dieter to help Sara back on her feet, Dieter ran back toward the camp yelling, "I'll meet you at the bridge."

"Dieter! Come back!" But he continued his sprint. Ruth slung Sara's arm around her shoulder and they moved as quickly as possible through the field. Another explosion knocked them to the ground.

"Go without me." Sara cried. "I can't do it."

"Yes you will! Don't even think like that. You run on that ankle now. It will heal when we're out of here." Ruth grabbed her sister's arm and they ran a little faster in the direction of the bridge.

"Ruth!" She turned at the sound of her name to see Dieter running toward them with Tomas.

"Tomas!" Ruth grabbed the boy, kissing his cheeks. "Sara can't walk."

"I'll take her on my back. Hold onto Tomas." Dieter grabbed Sara.

"Did you find Mama and Papa?" Ruth asked.

Dieter looked her in the eye. "Let's just get to the bridge."

They ran as fast as they could until they crossed the bridge, stopping just on the other side to wait for their parents and Greta.

"We will wait for ten minutes, as Papa said," Ruth told the group.

"I don't think that's possible." Dieter replied as he pointed beyond her shoulder. Ruth turned to see a Jeep coming toward them. It stopped a few yards away as soldiers jumped out with guns drawn, moving toward the group.

Ruth exchanged a quick look with Dieter and each grabbed a sibling to run into the woods. But Sara pulled away and ran toward the Jeeps.

"Sara!" Ruth grabbed for her sister, but the soldiers were almost upon them. Ruth turned away, knowing her father would be ashamed, but Dieter grabbed her and held her tight.

"Ruth, stop!" But she could not. She could not go back to the prison camp. She couldn't take it anymore. Sara had clearly lost her mind. Ruth could help no one. She struggled against Dieter crying, begging to be let go, and falling to the ground.

It was Tomas who caught her attention, running to her and hugging her tight.

"It's okay!" said the boy. "Ruth, stop! The soldiers are American!"

At last they were free. The war was over. Now she could find the rest of her family. And Vincenzo would find her.

"Everyone clean your desks. You!" Paul pointed to Stacey. "Get those pictures off your desk. And you!" He pointed at Mark, who's hair was spiked into a fauxhawk. "I want you working at your computer for the next hour. No leaving, no personal phones calls and no joking around." Paul looked frantic as he came into Sheila's office.

"Ann Joyce is going to be down here in fifteen minutes. You've got to make sure your staff behaves properly," he said.

"Why?" In the five years that Sheila had been here, Ann Joyce had never set foot on this floor.

"I don't know." Paul was practically sweating. "But we have to make sure everything is buttoned up and polished. This is the CEO of the company, for God's sake."

"I know who she is Paul. Did she say why she's coming down?" Sheila fought the urge to roll her eyes.

"No." Paul rocked back and forth on his left foot, chewing his thumb. "It's probably because Alessandra had her episode and now she wants to make sure we're not all a bunch of derelicts," Paul said.

"Maybe it's because Crystal shook down the HR department to keep quiet," Sheila replied.

"This had nothing to do with Crystal. And she didn't shake down the HR department, she made a deal with them at my advice, I'll have you know. It's more likely to do with Alessandra being a drunk and drug addict." Paul looked at his watch. "Ten minutes until she's here."

Paul stepped outside Sheila's office and pointed to Melissa's empty chair. "Where's your assistant?"

"She had to use the bathroom."

"Well, get her! I want all assistants busy and all sales reps out of the office, including you. Take your bag and go, but get Melissa first." He called as he rushed back to Baxter's office.

Great, thought Sheila as she packed up her laptop. I've got a million things to do and now I'm going to waste twenty minutes finding a seat at Starbucks. She was still muttering to herself when she went into the bathroom but stopped dead in horror at the scene before her.

In the middle of the bathroom floor, Crystal stood with one gold strappy sandal on her right foot and a silver stiletto heel on her left wearing an extremely low-cut dress that she hadn't been wearing earlier. Melissa was standing with her back to the door, holding a shoe box.

"What are you doing?" Sheila pushed the door to the bathroom shut so no one else could enter. Melissa turned but Crystal ignored her, balancing from one foot to the other. "Ann Joyce is coming to this floor in five minutes to meet Baxter. What are you doing?" Sheila asked again.

"Trying on my new clothes. I have a date tonight. I can't look like crap." Crystal continued to examine each shoe. "I think the

silver stilettos are the way to go for this one but let's try those."
She pointed at the shoes in Melissa's hands but Sheila rushed
forward.

"Did you hear me? Ann Joyce is on her way. Please tell me
you know who that is." Both women just stared blankly. "My
God! She's the CEO of the company! She's one of the most
powerful women in media. Melissa, get back to your desk right
now."

Melissa quickly put the shoes down and left as Crystal moved
past Sheila to the handicap stall. As the door opened, Sheila's jaw
fell. Hanging on the purse hooks were at least three different
bags. Clothes were draped over the railing and the side of the
stall and a few bags were on the floor.

"Where did all this come from?" Sheila said.

"I went shopping at lunch. What's the big deal? I'm sure Ann
isn't going to come into the bathroom and if she does, I'm sure
she won't care that I want to look good on a date." Crystal rolled
her eyes while examining the black designer dress in her hands.

"I'm telling you to get this crap back in your bags and get
dressed immediately. Ms. Joyce could walk in here any minute
and she most certainly will mind that you are trying on clothes
instead of working. Paul's been running around the office
making sure everything is perfect. You're going to get me, him,
and Baxter in a lot of trouble. What is wrong with you?"

"How will Baxter and Paul get in trouble?" Crystal finally paid
attention.

"Because it will look like he doesn't have control over his
staff if someone's playing dress up in the bathroom. Get it?"
Sheila said. "If anyone finds you in here, I'm not taking the
blame. Even Baxter won't be able to help you with this." Sheila
swung open the door and walked as quickly as possible to the
elevator.

*****

The visit from Ms. Joyce couldn't have gone well because Baxter and Paul were both frantic and from the smell of it, they had more than a few drinks with lunch. Sheila wrote as fast as she could to keep up with them as they spoke.

"She wants a presentation on Friday morning at 9 a.m. on the state of our business, so we need you to get all the information from the sales team. Stacey's going to put it all together tomorrow. Paul and I will present it on Friday."

"When's the last time you met her?" Paul asked Baxter.

"Last year, but Alessandra's met her a few times since." Baxter sat in his chair, looking nervous. "We really need your help here, Sheila. Paul and I have discussed how important you are to the team and the potential for promotion. But if you pull this off, we can make that happen quicker."

Sheila practically floated back to her office. She didn't know that Baxter was considering her for a promotion. This could solve her mortgage problem and help her get back on track. It would make life so much easier. Then she saw Crystal showing one of her new pairs of shoes to Susan and wondered if the money would be worth the aggravation. Damn Joe.

35

"Here's the stuff for the presentation tomorrow. Tell Baxter that I have really bad cramps and I have to go home, too." Stacey threw some papers on Sheila's desk.

"Stacey, you don't have cramps. You're just mad. Go take a break then finish the presentation." Sheila held the papers out to her.

"No! That bitch gets away with murder. It's time Baxter learned that if he's going to give her special treatment, then we all want it." Stacey slung her purse over her shoulder and stomped off.

Sheila walked to the pit where Mark sat typing, listening to his ear buds. Sheila motioned to get his attention.

"What?" He looked at her angrily.

"Whoa? What's with the attitude?" Sheila said.

"Attitude? I have an attitude? That's rich. I work hard here, you know. Just as hard as Melissa and Stacey, but Stacey gets to leave while I get asked to do more work? Why? Because I can't have cramps? Uh, uh." He stood and ripped his ear buds out of his computer. "I'm leaving, too. I may not have cramps, but I definitely have a huge pain in my ass!"

Sheila sank into her office chair defeated. She had planned to see her good friend, Jess Bancroft, for over a month. They had worked together during the late 90's until Jess went to the biggest online toy store where she made a fortune. Then she went somewhere else and made a bundle on that stock, too.

By the end of the Internet boom, Jess was worth a fortune and scooped up homes in New York, Nantucket, and Greenwich, Connecticut. She was always a breath of fresh air because she didn't worry about the little things. If someone didn't like Jess, she didn't care. She didn't waste her time gossiping or worrying. She moved forward every day of her life with an ease that made almost everyone love her. Those that didn't love her, hated her, but she didn't care. It was all good in Jess' world.

So what would she do with this situation? Sheila thought as she stared at the pile of papers in her hands.

"Bad news," Sheila said to Jess on the phone a few minutes later.

"What?" Jess said.

"My team of assistants revolted and now I have to spend tonight finishing a presentation for my bosses to present at 9 a.m. tomorrow. I can't go to dinner."

"Oh, Sheila, you're not going to waste your time with this. Meet me at my place at six with your stuff. I'll take care of it." Jess said.

"How? It's PowerPoint charts and graphs. You've never done this in your life," Sheila said.

"Just bring your stuff. Have I ever steered you wrong?" Jess replied.

"No, but Jess, who's going to do this if I don't?" Sheila said.

"Ginger, my assistant." Jess said. "See you at six!" And she hung up.

*****

Jess opened the door with a smile and a glass of wine, which she promptly handed to Sheila.

"Give me the stuff." Jess sat down at her computer

"I didn't know you hired someone. Where is she?" Sheila said, looking around the apartment.

"India. She's virtual and she's fantastic," Jess said.

"India? I thought India was for customer service reps," Sheila said. Her stomach dropped.

"Ha. Wait until you see what she does for you." Jess smiled.

With a few clicks, Jess had the documents scanning and a young woman popped onto her screen.

"Hello, Miss Jessica. How are you this lovely evening?" Ginger spoke with a lilting accent.

"Fabulous, Ginger. Thanks. I have a big project, a top priority, which I'm emailing to you now. It's a presentation that must be sent to me by nine o'clock tonight, Eastern Standard Time." Jess spoke to the computer.

"Yes, Miss Jessica. I have received the email. Let me open it now," said Ginger.

Sheila felt like she was watching an exhibit in Disney World. Like the talking presidents she had seen with her parents as a child. The memory made her smile.

"Miss Jessica, I have the documents in place. Would it please you to go through them so I fully understand what you need?"

"My associate, Sheila, will explain everything. I am also sending her email address so you can ask any questions this evening." Jess got up. "It's all yours."

In less than fifteen minutes, Sheila explained what she needed while Ginger made suggestions, apparently understanding everything even though they had never worked together. It was the best meeting Sheila had had with an assistant in five years.

"Well, Miss Sheila. I will send any questions to you. You will have your presentation by 9 p.m. Eastern Standard Time tonight, if not sooner." Ginger smiled warmly and signed-off.

"Sooner. She said she might finish it sooner. Where can I get someone like her?" Sheila asked Jess as they walked to the restaurant.

"I read about them in *Fortune Magazine*. I've been using Ginger for a year. She's incredible and dirt cheap," Jess said.

"I can't believe she understood everything I said. I don't just mean the language, but the actual information. Why isn't she working here?"

"Ginger received an MBA in New Delhi. She handles all my administrative stuff, all my databases and my personal stuff," Jess answered.

"Like what?"

"Hair appointments, balancing my checkbook, paying my bills, updating my Christmas mailing list. You name it, she does it, and with a smile. So let me ask you this; why are you putting up with shit from your assistants?" Jess stopped to look at Sheila with concern.

"I don't know what's going on, Jess. It's like this girl Crystal showed up and everything went down the tubes. She's got Baxter in some trance even though she's completely irrational and has no idea what we even do. It's like she thinks joking and flirting are actually work. I don't get it. Alessandra would have gotten rid of any sales person that sucked this bad, but even she puts up with it."

"It's the new generation. Every generation thinks they can do it better but this one in particular is only interested in the surface and how things look. They also have no shame so when you reprimand them, they get outraged. Then you see someone like Ginger who is professional and happy to have a job. Remember the assistant I hired two years ago? Not only was she completely uninterested in learning how my business actually worked, when I told her I wouldn't keep her past the ninety day trial period, her father called me! No wonder she's so stupid. He actually referred to his twenty-four year-old daughter as his 'Princess.' I blame the parents. It's pathetic," Jess said.

"Don't you feel bad for not hiring an American?" Sheila asked.

"Did you hear me? This has saved my business. I pay eleven dollars an hour, no benefit issues, no threat of being sued. And wait until you see the results. College graduates over the next five years, with the way this economy's going, they're screwed. You'll see." Jess said.

They arrived in time for their reservation and Jess ordered another bottle of wine.

"I better not," Sheila said, checking her phone. "In case this presentation doesn't turn out too well."

"You worry too much. Bring the wine," Jess told the waiter.

Just then, Sheila's BlackBerry vibrated with a new message.

"Miss Sheila —

Attached please find:

- *Your presentation.ppt*
- *Research documentation.ppt*
- *Client Media Spend.pdf*
- *Client Internet Spend.pdf*

I hope that I completed everything to your standards. If there are any issues, please email me so I can correct them by 9 p.m. EST.

In the event you need printed copies, please send me your address and I will arrange for the closest Kinko's to print, collate and deliver your documents. Please let me know how many copies.

All respect,

Ginger

"She's finished!" Sheila scrolled through the information in amazement.

"I'm telling you. This younger generation – screwed. And, it cost less than thirty-five dollars," Jess said.

The documents were perfect. Better than perfect. Ginger had given two presentations. One contained the information that Sheila requested. The second was a version with animated graphics and seamless transitions between the slides. Ginger also included competitive research which Sheila had never seen. Breathing a deep sigh of relief, Sheila poured herself another glass of wine and made a toast to Jess.

36

Sheila took another gulp of Pepto Bismal from the bottle she stashed at her desk before heading to the Executive Suite on the twenty-fifth floor. It was 8:40 a.m. and Sheila had been waiting nervously for over two hours to discuss the presentation with Baxter and Paul. Finally, Paul had shown up at her door.

"Hey, Sheila. Baxter and I think it would be best if you go into the meeting. You should go to twenty-five immediately." He raised his eyebrows caused Sheila's stomach to lurch.

"Is there something wrong? I've been here since 6:30," Sheila said.

"No. It's just..." Paul trailed off, rubbing his hand along the door jam. "Some of your thoughts need clarification. It's hard to make heads or tails of a few of the pages."

"Okay. I'm going." Sheila unplugged her computer and headed toward the elevator. "Ah, Paul. Aren't you coming?" She stopped as Paul walked in the opposite direction.

"No. Baxter and I think it's best that you handle this since you put together the presentation. You'll need to do some explaining to Ann to make sure you're in line for that promotion." He smiled and went around the corner to his office.

There must be something wrong with the presentation, Sheila thought, wishing she had something stronger than Pepto Bismal at her desk. Paul certainly didn't look happy about it. But what could it be? It all looked fine to her last night. Her stomach ached terribly. Sheila looked at her phone. 8:50. She wouldn't even have time to use the restroom.

As Sheila walked into the executive conference room on the twenty-fifth floor, Baxter was already standing in front of the floor-to-ceiling windows overlooking Central Park. For a brief moment, Sheila forgot her worries and stared.

"It's a beautiful view," Sheila said. Baxter turned, looking a lot calmer than Sheila had expected, based on Paul's attitude.

"Yes, this is the place to be. Maybe one day, you'll be in these offices." Baxter smiled. "But first, you need to shine on this presentation."

"Right." Sheila's armpits started to sweat.

"You sit here." He pointed to a chair. "I'll sit there and Ann always sits there. She'll be here at exactly 9:00 a.m." He looked at his watch. "Three minutes. Try to relax. You look panicked." He turned back to the window, leaving Sheila alone with her sweat.

At precisely 9:00 a.m., Ann Joyce walked into the room. She was a tall woman with thick silver hair. Although they worked in the same building, Sheila had only seen Ann's image in magazines. In person, Ann was even more impressive.

"Good morning, Baxter." Ann made no move to greet him and he scurried across the room to shake her hand, an act that was not lost on Sheila. But Ann was already looking at Sheila, who immediately stood and held out her hand.

"Good morning, Ms. Joyce. My name is Sheila Davenport, Senior Account Manager. I report to Alessandra Arrugio."

"Welcome." Ann looked her over then turned to Baxter. "Let's get started. You have exactly twenty-nine minutes left."

Sheila clicked through the slides while Baxter presented. He obviously understood the information, even adding his own anecdotes, which left Sheila wondering why she was there. Ann was listening quietly, looking passively at the information. Baxter must have wanted Sheila to meet Ann in preparation for her promotion. Sheila relaxed for a moment, thinking of the call she would make to straighten out her mortgage problem. Smiling slightly, she transitioned to the slide on competitive research and Ann shot forward in her chair.

"Where did this come from?" Ann asked gruffly, looking at Baxter unkindly.

"Well, Ann. This slide is Sheila's creation, so I'm going to have her answer your questions. As you may know, Sheila is our number one rep and has some limited managerial responsibilities, so I asked her to participate in the presentation. I think it best for you to see her capabilities in person. Sheila, could you explain this slide to Ann?" Baxter said as Ann turned to frown at Sheila.

Sheila stared at Baxter while silently kicking herself for believing he had included her because he was on her side. This was all a set up because he didn't understand the presentation. The information had looked right when she received it last night. Had she made a mistake? She shouldn't have shared that bottle of wine with Jess. Between that, this extra turmoil, and Ann Joyce staring straight at her, Sheila wondered if she might throw up right on the conference table.

"Well? Where did this come from?" Ann asked a second time

Sheila briefly pictured Crystal and the others re-telling how she had vomited all over the CEO of the company. This was the end.

No, Sheila decided, that was not an option. She had to control herself and answer.

"India." Sheila was so nervous; it was all she could say as her stomach gurgled loudly.

"Excuse me?" Ann looked at her through slitted eyes.

Sheila knew she had five seconds to start talking but she was petrified. Taking another breath, she wondered why she was so scared. Ann couldn't actually hurt her. She would just fire her and Sheila would have to sell her co-op and live in a box. Maybe even move to another country, she thought. Well, if she was going out, she might as well be proud enough to go in flames.

"I couldn't find the information I needed to estimate business for next year, so I contacted a consultant for Fortune One Hundred companies and used my own money to hire her research firm in India. They provided the information." Sheila was amazed at her own ability to stretch the truth, though Jess was a consultant.

"And how much did that cost you?" Ann sat back in her chair, still staring at Sheila.

"Thirty-five dollars." She stared straight into Ann's eyes while she spoke but from the corner of her eye, she could see Baxter gawk.

"Ann, I knew nothing about this. I assumed her sources were credible or I wouldn't have allowed her to put this in a presentation for you. I guess I should have given this assignment to Paul Lynch. I'm so embarrassed," Baxter said.

"You had no idea about this?" Ann asked Baxter. He shook his head 'no'. As Ann turned to look at the slide, a smile spread across her face and her loud, guttural laugh filled the room.

"Well, that's too bad for you, Baxter, my boy. I have this information but haven't shared it outside this floor. I thought you convinced one of your buddies to leak it." She sat back in her chair, laughing harder. "You got this for thirty-five dollars? I can't wait to tell the others about this. Good job." Ann smiled broadly at Sheila.

"How come you haven't suggested that Sheila cover until Alessandra returns? How come you only mentioned Paul?" Ann was now looking at Baxter again but the smile was gone.

"Well, Sheila's a tremendous asset to the team but she needs to concentrate on selling, so —."

"Selling? She got this research for thirty-five dollars and you don't even know what it is! We bought it for over two-thousand dollars! Without her input, the rest of your presentation is a regurgitation of what I already know. No, Baxter, this is the kind of person we want to promote internally because she brings value." Ann smirked at Baxter. "That said I want Sheila to cover while Alessandra is on leave. Not Paul."

Baxter pursed his lips together so tightly, they were white. "With all due respect, Ann, I can assure you that Paul has the senior experience to —"

"But Paul's not here is he?" Ann glared at Baxter, looking every bit as powerful in person as she did on the cover on Fortune magazine.

"Excuse me, Ann." Her assistant walked into the room. "Five minutes until your next meeting." Ann stood.

"Look, if you want to keep Paul as General Manager because you owe one to his father, that's up to you. But as far as the sales department goes, he's not up to it. So, congratulations, Sheila you are the interim VP of Sales until Alessandra returns." Ann reached across the table to shake Sheila's hand. "I look forward to hearing more from you in the next three weeks. And congratulations to you, Baxter. You brought the right person to the meeting."

Sheila could have sworn Ann smirked at that last comment but she was out the door so quickly that she wasn't sure. Sheila gathered her things in silence. Baxter and Paul brought her here to make her look bad. Then, in a fantastic twist of fate, she ended up taking over until Alessandra came back. Even her stomach had stopped hurting until she turned to face Baxter who stared right back.

37

Paul was watching his favorite TV show online with one earbud in his right ear. He then unplugged the keyboard and pretended to type in case anyone walked by. His office was next to Baxter's on the end of the floor that no one walked through. It was the same layout as his previous office with slightly different views of southern Manhattan because he was two floors lower, which really pissed him off. The whole point of moving offices is to move up and to the corner, but Paul had been next to the corner office for six years. Six long years.

Paul knew he was luckier than most. He had a big home, a beautiful wife, cute kids – though they drove him crazy on the weekends. But in the last few years, he really felt stagnant. Ever since the Internet came along, every company scrambled to hire an expert like Alessandra, leaving men like him to try and catch up. He could do her job, he snorted. For God's sake, Alessandra did the job while addicted to drugs and booze and sex, according to the health insurance documents he wasn't supposed to see. Everyone enjoys a line of coke once in a while, Paul thought as he stared at the computer screen randomly hitting letters on his keyboard, but not in the morning. What irritated him most of all, however, was the fact that Alessandra hadn't been fired.

Paul paused the TV show and turned to look out his window. It was this new management ethos. 'Love thy employee,' and all that crap which meant she'd get a second chance. It pissed him off more than moving two floors below his previous office.

In the past, Paul could scream at anyone and they jumped to get what he wanted. Or he made them cry when he couldn't get them motivated by screaming. Now he had to listen to people's problems and care about their feelings. It was worse than dealing with his wife, Lisa. As long as she was shopping or lunching with her friends and taking her prescription, she was happy. But Paul's income hadn't increased like he expected leaving her less to spend. At least he found a solution, though he still needed that promotion.

Lisa was also always ready for a party. But even that wasn't fun anymore, especially the last one with the screw up on Sheila's place setting. He had purposefully typed her email address wrong so she wouldn't get the invite. He had assumed she wouldn't be there. He never did find out who told her about the party.

Paul turned to the presentation that Sheila had done. Thank God he wasn't in that meeting. He hated Ann Joyce. She was as bad as Alessandra with her new way of thinking and big drive toward the Internet. Meanwhile, Paul's father had worked for this company for forty years, spending another five on the board, and Ann didn't show Paul any respect for it. He was Daniel Lynch's son. That should count for something, but it didn't. Not anymore.

Better to let Sheila look foolish trying to explain some of those slides to Ann, that's for sure. With a thrashing from above, Sheila would be more than helpful. Now that she was single, Paul knew he just needed to twist the knife a little and she would jump. Like this morning. He smiled remembering the panic on her face. He really had no idea if those slides were right or wrong, but he wasn't about to send Sheila to meet Ann with a lot of confidence. Between this and Crystal's antics, Paul had to admit that if he were in Sheila's shoes, he'd probably fail, too.

Although Crystal was a pain (a sexy pain), the plan was working well for him. Paul needed something to shake him out of his funk and Alessandra's job would do it. Turning back to the window, he smiled thinking how much better his view would be very soon. Until Baxter walked in and shut the door.

38

Mabel Brown was staring out her window surveying the neighborhood. The war had ended ten months earlier, but she was still uneasy. Her son, Brian, had come home a hero. He had become a man with an entire chunk of life she couldn't understand. As her eyes landed on the Königs' home, Mabel made a note that the lawn had to be mowed and the bushes trimmed so the house wouldn't become an eyesore for the neighborhood. All the neighbors kept vigil during the war, hoping for word from their friends. Now the war was over and the men were all home. It could mean only one thing. The neighbors simply waited for the day when a next of kin would claim the house and possibly give some answers.

Brian rarely spoke of the war. The few stories he had shared chilled Mabel to the bone. Hugging her arms around her chest, she comforted herself as she considered the possible terrors her dear friend, Eliza, might have known. She pushed the thought from her head as a car moved slowly down the street, stopping in front of the Königs' house. A man stepped from the car, so similar to Franz it had to be a relative. He even had the same walk, but this man was much younger. When he reached the house, he peered inside the front window. The young man then turned toward the car and motioned for the occupants to join him. Unable to wait any longer, Mabel took a pale pink sweater from her closet and went to introduce herself.

By the time Mabel stepped off her porch, two younger boys were also by the front windows of the Königs' home.

"Hello?" Mabel called, dreading to hear the words she knew must be true. She passed the parked car, carefully avoiding the gaze of some people remaining inside to give them the privacy they needed.

"Mrs. Brown?" a voice called.

Mabel turned at the sound of her name and stared at the young woman who had just emerged from the car. Mabel smiled sadly at the family resemblance and walked toward the girl.

"Yes, I am Mrs. Brown. It is nice to meet you." Mabel held out her hand.

"Mrs. Brown. It's me, Ruth. We are home."

Mabel stepped back in shock, clutching the neckline of her sweater. The last time that Mabel had seen Ruth, she was a twelve-year-old girl with pig-tails. This stunning woman of twenty looked more like Eliza's sister.

"Mrs. Brown? Are you feeling well?" said a male voice.

"Dieter?" Mabel turned to the tall sixteen-year-old who had been looking through the front window.

"Yes." Dieter was a replica of his father.

Emotions overtook poor Mabel, who began to sob. Seeing the family after thinking they had been dead for the past eight years brought overwhelming relief. Having seen this reaction at

Uncle Jacob's and again at Aunt Marta's, Ruth understood the emotions that Mabel was feeling probably better than Mabel herself. She went to Mabel's side and hugged her tight. When Mabel pulled herself together, Ruth reintroduced Mabel to the rest of the children. Sara, now eighteen, said 'hello' and hugged her old neighbor, happy to be home. Thirteen-year-old Tomas also said his greetings, but he had only been five when they left for Germany so he didn't remember Mabel or the house. Greta, now eleven, also had no memory of this place that everyone said was her home.

"Annabelle must be big by now," Mabel said.

Looking around, she immediately regretted the comment. Of course, Mabel thought, not everyone had made it. The thought numbed her as she looked for Eliza.

"Mabel!" Franz came from the driver's seat and enveloped his neighbor in his strong arms. They held each other tight, crying tears of joy. Now that Franz was in front of his own home, seeing an old friend, he realized all he had missed and how much harder it was to come home due to their losses in Germany. There was so much to explain that he couldn't even begin. He stepped back and laughed through his tears at Mabel.

"I am so glad to see you!" Mabel said. "You must be worn out. Why don't you go inside and I'll bring some tea and cake."

As Mabel walked to her house, her heart was divided by the pleasure of seeing the Königs and the sadness of knowing that some did not make it home, especially Eliza. Mabel had considered Eliza dead for years but seeing Franz and the children today made her ache for her friend all over again. They had spent many enjoyable times in the Königs living room. Mabel would sit on the sofa while Eliza sat in her favorite green chair often holding a baby. Mabel shut her eyes imaging the scene. She and Eliza would talk and laugh over tea and cake while their children played together. It was hard to believe that she was actually going inside Eliza's house and Eliza would not be there. Mabel dried her tears.

She put a cover on her cake and the teapot on a tray. She would have to come back for the cups and saucers. Those poor children wouldn't have any food, and possibly no money. She would feed them tonight and take care of them until they got on their feet.

As Mabel walked the familiar path to her neighbor's home, laughter spilled into the street.

Mabel paused a moment to compose herself. This was a joyous occasion and she would not spoil it with tears or questions. Not today. There would be plenty of time to catch up. Smiling bravely, she called out for someone to open the door. As she crossed the threshold, Sara rushed forward to take the heavy tray not a second too soon. Because in the big green chair Eliza sat holding a baby and poor Mabel Brown dropped to the floor.

39

Ruth had been twelve the last time she sat in her bedroom, which still held her roller skates and dolls. Being the oldest, Ruth roomed alone. Her bedroom had seemed grand at the time, a room of her own. Now the house, not to mention her past life, seemed much smaller than she remembered.

Her old friends were more than willing to befriend Ruth again and take her to socials, but Ruth just didn't feel the connection as readily as they did. Her girlfriends' lives had been altered but they hadn't left their homes. Ruth had actually seen the war and related more to the G.I.s, with their quiet acceptance of what they had seen and done, and their determination to move forward.

With Ruth's teenage years taken by war, she simply didn't relate to other girls her age. Coming home at age twenty, she was too old to go to high school, leaving her quite lonely during the days with her thoughts on Vincenzo.

A few young men in the neighborhood tried to court her, but she wasn't interested. Vincenzo had promised to come and she would wait. Until then, Ruth would help her parents get back on track financially. So, she announced to the family one evening, "I have a job interview in New York tomorrow."

Franz looked at his eldest daughter carefully. It broke his heart that Ruth was having such a difficult time adjusting.

The others, except Dieter, were in school, surrounded by people their own age and fitting into American life. Dieter was learning finance at his job in New York, with plenty of returning G.I.s to befriend and join on nights out. Franz wished Ruth would find a beau, like Sara, and consider marriage, but she didn't show any interest. Finally, he spoke.

"That is fabulous, Ruth. Dieter, would you accompany your sister on the train?"

"Yes, Papa. You'll have to come early, Ruth. I must be in the office at 8:30," Dieter informed his sister.

"Certainly," Ruth said, smiling with relief at her Father's support.

*****

Ruth got the job as dressmaker's apprentice on Madison Avenue joining two others in the shop.

Her boss, Edna Mandusky, was a different sort of woman, standing just over five feet tall and about as wide. All her graciousness was saved for her clients, whom Edna fawned over and pampered. When the shop was empty, it soon became apparent that Edna was an unhappy woman often berating her assistant, Louise.

Louise had been with Edna for the past four years. She was a sweet woman who looked to be in her late twenties. It was obvious that life was hard for Louise, which is probably why she put up with Edna's moods for so long. She never spoke of a husband, only a son and her mother. Being that Ruth was a fast worker and quite a good seamstress, Edna was pleased. But as usually happens, Edna's true colors came out after a few weeks.

"Who told you to buy this thread?" Edna stood over Ruth, holding a spool of silver bullion thread. "Do you know how expensive this is?"

"Yes, but I need it for the beadwork on the Sullivan's wedding dress. It's the only thread that can hold those pearls." Ruth continued with her needlework.

"I have been doing this for longer than you've been alive and I have never used this thread. No one's ever complained before. You do not make any purchases without my approval." Edna raised her voice.

"You did approve it. Last week. Maybe you don't remember." Ruth now looked at Edna.

Louise nodded, "I remember."

"Who asked you?" Edna slammed her hands on the work table sending a container of bobbins to the floor. "I am in charge here and I am not paying for this thread. I'm taking this of your wages. Let it teach you a lesson. And you, pick up this mess." She pointed to Louise who fell to the floor to get the bobbins.

"I don't need to be taught any 'lessons.' In fact, here's a lesson for you: it's impolite to speak to people this way and I won't stand for it," Ruth said calmly. After being in Germany, Ruth had no fear of Edna. "I quit. Make your own dress in your own shoddy way. I won't have my name on it." Ruth stood.

"Okay. Stop the dramatics and go back to work," Edna said. Ruth silently put on her coat.

"Did you hear me?" Edna said. "I'm not going to apologize more than that."

Ruth continued buttoning, then reached for her gloves.

"Fine. I'll give you an extra dollar a week. Now sit and finish the dress," Edna said. In the past six months alone, she had fired four women because of shoddy work. This girl was a genius and, frankly, better than Edna.

"Two." Ruth put her hat on her head.

"Two what?" Edna demanded.

"Two dollars more per week and I get a full hour for lunch or I leave," Ruth said.

"A young girl like you is pretty brave to make such demands," Edna said.

Ruth locked eyes with Edna.

"You have no idea what bravery is," Ruth said. She passed Edna on her way to the door.

Edna watched Ruth walk toward the door with her head held high and her shoulders set. This girl had chutzpah. Which meant Ruth would be able to handle the clients. An important talent as the last apprentice was unable to hold her own with some of the difficult clients and only lasted three weeks.

"Okay. Okay. I'll give you the two dollars and the extra half hour for lunch," Edna called as Ruth opened the door. "You have guts. I need someone the clients can't push around. So stay. I'll teach you how to make the most beautiful dresses you'll ever see."

And a business partnership was born while Louise stared from the floor, still kneeling among the bobbins.

40

"I'm not working with her." Scott gulped his coffee. "She's nuts."

"Scott, please. I don't need this right now. I know Crystal's a handful." It was too early on a Monday morning for Sheila to be exhausted.

"No, you don't. She texted me at two o'clock Saturday morning. The beep woke up my wife and the baby and I had to spend an hour convincing her that I'm not having an affair. Then I had to sleep on the couch." He stared evenly at Sheila. "I don't need this."

"Neither do I." Sheila reached for her Tylenol. "What did Crystal want, anyway?"

"Look." Scott slipped the phone from his holster.

Sheila stared at the message on the screen, horrified. She looked at Scott in stunned silence.

"I told you. My wife saw it and thinks I'm having an affair. Crystal's nuts and I'm not working with her," Scott said.

"Have you said anything to her?"

"I'm avoiding her because she's supposed to come to a meeting with me this morning and it's not happening. You need to tell her." Scott said.

"No, you tell her." Sheila wasn't about to start taking on Scott's problems. "You're a big boy, you know what to do."

"She's crazy, Sheila. Like *Fatal Attraction* crazy. She's constantly coming into my office showing me her outfits like I'm some chick – no offense. Then she'll tell me stories about her social life, which is out of control. I've told her I don't have time, but she doesn't get it. This —" Scott raised his eyebrows and glanced at the phone. "is the last straw. I need you to do it because you're in charge. She'll listen to you."

Sheila scoffed at the thought of Crystal listening to her. "No, she won't. She's out of control and I have to figure out how to handle this. I may have to go to HR, which will bring the wrath of Baxter."

"I'll back you up. I can't have my wife thinking that I'm messing around. She's all hormonal after the baby. I can only handle one crazy woman at a time so you have to handle Crystal."

"Well, you might not like the results if you leave it to me because Baxter's watching out for her. You'll have a better shot if you go to him directly since it happened to you," Sheila said.

"No way. I report to you. I'm not going to look like I'm skipping rank."

"Grow up and handle it, Scott. Either tell Crystal yourself or go to Baxter." Sheila turned to her computer hoping Scott would just leave.

Instead there was a quick knock on Sheila's door which opened as Crystal stepped into the room without waiting for an answer.

"Hi. I heard you were here. Do you want coffee before we go?" Crystal looked at Scott.

"Aah, Sheila?" Scott said, dumbfounded. "You want to weigh in here?"

Sheila finished her email with a few loud clacks and turned to give Crystal a lesson in office etiquette when her jaw hit the ground. As Crystal stood in the doorway, the light behind her made her plum lace mini dress entirely see-through. And as if that wasn't enough, she obviously wasn't wearing a bra.

"Well?" Crystal shifted to lean again the door jamb and the Grecian folds of her dress shifted, revealing the entire left side of her breast.

"She's all yours, Sheila." Scott stood to go but since Crystal was blocking the door, he could only look at Sheila helplessly.

Scott was right, Sheila realized. This wasn't something he could handle. Anything he might say could easily get him into a worse situation.

"Crystal, why don't you sit down so we can have a talk?" Sheila said.

"I have to get ready for my meeting with Scott," Crystal said.

"No, you should sit." Scott said. "Now."

Crystal happily obliged Scott with a smile. He walked past her and shut the door behind him.

"You're not going to the meeting with Scott." Sheila sat back in her chair.

Crystal's expression quickly changed from annoyance to outrage but before she could open her mouth, Sheila held up her hands and continued speaking.

"First, your dress is inappropriate. You can't represent the company like that. Second, when you send text messages at 2 a.m. to a male colleague telling him you're horny, among other things, it's a problem."

"You have no right to judge my clothes and that text is between Scott and me. Are you spying on us?" Crystal's upper lip curled.

"Stop being so dramatic, Crystal. Scott came in here because he doesn't want to go to HR. So please take this as a warning," Sheila said.

"Warning? You have a problem with my dress because it looks amazing. And as for Scott, he flirts with me constantly. He's always making sure I understand what's going on, something you don't do, and he even took me to lunch last week which he wouldn't have done if he didn't like me." Crystal leaned back in her chair, causing another shift in her dress.

"Crystal, Scott's not flirting, he's being nice. He went to lunch with Jenn yesterday. Have you been thinking he's interested in you?" Sheila said, averting her eyes.

"Why else would he buy me coffee? And help me? Plus, I see the way he looks at me. Whenever I ask him if my outfit looks good, he says 'yes.'" Crystal smiled confidently.

Unfortunately for Sheila, the Tylenol hadn't kicked in yet. In fact, her head hurt worse as she stumbled to find a way to help Crystal understand the truth without bruising her obviously delicate ego.

"Crystal, we're a team here and everyone helps each other. So when Scott buys you coffee, it's the same as if Jenn or I buy it. It's a morale boost. It doesn't mean there's an invitation for a personal relationship. Do you understand?"

"Maybe it's not an invitation for you but for someone like me, it usually is," Crystal shot back, folding her arms with a smirk.

"Well, Scott didn't appreciate your text so you need to stop. You're making him uncomfortable and it's putting a strain on his ability to do his job. And, once again, your outfit is inappropriate for the office. I need you to go home and change."

"You can't tell me to stop texting someone and you can't tell me how to dress. This is a designer dress that looks great. The only reason no one else is wearing it is because they can't afford it," Crystal said.

Well, everyone doesn't have a rich daddy, Sheila thought. Sheila knew Crystal's salary, which was very low, almost too low.

Even if Crystal went to Century 21, she wouldn't be able to afford these clothes. Someone was helping her.

"Well, this has been fun but I'm going to the meeting now. While I'm there, I'll ask Scott if he has a problem with my texting him." Crystal stood.

"Crystal, if you attempt to go to that meeting, you'll leave me no choice but to call HR. Please go home to change and come back to the office," Sheila said.

"You know what? I'll go to HR myself. You can't tell me what to do." Crystal walked out the door.

Sheila quickly called HR then walked to Scott's office.

"Crystal voluntarily went to HR. She doesn't think her outfit is inappropriate, so any help you can give me would be appreciated," Sheila said. "And, she's insisting that you flirt with her so get ready to defend yourself."

"Sure. What the hell is her deal, anyway?" Scott looked concerned. "I mean it's pretty bizarre that she never cares what you think."

"I think her father gives her money so she doesn't really need the job." Sheila shrugged.

"That's not it. I know a little bit about her family. The father basically ignores her because he hates the mother. Baxter's obviously watching out for her because no one would act like that unless they knew they couldn't get fired," Scott said.

"So where do you think she's getting the money?" Sheila asked.

Scott smirked and shrugged. "Do you think she has something going on with Baxter?" Scott's phone rang before Sheila could answer. "This is Scott. Hm. Yes. That's right. Sure." He hung up the phone and turned to Sheila. "HR wants to see me."

"Good luck," Sheila said.

"Hey, Sheila," Scott said quietly. "Can I give you some advice?"

"Sure."

"You've got to start standing up for yourself. This is only a job so stop being such a wimp with Crystal. Baxter can't fire you for managing your employee." He walked away, leaving Sheila in his office, wondering if that were true.

41

"It's perfect," the client said, turning left to right as she stared at her reflection in the mirror. "I actually look like I have a waist." She smiled triumphantly at herself. "You have a gold mine in this girl, Edna."

Edna smoothed the fabric over her client's shoulders. The dress did fit perfectly with precise stitching that lay flat and even. Edna herself could not have done better. The shoulders extended just enough to give the illusion of a slimmer torso, which this woman hadn't possessed since giving birth to the third of her six children many years earlier. And the hem set off her legs which, somehow had stayed slender.

Yes, the dress truly was a work of art. Edna considered herself an expert seamstress and even she could not figure out how Ruth had pulled this one off.

"Yes, Ruth does fine work but not without a lot of guidance, I assure you." Edna whispered conspiratorially so Ruth wouldn't hear. "I'll send Louise to help you change and box the dress."

In the past two years, Ruth had proven herself invaluable to Edna's business. Not only was she a gifted designer and seamstress, she easily handled the clientele who were sometimes quite difficult. Plus, Ruth didn't mind working long hours.

Society women now flocked to Edna's to get her one-of-a-kind gowns which Edna had no problem promoting as her own work. The clients knew Ruth's contribution because she dealt with them closely in the design process, so Edna quietly made a point to tell them that she was teaching Ruth, though it was completely untrue.

The bigger question on Edna's mind was Ruth's lack of a life, specifically a love life. Working in a boutique such as Edna's didn't provide the opportunity to meet a man. Edna wrinkled her nose at the thought. Men. She really had no use for them. Never did. Now that she was older, no one bothered her about it, assuming she had lost her chance. It prevented a lot of problematic conversations.

Although Ruth didn't strike her as having the same opinion of men, the girl really was a mystery. All day long, Ruth created beautiful gowns – especially the wedding dresses – and never displayed any jealousy or wistfulness. Nor did she talk about herself. She did her job and business was booming.

In fact, business was much better than before the war. Women wanted to look good for their men and New York's night life was bustling. Cotillions and fundraisers were back in vogue, but best of all were the weddings. One wedding party usually brought the dress for the bride plus six or seven bridesmaids' dresses and another for the mother of the bride. The profits on a wedding party alone gave Edna a nice cushion for retirement.

"Louise, wrap the last client's dress," Edna snapped at the girl as she entered the back space. She then turned to Ruth. "We have the McCready party coming for the final fittings. Is everything ready?"

"Isn't it always?" Ruth didn't look up from her needlework. On her table lay a dark violet fabric in the midst of being transformed by an intricate bead pattern into a rich and silky bodice. She really is worth every penny, Edna told herself once again.

*****

"Oooh!" The group of young women cooed at the bride-to-be as she stepped from the fitting room in her wedding gown. She smiled happily at her mother then turned for the group as best she could with a six-foot train behind her. Ruth re-lay the train along the floor.

"It's beautiful!" Mrs. McCready wiped tears from her cheeks at the site of her daughter. Pearls had been hand-sewn along the edge of the fabric. Every four inches a swirl of pearls, rhinestones and sequins cascaded from the edge of the train to the center where they met in a dazzling bouquet of flowers. But the bride-to-be just couldn't keep still.

"Oh, Mother! Look at me!" From most people, this would have seemed conceited. But the bride was, unfortunately, a very plain girl who had really never looked pretty a day in her life. Her features were pleasant enough, but her face was quite easy to overlook. Her figure matched. From her shoulders to her hips, she was slender and rather boyish with virtually no breasts or muscle tone to add any sex appeal.

It had been a challenge, but Ruth had found a way to drape satin across her chest giving the illusion of a fuller bosom. The fitted bodice then gave way to a slightly fuller silk skirt at the waist which fell in deep, rich folds, creating hips for the girl. A toile skirt would have made her look ridiculous, contrasting harshly against her slightly asexual presence.

Watching Ruth put the final touches on the dress was like watching a master. The slightest pull here, a gather there, and the bride looked magnificent.

"I can't thank you enough," she said with a hug.

As Ruth smiled at the compliment, the bell on the front door jingled. She glanced at a tall, willowy blonde in a chic wool suit speaking to Edna. Something about her made Ruth's blood run cold.

*****

As soon as Ruth finished with the McCready party, Edna called her to the front of the store with a smile.

"Ruth." Edna was most charming which could only mean this lady planned to spend a lot of money. "I'd like to introduce you to Annette Malfique. Annette is getting married in six weeks and has come to us for her wedding dress."

"Yes, I have heard of your work," Annette said in a sophisticated French accent. "That dress you were finishing. Did you do that beadwork?" Annette gazed at Ruth with pale blue eyes heavily fringed with blond lashes.

"Yes," Ruth answered.

"Well, then, you must make my dress." Annette smiled and clasped her hands under her chin.

"Wonderful! And how many in your wedding party?" Edna asked expectantly.

"Their dresses are being done elsewhere," Annette said. Sensing Edna's disappointment, Annette smiled again. "I also require a trousseau for my honeymoon. We are going to Brazil." Edna smiled graciously once again.

"But there's no time," Ruth said, stopping both women momentarily.

"Of course there is, Ruth." Edna smiled at the girl.

"I'm sorry, but I have nine dresses to finish in the next four weeks. I'm so sorry." Ruth looked at Annette. The truth was Ruth simply did not like this woman. She couldn't figure out why. In fact, when they shook hands, Ruth had wanted to wipe her hand on her skirt.

"Well, I will pay." Annette waved her white gloves as if to make the conversation fly away. "How much?"

Of course, thought Ruth. Annette has enough money to get everything she wants with no care for anyone. Before she could speak, Edna jumped in.

"Six thousand dollars in order to rush material delivery and hire more embroiderers," Edna said, expecting Annette to haggle. Instead, Annette simply smiled elegantly.

"Here is what I will do. I will pay eight thousand dollars but I will only accept Ruth to do the work. I will come back tomorrow morning at 9 a.m. for a fitting. Do we have, as you say, a deal?"

*****

"I heard you are the best seamstress in the city. Where did you learn?" Annette asked Ruth as she stood on the pedestal in her lingerie.

"I made all the clothes for my family." Ruth continued taking measurements. This would be an easy fit as Annette's long, lean shape was quite perfect.

"Such hard times during the war, no? I was here, but visited France last year. The country is destroyed, as is most of Europe. My fiancé was in Germany, not as a soldier but he has the most atrocious stories. Being an American, you wouldn't understand. Everything here is so removed."

"Yes, it is." Ruth sighed.

"My poor fiancé has nightmares. He saw people suffering greatly. I know he feels that he should have done more to help. But what could he do?" Annette stared at her reflection in the mirror as she spoke. "You will see when you meet him."

Ruth finished as quickly as possible and promised to send sketches by the next day.

Ruth still couldn't concentrate hours after Annette had left. While Annette spoke, Ruth wanted to interrupt and tell about her years during the war to show Annette that she had suffered too. She had kept quiet because portraying oneself as the biggest victim is a dangerous road to travel. Plus, Annette would most likely not care that Ruth had been separated from her love while Annette was reunited with her fiancé after the war. It just seemed too unfair.

All Ruth's friends were married, every last one of them. They had either married their high school sweethearts as soon as the war ended or married a returning G.I. they had met at a dance. That's where Sara met her fiancé, David. Ruth went to the dances mainly to chaperone her sister and keep her parents from worry because she had no interest in any of the boys. They were sweet and earnest, wanting to forget about the war by finding a nice girl and settling down. But they were nothing compared to Vincenzo.

Where was he? Ruth wondered. Was he hurt? Did he suffer? Or was he home, earning money to travel to the U.S.A.? That was Ruth's best scenario; that Vincenzo was putting his life back together, making sure his family was supported so he could come here and marry her.

A smile crossed Ruth's face at the thought of her own wedding. She knew what her dress would look like, as every dress she sewed at Edna's was practice for her own. It sustained her. But time was going by and Ruth hadn't heard anything from Vincenzo. She knew Italy was in bad condition. Since Vincenzo's father was most likely dead, he may be destitute with his mother and sister to feed.

Ruth couldn't stop thinking about Vincenzo, even during dinner that evening. As she scrubbed the pots and pans, she imagined Vincenzo, the slant of his face and depth of his voice. The strength of his hands.

"Is something wrong?" Eliza continued drying the plates, eying her daughter carefully.

"No." Ruth scrubbed a pan furiously, determined to remove every bit of gravy.

"You seem upset. At least with the pan." Eliza gently touched her daughter's shoulder and tried to catch her gaze.

Ruth dropped the pan in the soapy water as tears began rolling down her face. Holding onto the edge of the sink for support, she let herself feel for the first time in years.

"I'm sorry. I know I shouldn't pity myself but I do." Ruth gulped for air. The loneliness was too much. The pain of it was heightened by the conversation with Annette. It gnawed at her somehow.

"It's natural to have feelings, but they're not facts. You won't be alone forever." Eliza knew that Ruth was waiting for Vincenzo. They all knew. Eliza couldn't fault her for that. Vincenzo had been Ruth's first love and he had been taken from her. "It's time to begin to heal, Ruth. Holding this wound is keeping you back."

"Hearing my client talk about Germany and her fiancé brought back so many memories. I still miss him," Ruth cried.

"Vincenzo loved you and he didn't leave of his own will. I know he asked you to wait and you have, but he may never come. Remember him as a good man in your life and move forward. Take pride knowing that Vincenzo loved you and thank God for sending him to you."

Tears rolled down Ruth's face as she listened to her mother.

"It won't be easy to let go but it also doesn't have to be torture." Eliza held her daughter tight, rubbing her back as she sobbed. There was no more for Eliza to say now. No one knew what had happened to Vincenzo and pretending would only prolong Ruth's anguish. "When this woman's trousseau is done, you should take a vacation. You and Sara together. You need a rest."

Ruth nodded in agreement while Eliza prayed that God would give Ruth the strength to find her way.

42

"Namaste is a dump!" Susan looked at Sheila in distain. "Are you kidding me? You're never going to meet someone there. Valley Spa is right up the street. Go there, for God's sake."

"Really." Stacey was throwing the rest of her bagel in the trash. "A friend of mine went to Namaste and left in the middle of the night because it was so hot. I mean, who doesn't have AC? You have got to do better than that if you want to find a boyfriend, Sheila."

Walking back to her office from the Monday meeting, Sheila wondered why she had bothered saying anything. Namaste was a great place to relax and that's what she needed, not a weekend in Vegas or a luxury spa she couldn't afford. In fact, she had wanted to visit Namaste for years but Joe would never go.

"Vegetarian food and no alcohol? Forget it. Any and all travel requires cocktails and burgers," were Joe's exact words. Even though they would have their own room, the fact that there were people willing to sleep in dorms just freaked him out completely. "Come on, Sheila. These people must be weird if they're willing to sleep in a room with strangers. It's not normal." Joe had pushed the brochure aside while they ate dinner. "But we won't be in a dorm. We'll have our own room. It will be nice to get away from everything." Especially you and your BlackBerry, Sheila had wanted to say. "No." Joe shook his head. "The Berkshires are for old people and people who can't handle the real world. If you want to go somewhere for a long weekend, we'll do the Hamptons or Nantucket. Jeremy has a place in Sconset. We can meet up with him and his family. I'll arrange it all."

And that's what they had done. For three days, Sheila made small talk with Jeremy's wife, who was constantly interrupted by her three small children under the age of four, while Joe spent the weekend on Jeremy's new forty-two foot sailboat. Every night after dinner, Jeremy's wife was too tired to go out so the boys went to Main Street for drinks and Sheila stayed behind for 'girl time' which meant putting three children to bed. While Joe had had a nice, relaxing weekend, Sheila was exhausted and bored.

Sheila shook her head to stop herself from wondering if Joe had been cheating then, too. Those thoughts brought her down a slippery slope. Many times, Sheila replayed moments from their relationship and tried to figure out if Joe had been cheating but it only ended with her in tears. She finally bought an egg timer after reading a popular relationship blog that recommended setting the timer to allow sixty seconds to think about your former love, and then switch thoughts. She was willing to try anything to get rid of the pain.

This is why a trip to Namaste seemed so perfect. Sheila stared at their website. True, the people weren't glamorous, but they all looked happy. There was a workshop offered next month, *Find*

Your True Happiness, which promised to "guide attendees through a personal journey of spiritual and practical development to their true path in life. Stop living for others and find your true happiness."

Thinking about Susan's comment, Sheila clicked to Valley Spa's website. Everything in it looked beautiful, especially the people. Sheila tried to remember the last time she had looked or felt that happy when Baxter called and asked her to his office.

"I heard you're taking a vacation. Some commune in the Berkshires?" He raised an eyebrow at her.

"No. I mean, it's not a commune, but I am taking a vacation at a yoga center in the Berkshires."

Baxter waved his hand at her and sat back in a leather chair. He studied Sheila's face as if trying to figure out if she was worth more words.

"Look here, Sheila. You and I have not always seen eye to eye. Maybe we should make a fresh start. Ann Joyce seems to like you so I'm going to help. You can't tell your employees you're going to some freaky place in the middle of nowhere for a vacation. Your sales team needs a leader. Someone they aspire to be. Someone who goes to L.A. and has lunch at The Ivy or goes to an expensive singles retreat and comes back with great stories about sky diving and getting laid. Not someone who needs to spend a week moping and trying to 'find' happiness. You should already be happy. Do you understand what I'm saying?"

Sheila simply sat in her chair, hoping the conversation would end quickly.

"You're a great sales person, Sheila, but not a great manager. It's because you don't give anyone a reason to look up to you. You have no power." He sat forward in his chair, leaning his elbows on the massive desk. "Do you think anyone would have told me about Alessandra's vacation plans?"

Sheila shook her head.

"That's because Alessandra would be going someplace cool and everyone knows she would have killed them for talking about her. No one's afraid of you. They're ratting you out so they can either get your job or get rid of you to get someone they like better." Baxter now walked around the desk motioning for Sheila to get up and walk toward the door with him. "I recommend you forget the meditating and concentrate on having fun this vacation. Then come back and tell us all about it. Here's the number for Charles Fitzpatrick in the Corporate Travel department. He's waiting for your call to book a vacation somewhere cool. Think Ibiza. Understand?"

"Yes, I understand," Sheila said as Baxter turned back to his office and closed the door in her face.

Sheila went to lunch with Baxter's words bouncing around her head. Did her team really hate her? Were they making fun of her behind her back? Why would they care if she wanted to meditate? When Alessandra was around, everyone complained that they wanted a boss who was calm and rational. Sheila was both of those things, but they didn't really care. They still hated the boss.

Walking down Broadway, Sheila realized she had eaten her lunch alone every day for the past week. Maybe Baxter was right and she did need to loosen up. She scrolled through the numbers in her phone, looking for someone who could be a good last minute lunch date. Someone who wasn't going to stab her in the back. Twenty minutes later, Sheila was eating her lunch and chatting away.

43

"Why do you care what they think?" Ruth finished the soup Sheila had brought. The mid-day visit was unscheduled and lovely, especially with the cupcakes waiting for dessert.

"Because they're just so judgmental. It's like mean girls in high school - once they target you, they keep attacking until you have a nervous breakdown," Sheila said.

"Well, I don't know about girls in high school but I do know that it's your life and you shouldn't be so concerned with what people think," Ruth said.

"It just seems that they have a rulebook that I didn't get. They all like the same things and go to the same places and I'm always on the edge. Joe was the one who knew what was cool.

Maybe I need a life coach." Sheila restrained herself from taking a second cupcake.

"No, you need to find your own way." Ruth looked Sheila straight in the eye. "If they're all going in one direction and you're always going in another, maybe you're just in the wrong place."

"I'd love to switch jobs, but I've got a chunk of commissions coming at the end of quarter." She didn't tell Ruth that it would all go to paying the HELOC because she was too embarrassed to tell Ruth about her financial problems.

"I'm not talking about jobs or money. I'm talking about your life. Maybe you're not supposed to be in that industry. Maybe you shouldn't be in New York. There is more to the world than Manhattan, you know." Ruth took a cupcake. "I don't know the answers and that Baxter certainly doesn't either. But I do know if you keep living for other people, you'll never find out." Ruth sat back. "See, that's the thing with freedom; it takes more courage than people realize."

Sheryn MacMunn

44

For the second time, Ruth dreaded a day of work. Annette was coming for a final fitting. The trousseau was ready but the train of the wedding dress needed to be finished. Ruth was usually happy to see her creations go out the door to be enjoyed. But not this time. Each outfit in Annette's trousseau had been a hardship. It hadn't made Ruth compromise on her workmanship, but it had been tedious.

Ruth worked on Annette's wedding dress in the back room almost constantly since they were so far behind. It was crowded in the small space due to the large train laid on the floor. The lights were also a problem.

In the front room, the lighting was soft and rosy to create a warm, friendly atmosphere. After all, it's stressful to know you'll be almost naked to be measured and examined by a virtual

240

stranger. It's a vulnerable time. So Edna created a sitting area for women to contemplate their style before moving to the fitting area, which was kept warmer with bulbs shining a soft, rosy glow that highlights most skin tones. Even the mirrors were draped with a white curtain so the customers weren't forced to stare at themselves while being measured. Edna had seen one too many women fixate on their hips or thighs and mentally magnify that area to twice its actual size.

But the light in the back room was harsh and sometimes blinding. When Annette's wedding dress had been propped on a mannequin, Ruth was shocked to see the silver bullion thread shining brightly. It hadn't been apparent in the light of the front room. Ruth had also stitched the cuffs with that thread and those lines reflected a sparkly shine in the bright light.

The fitting room was now free so Louise and Ruth moved the dress, which took a considerable effort. At last it was ready to go but Ruth wanted a bright light to show Annette the magnificence the bullion thread would give her dress if the sun was bright on her wedding day.

The bell on the door jingled. Ruth heard Annette's voice mixed with Edna's in that fake greeting only women of a certain class can do. Ruth turned to greet Annette, relieved this project was almost over. As Ruth helped Annette try on every outfit, Annette's enthusiasm overflowed. After she was dressed once again in her own clothes, Louise turned on the lamps as Ruth showed Annette the details of the silver bullion threadwork on the wedding dress.

"It is better than I imagined." Annette smiled triumphantly at the dress. "You're sure it will be finished tonight?"

As Ruth started to answer, the air was suddenly sucked out of her lungs with the jingle of the bell. The hair on her neck stood up as a deep chill ran through her body. The blood ran to her toes and she momentarily froze.

"Are you feeling well, dear?" Annette asked but Ruth didn't hear her. Picking the sharpest scissors from her case, Ruth turned slowly to face the door.

"Ruth?" Annette looked concerned.

Ruth couldn't answer. She just stared at the door. It was him.

45

"**R**uth, meet Annette's fiancé, Rolf Syndeman." Edna smiled broadly. "So this is the wonderful seamstress my Annette speaks of so highly. It is an honor to meet the woman who has made Annette so happy!" Rolf walked to the back of the shop smiling in celebration. "It is a pleasure to meet you, Ruth."

Ruth stared at those blue eyes. She had dreamed of those eyes, fearing them. "We have met. Do you not recognize me, Captain Syndeman?" Ruth stared.

"I believe you have me confused with someone else. I am not a captain, my dear." Rolf laughed in Edna's direction.

"You were. You were a Captain in the Reich. I am Ruth König, Captain. You remember my father, Franz?" Ruth stepped forward.

"Ruth, I never knew you had such an imagination." Annette approached, languidly putting her hand on Rolf's arm. "My poor fiancé often has to defend himself against those who think every German is a Nazi."

Edna stepped between Ruth and the couple. "Ruth, why don't you go in the back and help Louise put the rest of Annette's trousseau together so these lovely people can leave. Then I'll come back and make you some tea."

"No! He is lying." She turned to Rolf. "Because of you, my baby sister died. Because of you, I was almost killed in the internment camps." Tears started flowing down Ruth's cheeks. "Because of you, I lost the man who loved me."

"I don't appreciate these accusations, Miss Mandusky. Especially when I am paying so handsomely for your services. This is an outrage," Rolf said to Edna.

"Ruth, you really must stop." Edna loomed closer.

"Ha! You think I am afraid of you? After what I have seen? Thanks to him?" Ruth glared at Rolf. "Admit it. Admit what you did. Your fiancée deserves to know what she is getting for a husband."

"Ruth!" Edna was truly shocked and a little nervous. Had she lost her mind?

Rolf looked at Ruth and spoke in German, "Watch what you say, young lady. These accusations can get you into trouble."

"I am not afraid of you. You are in my country now. You are nothing without your uniform." Edna's jaw fell when Ruth spoke German fluently.

"We'll see about that." Rolf turned to Edna and switched to English. "Your girl is quite overcome with emotion, so I will leave now. You will receive payment when the wedding dress is finished and delivered in perfect order."

"Yes, yes. Of course, sir. I do not know what came over the girl. She has such a vivid imagination," Edna said, opening the door as Rolf took Annette's boxes from the counter.

"Make sure the wedding dress is delivered tomorrow by 9 a.m. and I expect you to assist at the wedding not her," Rolf said to Edna as he stepped through the door. He then looked back at Ruth and spoke in German. "I handled so many families like yours, it's difficult to remember them all. However, I do have to say that your family was one of my most interesting cases. Especially at the end when your boyfriend ran after you, promising true love. Tell me, has he found you?"

Rolf smiled cruelly and turned. Ruth following quickly behind.

"What did you do with him? Where did you send Vincenzo?" Ruth grabbed his arm. "Tell me! You are an animal!"

Rolf shrugged his arm from the girl's grip and continued walking to his car. Edna ran to hold her back

"You have no right to be in this country!" Ruth screamed in English. "I will tell everyone what you did! That you are a Nazi!"

Annette stepped onto the sidewalk, facing Ruth squarely.

"Control yourself. You look like a fool" Annette hissed while putting on her gloves.

"Annette. You must listen. Your fiancé is not who you think he is. He is a monster who was a Captain for the SS. He is an evil man who killed many innocent people. You have no idea what he has done," Ruth said.

Annette leaned forward and, in perfect German, said, "Yes, I do."

46

"Sheila, do you have a minute?" Paul and Crystal were standing outside her office.

"Sure. Come in." Sheila motioned for them to sit at her table.

"Crystal and I have been having an interesting conversation about team spirit in this office," Paul said.

"Really? Does Crystal want to be a better team player?" Sheila kept staring at her computer.

"Sheila, Crystal needs some guidance today and Scott and Susan aren't here. That's leaving the most junior person on our staff unable to get what she needs," Paul said.

"Well, I can't have sales people sitting in the office to train Crystal. I'm here and the assistants can help, so what does she need?" Sheila looked at Paul, annoyed.

"We need coverage, which means everyone should be in here five days a week. It's not just for Crystal, it's for everyone," Paul said.

"That's not possible. Jenn has Fridays off —" Sheila said.

"Which is totally unfair," Crystal started but Paul put his hand on her arm. Sheila studied the two of them.

"See, that's just it. Jenn's not here and it's upsetting the apple cart. We need people sitting on the bench from time to time. It's not okay to be home because it's convenient for Jenn's family. We're a family, too," Paul said.

Not the lame sports analogies again. Sheila took a deep breath to avoid exploding while Crystal sat back with a satisfied grin.

"First of all, Jenn's not working from home, she's off on Fridays. Second, it's not Jenn's duty to train Crystal, it's mine. So until Crystal comes to me with a real problem, I can't help her," Sheila said.

"I do have a problem. I want flex-time. So what if I don't have kids? I can get my job done in four days just fine." Crystal crossed her arms and pouted.

"Crystal, you're not making your number now. I can't see how a four-day work week will help. Do you, Paul?" Sheila said.

"Sheila, you're not understanding Crystal." Paul leaned back in his chair, stroking his tie. "You see, when I came up through the ranks, it was important for people to be together and create a family with their co-workers. Trust was built through exercises as a group. I once had to fall backward into the arms of a co-worker I didn't particularly like and you know what, Sheila?" He looked at her with wide eyes and threw his hands in the air. "He caught me! From that day on, I trusted him completely. That's why Jenn needs to be in the office. So Crystal can see that we are here to catch her when she falls."

"So you think Crystal's falling a lot? Crystal, do you agree with Paul? Because that would be a problem," Sheila said.

"That's not what I mean, Sheila. I'm saying that the situation is clearly sending the wrong message to the young people," Paul said.

"What young people?" Sheila.

"The assistants, Crystal. They are impressionable. You need to mold them into strong corporate employees who are loyal to our company. We're a world-class brand, Sheila, and we need to act like one. You need to show them how to do that. You need to trust, too. These young people will follow if you lead. Watch," Paul said, bouncing out the door like an excited puppy.

"Melissa, stand up for me." Paul smiled eagerly, standing in front of Melissa's cubicle.

"Aah." Melissa looked Sheila for help. When Sheila shrugged, Melissa stood uneasily.

"Melissa. What would you say if I told you that I want you to fall back and I'll catch you?" Paul asked.

"No way." And she sat down.

"See, that's what I mean." Paul turned to Sheila. "Melissa should feel safe enough to say, 'Sure. I know you'll catch me.' That's why we need some changes."

"What changes?" Stacey asked.

"Nothing." Paul waved her away.

"Wait a sec." Stacey walked to Melissa's cubicle. "You want Melissa to fall into your arms, which is harassment by the way, but you won't tell us what you want to change? Why should we trust you if you're going to change something but won't tell us what it is?"

Paul opened and closed his mouth a few times. "Stacey, trust is knowing that I'm here to take care of the team. To make things better."

"Then tell us what you're changing." Stacey raised her eyebrows.

"What's changing?" Mark said as he came back from lunch.

"We don't know. Paul won't tell us but he does want Melissa to fall into his arms so he can catch her," Stacey said.

"Gross." Mark sat in his chair.

"I'm talking about building the team spirit here. When I was a young employee, the company sent us to team building events.

We'd climb rocks and canoe to build our strength as a team."
Pete beamed at the group.

"Sounds awful." Stacey looked scornfully at Paul.

"Painful. When was that? The eighties?" Mark shuddered.
Paul's face fell. "Wait a second, guys. Learning to trust your
team is important and builds bonds that last a lifetime."

"Lifetime? I don't plan on working here for a lifetime. I don't
know anyone my age," Mark looked at him pointedly, "who's
been at a company more than three years."

Paul went back to Sheila's door. "This needs to change. This
is why everyone, including Jenn, needs to be in the office five
days a week."

"Jenn's coming in five days a week?" Melissa looked worried.
"She doesn't have a nanny on Friday. What's she going to do
with her kids?"

"That's not your concern, Melissa. Doesn't it upset you that
you are working while she's probably still in her pajamas?" Paul
said irritably to the group.

"No!" came the unanimous reply.

"I thought you were trying to build trust," Stacey shot out.
"How is messing up someone's life going to do that?"

"Then, we should all take Friday off." Crystal said to the
team.

"So this is your idea?" Stacey glared at Crystal.

"Well, why shouldn't I have Fridays off? I have a life, too,"
Crystal said while Melissa slid her phone off her desk and started
texting.

"Stacey." Sheila had enjoyed seeing Paul's approach fail but
this was getting out of control. "Paul's just putting out some
ideas which I've already vetoed."

"You can't veto me, Sheila. I am the General Manager and I
have the power to do what's needed to make the company more
profitable," Paul said.

"And I for one would feel better if there was more trust here.
So I support Paul." Crystal stood behind him and smiled.

"Then let Paul catch you," Mark said.

"Excellent idea. Come on Crystal; let's show them how a trusting relationship can work. Turn around," Paul said as Melissa's desk phone rang. She answered it immediately, turning her back on the group.

Crystal tried to hide her disgust at the thought of falling into Paul's arms in her pencil skirt. All she wanted was to get Fridays off and now she had to let Paul catch her? This was not part of her plan.

"Crystal, you're not setting a good example by not falling for Paul," Mark cajoled.

"Come on Crystal. Now's your chance to be a leader." Paul stood with his arms outstretched.

"Yes, Crystal, you need to show us how dedicated you are to building trust." Sheila enjoyed the glare Crystal threw in her direction.

"Paul?" Melissa said. "Jenn's on the phone. She needs to speak to you."

"She'll have to wait. Tell her we're in the middle of some team building exercises. Turn around." Paul motioned to Crystal.

"You should take Jenn's call," Crystal tried to stall.

"He will, after you fall into his arms, Crystal," Stacey mocked. "Jenn can wait."

"Crystal," Paul said with a slight edge. "You have to fall. Now."

"Fine." Crystal turned. How hard could this be? she reasoned. If this is what it takes to get Fridays off, she'd suffer through it.

"Okay, Crystal, now you count to three and fall. I'm here for you." Paul was a little too happy.

"Paul, Jenn is waiting. She said it's very important," Melissa said.

"Not now. She has to get in line behind Crystal." Paul squatted slightly and took a deep breath.

"Okay. One." Crystal stood straight, thinking how she could go to the Hamptons a day earlier every weekend.

"OK. I'll just put her on speaker." Melissa pushed the speaker button on the phone. "You're on, Jenn. He can hear you."

"Hey, Paul." Jenn's voice rang out clearly. "So glad you're working on building trust in the office. I love building trust."

"Two." Crystal shut her eyes and pressed her legs together, thinking how she could get her hair blown out before the Friday rush. She took a deep breath. "That's great, Jenn. We'll talk about it when you're in on Monday." Paul repositioned his feet, wondering what Crystal's slender frame would feel like in his arms.

"Actually, you need to talk about it now." Jenn's voice rang through the pit. "See, I called my team in HR and they're not so happy with your changes to my work schedule. Deborah Adams wants you in her office. Immediately."

"Three!" Crystal let out her breath and leaned back just as Paul turned to grab the phone, leaving her to fall into thin air.

47

"I will not finish it." Ruth said.

Edna knew Ruth could be stubborn but how on earth could she refuse such a large amount of money?

"I am offering a thousand dollars! You can save your parents' house with that much!" Edna said.

"I don't want his money! My parents wouldn't want his money! It has blood all over it!"

Edna's nerves were frazzled but she knew better than to speak. In the time Ruth worked in her shop, she had revealed very little about herself. But Edna was nothing if not a gossip, so she knew more than Ruth realized.

"I have an obligation to finish that dress for Annette. If it is not finished, I will not get paid." Edna was trapped. Her clients knew of Ruth's skill so it wouldn't be difficult for her to find work but Edna's reputation would be ruined. Plus Edna did need her. But the trick of every small business owner who has a star is to make them believe that the business will be fine without them.

"I never would have taken the account if I had known about Rolf's past but it is done, Ruth. They will get married with or without that dress and the wedding will be in all the papers. At least you will make a name for yourself and never have to worry about money with the kind of clients we will get. If you don't finish the dress, you will get no publicity."

"Publicity is not the most important thing in the world. There is something called integrity that we need to think about. Other people should know the truth about him," Ruth said.

"No one needs to know anything. I have a business to run and I will run it my way. If you have a problem with that then you can go home or finish the dress. Your choice." Edna walked to the front of the shop.

The girl had her convictions. Who could blame her? She was young. But the war was over and everyone needed to make a living. Something Edna understood all too well. She reached for the flask she hid under the counter, right next to the money, and took a swig of bourbon. As the alcohol burned her throat, it helped wipe away her own memories of war.

*****

"I'm going to fight in the World War. Everyone is doing their part. Your part is to be brave and take care of Mother. I'll be home as soon as I can." That was all Edna's father had said when he walked out the door, never to return. The tears began stinging her eyes, so Edna took another swig as the memory of her mother rushed back. The poor woman had laid in her bed, sick and hungry because they had no food. It had been up to Edna to support them, leaving her to do whatever it took to make money as a young girl in Indiana.

As soon as her mother died, Edna moved to New York and began using different skills to earn a living.

This time, instead of making money working directly with men, she focused on their wives. Wealthy women who needed pretty clothes for all their many events.

Another gulp and Edna was able to push that life in Indiana from her memory and come back to the present where her gaze focused on her ledger. The three thousand dollar debit glared at her.

Oh that girl is young, Edna thought, closing the book and reaching for her flask. If it were me, I'd take his money. After all, it is really the only thing that matters.

Gathering her things in the back room, Ruth stopped when she saw Louise motion to her.

"Money isn't everything but we all need it to survive. It would be a shame not to take advantage of the situation, especially since so many people will see the dress." Louise peeked toward the front to make sure Edna was out of earshot. "Edna will get all the money because she will finish it. You are now free from that man. Think of the money as Edna's and what you could do with it to get freedom from her. I wish I could. Plus, the world will never know who Rolf Syndeman is unless you tell them." Louise put a roll of the silver bullion thread in Ruth's hand. "I would reconsider if I were you."

Then Louise turned on the lamp and left Ruth to stare at the half-finished handiwork sparkling on the train.

48

"**Y**ou could be in over your head, you know." Jeff Levine, the head of Creative Services for Shearson Media, looked at Sheila over his Cobb salad.

"I know." Sheila sighed, unable to eat.

Jeff and Sheila had been friends since Sheila had come to New York, working together at her first job in the city. They had never been close friends but they used to go clubbing, analyzing one another's dates and generally helping each other out. Unfortunately, Joe had never warmed to Jeff, which Sheila suspected had to do with Jeff being gay though Joe denied it.

"He's just so corporate. I don't trust him," Joe had said. Of course, that was before Joe went to grad school and became a banker.

As a matter of fact, Jeff was the one who got Sheila an interview for the job at *Goodliving.com*. He recommended her highly for the position which had been a godsend. When Jeff met his partner, Bob, he and Sheila had less and less time for each other but they always stayed friends. Sheila felt bad calling him for help after not speaking for so long, but Jeff had been with the company for almost fifteen years and he knew where all the bodies lay.

"Listen. I don't know any other way to say this." Jeff picked up his fork. "You need to get a handle on your staff. It doesn't matter if Ann Joyce likes you. If your staff is a problem, you're going to pay. And Baxter hates anything Ann likes so don't be surprised if he isn't helpful." He took another bite and let Sheila digest his words.

"They just won't listen. I mean, every one does something outrageous, it's like the next one has to outdo it. And that Crystal just winds them up somehow," Sheila said.

Jeff put down his fork. "Sheila. I'm always more than happy to help. But there comes a time when you have to start being the mentor. You can't be the Interim VP of Sales and act like you don't know what to do. Even if you are completely clueless, you have to act like you know what you're doing. And if you make a mistake, well, you blame the people under you." Sheila opened her mouth to protest but Jeff held up his hand.

"I know you don't want to hear this, dear heart, but it's true. That is just the way it is and it is this way because it works. That being said, I asked around to see if anyone has made any big waves in HR and aside from Crystal, Mark has a few items in his file. So, I'll help you deal with him," Jeff said.

"What are you going to do?" Sheila asked.

"Just leave it to me. But sweetheart, I can only do this once. The rest is up to you."

49

Mark nervously walked toward Evan Cutone's office. He had no idea why Evan, the Art Director of *Victory Magazine,* wanted to see him, but Mark knew he was gay and gorgeous so he had some secret hopes. As he entered the office, the door shut to reveal Jeff Levine sitting in a chair.

"Hey, guys," Mark said. "Wow. I didn't know it was a party." He smiled.

"Shut up and sit down," said Jeff. "We're here to give you some friendly advice."

"Okay." Mark was confused.

"You've been making waves in HR and we don't like it," Evan said in his quiet, cool tone.

"You're making us all look bad." Jeff sneered at him.

"So, let us tell you what you're going to do." Evan looked Mark over as if he were insignificant. "First, stop wearing the see-through shirts and mandals. It's inappropriate."

"Why? It's my right to wear —"

"Oh no, please don't go there." Evan put his fingers against his temples. "I just cannot hear another child talk about their rights. What the hell have breeders done to these children to make them think we care?" He looked at Jeff wearily.

"No one gives a fuck about your rights." Jeff rolled his eyes. "It took a very long time for us to get where we are in this company. In many companies, as a matter of fact. Every time you act like it's Saturday night on Fire Island, it reflects poorly on all of us."

"Well, that's not my fault. It's homophobia and I plan to fight it my own way. Plus, I look great in that shirt. It shows off my stomach fabulously." He smirked cutely and pulled up his shirt to show perfect six-pack abs.

"Oh my," Evan said.

They were beautiful, but Jeff glared to remind Evan of the business at hand and snarled. "Focus."

Both men leaned toward Mark with menacing glares.

"It's not homophobia to expect an employee to keep his nipples covered and not paint his nails in the office," Evan said.

"But the girls do it." Mark looked scared now. This was not the friendly meeting he expected and he certainly didn't want to make any enemies, especially with Evan, who was rich and single.

"They're not gay men," Jeff almost shouted, but he regained his composure quickly. It wasn't this kid's fault that Jeff had had to fake being engaged during the eighties and most of the nineties.

Evan quickly jumped in. "Here's the deal. Go get some decent clothes for the office and start acting respectable. You do that and we'll get you a promotion. Keep acting like it's the Pride Day Parade – we'll have you fired."

"You couldn't!" Mark was horrified.

"Could and will." Jeff threw back. "Do you understand?"

"Yes." Mark looked like a kicked puppy. Although he honestly wasn't sure they could fire him, he knew they meant business.

Jeff got up and walked out of the office, finished with the episode. Evan leaned back in his chair to watch Mark pout.

"Now, now. Be a good boy and maybe we'll meet at Gobar to discuss those abs. Until then, don't make even one mistake." Evan smiled sexily and shooed Mark from the room.

Mark stepped on the elevator dreamily thinking of Evan's last words. Oh, yes, he'd behave. If not for the promotion, to meet Evan outside of this wretched building.

50

Walking to the outside garden of Golden Hills Rehabilitation Center, Sheila couldn't help but wonder if she could stay here for twenty-eight days herself. The grounds were beautifully manicured, stretching for acres. It seemed like a nice place until she noticed the people crying, arguing, or just wandering around looking miserable. Maybe this wasn't such a great vacation spot after all.

Sheila had tried to say 'no' when Alessandra called a few days ago and asked her to visit, but somehow she ended up renting a car for the drive to Connecticut, on a Sunday no less. It was the right move, she reasoned since Alessandra would be coming back to work soon. As she continued walking the grounds, Sheila wondered what Alessandra's mood would be. Please let it be decent, she prayed.

"Hey!" Just hearing Alessandra's voice made Sheila's stomach flip. Turning around, Sheila realized she had walked right by her.

"Hi," Sheila said, a little put off by the person sitting on the wicker chair. Alessandra wore a plain, long sleeve, white t-shirt with jeans and a ponytail. She looked like a child, sitting so still in the large chair. And her eyes were different. There weren't daggers coming out of them. Sheila nervously sat in the chair across from Alessandra and took out her notepad and pen.

"Sheila, put down the notebook. I didn't ask you here to work." Alessandra sighed.

"Ah, okay. How are you? You look good." Sheila tried some small talk.

Alessandra rolled her eyes. "I'm in rehab. I can't drink anymore or do drugs and for six hours a day, I have to sit in group therapy." The accompanying look let Sheila know this wouldn't be a heartfelt reunion.

"Okay. Glad we got that straight. So, what did you want to talk about?" Just let me out of here, Sheila thought.

Alessandra looked away to the grass and trees in the distance and just stared, making Sheila very uncomfortable. She had never seen Alessandra still or quiet. Maybe they were just allowing her to take different drugs. It was a full two minutes before Alessandra spoke.

"I assume you're familiar with the Twelve Steps of Alcoholics Anonymous." Alessandra gazed at Sheila. "Well, I'm working on Step Nine, which means I need to attempt to make at least one amend before I leave. I already had to do this with my family which wasn't pretty. Apparently, making business calls in the limo during my dad's funeral wasn't appreciated. Now I have to do one outside the family and I've chosen you."

"Okay. Do I just forgive you or is this like Earl, where you have to do something?" Sheila asked. The thought that Alessandra was going to apologize to anyone was unfathomable. Knowing Alessandra wanted to apologize to her almost knocked Sheila off her chair.

"I wish it were that easy. I've done something wrong and I'm going to help make it right." Alessandra tucked her legs under her and crossed her arms. "I know I could be hard at work and I know I was awful to some people, including you." Then she looked at Sheila. "But I need to hear what it was like to work for me. I'll listen to whatever you need to say."

"Alessandra, you're trying to get sober. I really don't want to upset anything —"

"Sheila." Alessandra suddenly leaned forward in her chair. "I need you to tell me. I mean it. I didn't bring you here to bullshit me. I need the truth."

"But you were there. You know the truth." Sheila desperately tried to back out of this situation. She knew that Alessandra once had someone transferred to another department for eating a donut in a meeting. Sheila needed her job.

"No. I don't." Suddenly Alessandra's eyes were round with worry.

"You mean you don't remember any of it?" Sheila asked.

"I remember bits and pieces, like the presentation in New Jersey. I remember getting there and being there but I don't remember the ride home. I took something in the bathroom." Alessandra sat back, defeated.

"Oh, Alessandra. This will take all day." Sheila was already starting to get hungry and, quite frankly, wasn't sure she wanted to be the guinea pig in this experiment.

"Please, Sheila." Alessandra grabbed her hand. "I need help and there are things you need to know, too."

Sheila looked for some sort of guard or doctor. Surely this must be a mistake. This woman holding her hand looking scared was the biggest psycho Sheila had ever met. There was no way that this was going to be good for Alessandra's sobriety or Sheila's career. For the first time, Sheila was going to say 'No!'

"Alessandra, although this is a beautiful garden and your 'Steps' sound nice, when we're back at the office, you'll hate me. Since Joe left, I really need my job. So, I'll just forgive you and we'll move on." Sheila tried to pull her hand from Alessandra's grip.

"Sheila, I appreciate your honesty and I certainly don't want to make you do anything you don't feel comfortable doing." Alessandra stared at Sheila and smiled.

"Thank you, Alessandra."

"But you're not going to have your job by the end of this month. So I still need to tell you what I've done to you. All you need to do is listen."

*****

Driving home four hours later, Sheila was exhausted. Alessandra had told her all about Baxter's plan to get rid of Sheila by the end of the quarter and that Jenn was also on the chopping block because they earned the most. Apparently, there was even a spreadsheet showing the profit from firing the two women. That's what her contribution over the last five years boiled down to; Sheila was now a number on a spreadsheet. A number which was too high, so she had to go.

At first Sheila cried. So many people were in tears that no one even noticed. Then she opened up to Alessandra about Joe taking most of their joint account and her impending mortgage problems due to Joe not paying.

"Christ. I thought I had it bad." Alessandra gave her tissues. "You're a mess. But hey, at least you can drink. Just not here."

"What am I going to do? I expected a quarterly bonus to get out of debt and then I could look for another job. Now I'm stuck." Sheila started crying all over again.

"Good God. You're not stuck. Sheila, please don't take this the wrong way, but you have GOT to grow up. I'm telling you this to help you and you're crying. You have to start thinking smarter, especially now," Alessandra said.

"I have to think smarter now? Why did you ask me here anyway? Why am I the one you chose?"

"Because I screwed you over and I can help you. You are a nice person, Sheila, but it's going to be used against you at this level. Please start looking for the clues. Add them up. Why would Baxter, who's been with the company for thirty years, suddenly let a twenty-seven year-old woman run amok in the office? He loved you! You were his star. Please, let's just talk so you can go into this prepared. You really need to do this right."

"I think he's having an affair with Crystal. That's why she gets away with murder," Sheila said.

"No, that's not it." Alessandra laughed. "He brought in Crystal because he knew that she would make you look bad. Makes it easier to build a case against you. Plus, he can pay her next to nothing which will help solve his other problem."

"And what problem is that?" Sheila sniffled some more.

"Baxter's been embezzling from the company and if he doesn't get the money back before the end of the year, he's going to get caught, as well as Paul. And guess who Baxter's banker is?"

"I don't know," Sheila shrugged.

"Crystal's father. Now can you now please stop crying and listen to how to save yourself?"

Sheila blew her nose and started taking notes.

Alessandra told Sheila her passwords so Sheila could access old emails and important documents on Alessandra's computer. Then she told Sheila to go to her desk and get a yellow envelope titled "Co-op Board" that was the proof Sheila needed to make sure Baxter backed down.

"I didn't have time to take it home when 'my incident' occurred with HR and Paul was watching my every move," Alessandra explained.

"Why is it titled 'Co-op Board'?" Sheila asked.

"Because no one will look at a file that boring. I called the doorman in my building. The key to my office will be waiting for you this evening. Here's the number for my lawyer. Get in touch with him. He'll know what to do."

When visiting hours ended, the two women still couldn't bring themselves to hug.

"Well, I guess this is it. Hopefully, I'll still be there when you return. If I get this right," Sheila said.

"I won't be going back." Alessandra shook her head.

Sheila's face fell with concern, which made Alessandra laugh.

"Sheila, look at the clues! I'm in rehab. Something's wrong with my life and I need to fix it."

"What will you do?" A few hours ago, this would have been a dream, but now there was no vengeance left or fear. Just a need for peace.

"I'll be fine." They shook hands and Sheila walked away.

"Hey, Sheila?" Alessandra's familiar scream rang across the yard.

"Has anyone told you how annoying your voice is when you yell like that?" Sheila turned with a smile.

Alessandra laughed and shrugged her shoulders. "Remember that this is a game to them. Play it to win."

51

"**I**'ll finish Annette's wedding dress. But I want the entire two thousand dollar bonus," Ruth said.

Drawing herself up, Edna realized she was quite drunk and didn't want Ruth to notice. She thought she had been alone. Well, Louise was in the back but she didn't count.

"I already decided to do it myself." Edna slurred through a drunken gaze.

"Don't be foolish, Edna. You're drunk. You'll ruin the dress. I'll finish it tonight so you can deliver it tomorrow. However, I want the money now."

"I thought money didn't matter," Edna mocked sloppily. "I thought you were above us all. Now you expect me to be happy that you want to fulfill your commitment? And I am not drunk." But she could feel herself sliding to that dark corner where she becomes mean. Even in her drunken state, she knew she had to stay calm. She began to perspire a bit.

"I'll give you a thousand dollars and no more. And you will finish that dress tonight! You made a fool out of me today. I shouldn't have to give you anything. It's because I'm generous and feel bad about what you suffered that I'll do it."

"You will give me two thousand dollars or I leave. And Edna, if that dress isn't perfect, they won't pay you either." Ruth said calmly.

"Fine!" Edna reached into her small safe and counted the money, which took three attempts to get right.

As Edna put on her coat, she yelled for Louise who didn't come. What was happening here tonight? Edna thought as she struggled with the buttons on her jacket. "Louise!"

"Yes?" Louise was next to her.

"You are staying to help Ruth tonight. I am going home to relax from the stress of this afternoon," Edna slurred.

"She'll have to pay her babysitter extra to stay," Ruth called out.

"What do you care?" Edna threw back. "It's none of your business."

"You need to pay her extra to cover her babysitting costs."

"I do not." Edna huffed at the thought, practically falling into the wall as she turned to stare at the women.

"You need to pay her twenty-five dollars," Ruth said.

"What did you say?" Edna screeched at the absurdity of Ruth's request.

"It's not fair for her to pay her sitter extra because of your scheduling error. You are making a fortune off this assignment. You can afford to pay her," Ruth said.

Edna's nostrils flared as she locked eyes with Ruth. In addition to the perspiration, a pounding headache had already begun. She breathed heavily as she considered her next move.

"Oh, you are a precious one. First you take my money, now you expect Louise to follow suit. No, she is not worth it to me. I can find a dozen stupid women like her and she knows it, which is why she didn't ask herself." Edna felt her body relax as she opened the door.

"Let me rephrase it: I won't stay unless you give Louise the twenty-five dollars."

Louise came forward and grabbed Ruth's arm but Ruth shook her off.

"Are you behind this?" Edna leered at the girl.

"No." Louise stood behind Ruth shaking so badly, Ruth felt it on her own skin.

"Of course not, because you're gutless." Edna re-entered the room.

"Edna, I'm warning you." Ruth raised her voice for the first time ever in the shop with a timbre so forceful that Edna stopped in fear.

They stared at each other but this time, it was Ruth who glared while Edna tried to compose herself.

"You want her to have twenty-five dollars, you pay her out of your money. I'll tell you now, she's not worth it."

"Yes, she is," Ruth said.

"Then why doesn't she ask herself? Because she knows she's pathetic. I'll bet you fifty dollars that she won't ask me herself. So, you can either pay her yourself or bet me, either way you'll lose." Edna smiled drunkenly at Ruth.

"I'll take your bet." Ruth turned to Louise, giving the girl a view of two faces. Edna's was drunk and cruel, Ruth's solid and sure. But Louise was afraid. She knew Edna's rages and was pretty sure Ruth would quit with that much money, leaving Louise alone to face Edna's wrath. Ruth could easily find another job with her skills, but Louise believed the nasty things that Edna had told her over the years. She believed that she was, in fact, useless.

Louise had never been a confident woman but with her husband dead from an accident and her son needing special care, she had been forced to take care of things as best she could. The war had actually helped Louise as women were put to work for the cause for a decent wage and there had been day care. Louise had been able to pay for doctors and even save a little. But now, good paying jobs were hard to find for a woman. Her savings dwindled as doctor visits for her son became more frequent. Between her pay and what her mother earned from odd sewing jobs, they scraped by. Twenty-five dollars would be a huge relief, but the thought of losing her job turned her stomach into knots.

"See." Edna smiled confidently. "I told you she wouldn't ask. That's why her son is sick, because he has to rely on her and she's weak. Where's my —"

"I want fifty dollars or I go home," Louise declared loudly. Her hands clenched by her side. It was one thing for Edna to insult Louise's work but to insult her as a mother was too much. Even if Edna was difficult to deal with for a while, Louise couldn't go home and tell her boy that he couldn't have more to eat because she had been afraid. No, Edna was mean, but her son needed everything Louise could possibly give. The pain would be worth it.

"You little traitor." Edna moved forward.

"Enough!" Ruth warned. "Give us the money and get out or this dress won't be finished and you will be ruined."

"No, you are finished." Edna opened her purse and fumbled for the bank deposit envelope. "Here!" She threw bills at the women, producing a lame effect as they floated on air.

"Do not think you have won. When this dress is finished, I want you gone." She stood inches from Ruth's face then stormed from the shop.

Ruth bent for the bills and handed it all to Louise.

"Let's get to work. We really don't have much time," Ruth said.

52

Edna couldn't get over how stunning Annette looked. The woman was flawless in the gown.

"You are beautiful," Edna gushed while David Sullivan, Annette's hired photographer, snapped photos of Annette looking at herself in the mirror as the natural light flowed through the floor-to-ceiling windows in her Fifth Avenue apartment.

"Thank you, Edna."

Ruth's outburst from the other day was not mentioned and, as promised, she did not join Edna. Edna knew Annette would not want to ruin her wedding day talking about what happened. The woman was driven, so it was quite possible that she hadn't given Ruth a second thought. But Edna could not help thinking she must get Ruth back on board, especially after seeing the finished wedding dress. Annette informed her that there would be at least seven society photographers at the church. Edna became heady with the thought of all the wealthy women who would see her work in the pages of the newspaper and magazines. Two bridesmaids already mentioned scheduling appointments. Well, she would simply offer Ruth a raise but she would fire Louise.

It took a full half hour to get into the limo that would take them to Darien, CT for the ceremony. The church looked more like a cathedral, sitting on a massive amount of land with large trees. As they pulled into the church parking lot, Edna jumped from the Mercedes to assist Annette.

Keeping pace with the bride was difficult as the train wasn't simply bustled. It was rolled from the sides, then the bottom end bustled inside-out to fully protect the beading. Edna held the dress mid-air to prevent dirt from getting anywhere on the hem.

She wished she had put on her sunglasses as she hurried down the path. Although the sun was hidden somewhat behind light, fluffy clouds, her eyes watered. Please Lord, let Annette stand near a shady tree, Edna silently prayed as beads of sweat rolled down the middle of her back and pooled under her armpits.

Her prayers were answered as David motioned them to the arboretum for their first shoot. Edna expertly arranged the dress and ducked into the shade of another tree while the photographer arranged the bridesmaids.

Edna breathed a little easier hidden in the shade as she located her sunglasses within her purse, next to her flask. The sunglasses made everything as dark as night. Staring at the chaos of the photographer organizing the bridal party, Edna couldn't help but replay the scene with Ruth and Louise. Even though the two thousand dollars disturbed her to no end, Edna still made plenty on this client. What really galled her was that Louise had stood up to her. In all their years together, the woman hadn't opened her mouth. Oh, well. Edna truly felt sorry for Louise as her son was sickly, but that girl had no idea how easy she had it, working in the shop. Edna only had one option to support her mother in Indiana.

Edna shook herself slightly. She couldn't think of that now, so she took a drink from her flask to push back the memories. The wedding would begin at noon, so the bride had to be inside soon to hide from her guests, giving Edna a reprieve from the heat for a few hours. She looked forward to cooling off in the backroom.

David broke her out of her revelry. "This natural light is perfect. Since I didn't have to set up the flash, we saved some time. I recommend we go into the church to keep the bride from sweating in the dress.

Edna was already moving, folding the train as the bridesmaids moved toward the church.

"I want the society photos in the church to be spectacular," Annette instructed Edna. "You must be sure to lay the train perfectly to capture the brilliance of the beads with that silver thread."

"Of course, Annette." Edna went to the photographer with Annette's wishes while the bridal party relaxed and enjoyed their refreshments. At exactly 11:55, Edna was summoned by the photographer to carry the train.

As the bride walked down the aisle, everyone watched in awe. Edna stood in the back, watching with pleasure. A woman leaned to her husband to comment at Annette's dress, filling Edna's head with dreams of a bigger shop and her name in lights, too.

David made it to the back of the church, having snapped photos of Annette as she walked down the aisle. Annette was now at the altar with Rolf waiting for the society photographers to take pictures before the ceremony began. Edna move quickly down the aisle to arrange the dress, then slipped to the left out of the camera's view. It was a much better spot to see the crowd's reaction, and everyone looked pleased.

The photographers quietly walked down the aisle and took their places, having been instructed by Annette to not block each other. Edna settled back to watch while the cameras began to click and flashbulbs sent blinding bright light through the church. Suddenly, gasps filled the church and people covered their faces in shock. The photographers stopped working, taking their cameras from their eyes. People started to whisper.

Edna stepped forward to see what had happened. Was there dirt on the dress? Had the dress hit a small puddle or patch of dew that ruined the silk? Edna stared but saw nothing.

"What is it?" Annette asked crossly but Edna didn't see any problems. The entire church now looked at Edna expectantly.

"Well?" Annette demanded.

Edna stepped into the aisle to examine the dress and saw nothing. The train lay perfectly with each fold evenly spaced. The beadwork was intact and spread without a wrinkle on the floor. Turning to the photographers, she shrugged.

David moved forward and turned on his flash, temporarily blinding Edna. After a few blinks to get rid of the white spots floating in her vision, Edna turned back to see the problem clear as day. She stood in shock, not knowing what to do. Seeing an opportunity, the photographers started taking her picture as she stared at Annette's dress which was covered in glittering swastikas that Ruth had embroidered into the train, using that damn silver thread.

53

Sheila had finally made it to see her financial planner where she sat uncomfortably facing Barbara's wrath.

"What do you mean, he took the money?" Barbara's eyes narrowed.

"When Joe left, he took money out of our joint account and wrote that I have equity in the co-op, so we're even," Sheila said.

"Are you joking?" Barbara's jaw was practically on the floor.

"No, he really did it." Sheila was mortified.

"And you've done nothing?"

"What can I do? It's gone. He's gone. He won't answer any of my calls." Sheila should have known better than to expect sympathy from Barbara.

"Get it back." Barbara scribbled on a piece of paper and pushed it across the table. "Here's the lawyer I used when Brian left. You need to get everything back that you put into that account. He doesn't get to decide what's fair."

"I just want to move on, Barbara. I have bigger problems."

"This is one hundred and twenty-five thousand dollars! You earned half of it and he stole it! You cannot walk away from that. How many years did it take to save it?" Barbara said.

"But Joe did pay half the mortgage for years and I own the co-op, so I see his point."

Barbara held her breath for a few seconds. "Sheila, he paid half the mortgage and in return got a place to live. If he hadn't lived with you, that money would be in a landlord's pocket. He dumped you for his assistant and you're still putting up with his bullshit."

"You're out of line, Barbara. This is a personal matter."

"No! The heartache is a personal matter. The money is life or death, especially now that you're single. He's banking on the fact you won't fight him and he's now buying a co-op with his fiancée using your hard earned cash." Barbara stared heatedly at Sheila who numbly looked back, not quite understanding what she just heard.

"That's right. I got a call because a mortgage broker needed Joe's statements and tax information. He's using your money to get a mortgage. And doesn't he have a boat?"

"Yes." Sheila tried not to cry.

"Well, that boat is communal property because he took money from the joint account to buy it. So let's review here. You owned the co-op when you met him. He needed a place to live and moved in with you, paying less rent than he would have anywhere else. He took a year off to get his MBA, paying the school with the HELOC money while you supported him. He bought a boat with your money. Now he left you for his assistant and stole your savings. Why am I the one who's mad?" Barbara leaned forward, truly looking concerned. "Do I need to know anything else?"

Sheila started crying, fearing Barbara's reaction.

"Yes. He stopped paying the mortgage months before he left, so I had to use the rest of my savings to pay seventeen thousand dollars on the mortgage. If I don't come up with sixty-one thousand for the HELOC, the bank is going to foreclose on my co-op."

"You need to call my lawyer immediately." Barbara took out her cell phone. "I'm dialing for you."

"No, don't. I can't talk right now. It's too much." Sheila stuffed her papers in her bag and stood. "Plus, I already have the name of a lawyer who can help."

"You have to handle this, Sheila, or you'll lose your home. Promise me that you'll call your lawyer tomorrow and then you'll call me. I'll deal with the bank but this has to happen quickly." Barbara sat back, looking at her copies of the papers. "Have they contacted your co-op board?"

"Would they?"

"Definitely. I really hope we're not too late."

*****

How could she be so stupid? Tears flowed down her cheeks while Sheila walked home. She had been a great girlfriend. Sure, she wasn't perfect, but Joe had no right to do what he did. Sheila had blindly accepted everything Joe wanted, even when he was dumping her.

Barbara was right. Just because Joe said something, doesn't make it right and it didn't mean that Sheila had to do it either. What could happen if she said 'no?' She stopped as the realization hit her.

If she said 'no,' it would mean the relationship was really, truly over because Sheila never said 'no' to Joe. In all those years, Sheila had gone along with Joe because she assumed he wanted the same things she did – a family and a long life together. Through their entire relationship, Sheila never gave Joe a reason to care about what she thought because she went along with everything he wanted, even the damn butter-colored paint on the walls in the co-op. She hated that color. For the past five years, she'd lived with a color she hated just to make him happy. Now, for the first time, Sheila needed to stand up for herself. But it meant, in some way, that she was admitting Joe wasn't coming back. She leaned against a building to catch her breath. It was very obvious that he wasn't coming back and he had left her with nothing. That's not love. That's a complete lack of respect, which seemed to be a recurring theme in her life right now. It had to stop. Sheila was living her life in fear of Joe, her job, and her mortgage.

Finally reaching her building, Sheila smiled weakly as Rudy opened the door for her. It was no use trying to hide her tear-stained face.

"I'm so sorry." Rudy touched her shoulder gently. "Your floor will never be the same."

"I'll be all right." Sheila smiled weakly, grateful for the support. As she waited for the elevator, an odd thought struck her. How did Rudy know about her mortgage problems? Sheila's head swam as she realized that the bank must have sent a foreclosure notice to the Board. Sheila walked back to the lobby where Rudy was now talking to the President of the Co-op Board, Mrs. Patricia Birken.

Mrs. Birken, as she liked to be addressed, was an elder member of the building who liked to gossip. She must have told Rudy that Sheila was going to lose her co-op. It would be all over the building soon. Oh, my God, I'm homeless. Mrs. Birken rushed to Sheila as the tears started again.

"I thought you would be very upset." Mrs. Birken held her hand. "I'm so sorry."

"I thought I had more time." Sheila wiped her nose with a tissue, overcome with emotion again.

"Let's sit." Mrs. Birken led her to a sofa in the corner of the lobby. "It's hard when something like this happens in a building such as ours where everyone feels we are a close knit community. When you're my age, you realize that it's for the best when it happens quickly." Mrs. Birken rubbed her back gently.

"It's just that I had a plan to fix everything. I was getting close." Sheila cried.

"From what I understand, nothing could have been done." Mrs. Birken looked at her intently. "You can't blame yourself."

"But I just met with my financial planner who said I might have had a chance. Please, Mrs. Birken. Please don't make me leave my co-op. I just need thirty days and I'll take care of the HELOC," Sheila whispered. "I just can't believe the bank contacted you already."

Mrs. Birken didn't quite know what to say. This situation was so difficult and getting worse.

"Sheila" Mrs. Birkin said gently. "I'm not making you leave your co-op."

Relief spread through Sheila's body at the news. It had been such an emotional meeting with Barbara, she had automatically assumed the worse. She smiled, feeling a little embarrassed at her outburst.

"My dear." Mrs. Birkin held Sheila's hand tighter. "Ruth died this afternoon."

54

Sheila stared at her bedroom ceiling, unable to stop crying for more than a few minutes. In the two days since she heard the news, Sheila had stayed in bed. Even when her phone rang, Sheila let it go to voicemail, even when she knew it was someone from work. She hadn't gone in yesterday and emailed Melissa again last night that she would not be in for the rest of the week to attend the wake and funeral over the next two days. It didn't seem possible that Ruth was gone. She hadn't been sick. Even with her cane, Ruth seemed, to Sheila anyway, like someone who could conquer anything. Curling into a ball, Sheila pushed wads of used tissue to the floor, which wasn't far since she still hadn't bought a new bed frame or dresser set. Her clothes sat in laundry baskets because she couldn't decide what to buy. Sheila had loved her bedroom set, which Joe now enjoyed with Taylor.

What would Ruth do? Sheila thought, cuddling her pillow. I'm sure she wouldn't be living like this. Sheila stared at the laundry baskets along the wall, wondering what was really stopping her. Yes, the money was a problem, and she wouldn't qualify for financing with her credit score destroyed. But there were other options. She could at least get something in a thrift store at a decent price. That's what Ruth would do.

Sheila looked at her phone. 1:30 pm. I really need to get a grip, she thought, remembering her last conversation with Ruth.

*****

"I can't believe you had the courage to do that!" Sheila was amazed that Ruth had defaced Annette's wedding dress. "I would never have thought of that."

"Well, I can't take all the credit. Louise gave me the idea to use the thread. You see, Sheila, when I stood up for myself, Louise gained courage, too, and was able to share her idea. High tide raises all ships, you know," Ruth said.

"I don't understand," Sheila said.

"Action causes reactions. Because I stood up to Edna, Louise did, too. Then she wasn't afraid to help me finish — and ruin — Annette's gown. I used the money from that gown to open my own shop and I hired Louise, who was like a whole new person. We had a very successful partnership that led us to places I never knew existed," Ruth said.

"Like what?" Sheila said.

"That's for another day, my dear. What I really want you to understand from all of this, Sheila, is that people who take positive actions create positive events. People who take negative actions sink and drag down everyone around them. It's happening at your office and it's the same with personal relationships," Ruth said. "I don't want to hurt you, Sheila, but being with Joe's negativity for so long, it dragged you down. I

280

know because I met you before you knew Joe, when you first wanted to buy your co-op. You were delightful and full of promise. You need to get that back."

"You and I met years ago, Ruth. I'm thirty-six now."

"Oh, Sheila." Ruth waved her hands dismissing the words. "I'm eighty-six. You're a baby in my eyes, a baby with her whole life ahead of her." Ruth smiled. "If I had given up at thirty-six, I wouldn't have met Bill or had my son and then I would have truly missed the best chapters of my life. Don't let that happen to you, my dear. Don't give up before the miracle."

"And when, exactly, is that miracle going to happen? Because I've been waiting for a few months now and haven't received any signs," Sheila said, sinking into the red velvet couch like a child.

"The miracle will happen when you start moving toward it. It won't just be laid at your feet, Sheila. You have to work for it one step at a time. And the steps don't even have to be perfect. You just have to take the action and learn from it. You do that and one day you'll realize you're in the middle of your miracle," Ruth said.

*****

Sheila took a shower and got ready to go furniture shopping. She even ate something. On her way out the door, her phone rang again and the office number popped on her screen. She hadn't been to work in two days. Sheila stared at the phone deciding whether to hit 'accept' or 'reject'. As the ringing continued, Sheila remembered Ruth's words and decided she couldn't get sucked into the drama right now. She had to take care of her bedroom furniture and for some reason, she felt it had to be done immediately.

Sheila got nervous as the call went to voicemail. No, she wouldn't do this. She had to break this pattern. But the pull to avoid a mess was too strong. I'll just check voicemail, Sheila decided, going to her desk. As she sat, a piece of paper caught her eye. Sheila smiled, taking this as a sign from Ruth. Instead of checking her messages, she dialed the number on the paper and scheduled an appointment with Alessandra's lawyer.

Going out the door to finally buy some furniture, Sheila figured that even though she had no idea what she was doing, meeting the lawyer could be one step closer to a solution.

55

The day after Ruth's funeral, Sheila was at the law firm of Phelan, Oxley & Schiff, being ushered into the most beautiful office she had ever seen. She had considered making the appointment for next week, but she really had to move on this. Sheila had to keep moving, period. The new furniture was in her bedroom, an eclectic set of antique furniture that Joe would have vetoed but she loved. In fact, Sheila had felt better when she woke this morning.

Maybe one day, she would have an office like this. A spotless mahogany desk took center stage in the room with two commanding U chairs in front. An inviting maroon couch took up most of the back wall with a coffee table and chairs. The credenza looked handmade and displayed sculptures, awards and books. She went to the wall of windows to admire the view. She was on the thirty-second floor and could see all of Central Park. It was gorgeous.

"Hello. Sorry I'm late. I'm Attorney Phelan. You must be Sheila Davenport." When Sheila turned, she was looking right at Tristan, the guy she had flirted with at Morgan's engagement party. "Have we met?"

"Yes, at Morgan and Dylan's engagement party," Sheila said.

"Right. You're the Maid of Honor. It's going to be a fun wedding." He gave her a gleaming smile.

"Yes, it will be."

"Well. Let's see how I can take care of this mess for you." He got right to business. They sat at his desk while Sheila relayed all the information she had from Alessandra. He took notes and then the questions began.

"How bad will it be to lose this job, financially speaking? Are you being supported by anyone?" He looked at her with concern.

Sheila hesitated, not wanting him to know she was practically destitute. But since he hadn't remembered their flirtation at the party or bothered to call her, she decided to tell the truth, minus the heartbreak. Though she did tell him about the money.

"Well, we'll have you speak to one of our divorce attorneys about getting that money back, which shouldn't be a problem. But I have to be honest, employment cases are never easy. You do have documentation, which shows your impending firing isn't really based on performance. But they have done analysis to show that eliminating your position benefits the company and the shareholders, which is good business." Sheila winced at that and Tristan smiled kindly. "Sorry to be so cold. I need anything that can be construed as harassment and any additional documents you can find. Is the other woman suing?"

"Jenn doesn't know yet. I'm going to tell her tomorrow. Don't I have a case because I'm being replaced by someone younger?" Sheila said.

"No." He shook his head. "If you were over forty, then you would be in a protected class. Although we haven't discussed your age, I can tell you're far from it." He smiled sweetly at her, making Sheila melt a little.

"Well. I've got to get to my next meeting." Sheila began putting her copies in her bag and continued. "I'll call you if I find anything else or if I get the ax, whichever comes first." As she stood to shake his hand, her purse swung off her shoulder, knocking over her coffee. When she tried to pick up the cup, she banged her knee on the side of the coffee table.

"That looked painful," He said, looking worried.

"No, I'm fine. I'll make another copy of those papers and send them tomorrow."

"Sounds good. Are you sure you can walk?" He moved around the table but she held up her hand and smiled.

"I'll find my way out. Thanks for your time. Sorry for the mess."

Sheila made the five steps to the door gracefully, then hobbled as fast as possible with an aching knee to the elevator. She leaned again the wall, trying to breathe through the pain, when she heard him call her name.

"Yes?" She straightened and turned with a smile.

"I need your home number."

"Sure." She took the pad and wrote. Maybe he did remember their connection from the party after all. This day was looking up.

"You only left your business info, so —" He stopped and delicately said, "I'll need this in case you're fired sooner than expected." As if on cue, the elevator door opened and the throbbing in her knee began again.

56

Standing at Starbucks with a swollen knee, Sheila scanned for an empty table while Jenn got her coffee.

"Don't take this the wrong way, but are you sick?" Sheila asked.

"No. Just tired. You've never seen me before 9:30." She smiled weakly. "So, what's up? Why all the secrecy and why are we here at 8:30 in the morning? Did you meet someone? Are you getting laid?" The color returned to her face at the thought of promiscuous sex.

A mother with a baby made a point to scowl and throw a dirty look in their direction.

"Give me a break, the kid's three months old! I'm a mother too. You need a life," said Jenn. "What?" Jenn looked at Sheila's shocked face.

"Nothing." Sheila sipped her latte, re-evaluating if this was a good time to tell Jenn her news.

"I'm sick of these moms who think everyone has to be a saint around their precious kids. Easy to be a saint when you don't have to work and can spend every second with your kids. God, I'm so jealous." Jenn looked out the window miserably. "Why are we here? I could still be in my pajamas with my kids."

Sheila took a deep breath and told Jenn about her conversation with Alessandra, causing Jenn to swear a lot and loudly.

"Okay, we're leaving." Sheila smiled at the mother next to them as she led Jenn outside.

They walked around the block at least four times so Jenn could get all the info. Then it was time to head into work, but Jenn was still fuming.

"Jenn, what are you going to do? Remember, you can't say a word," Sheila said.

"I won't." She stopped to text her husband. "But I'm not losing this job."

Seeing Jenn angry was impressive. Sheila wished she could be like that instead of getting flustered and knocking things over.

"Think we should go up separately?" Sheila asked when they reached the building.

"Who gives a shit what they think?" Jenn said. When the elevator doors opened on the fifteenth floor, Jenn hit the button for twenty-one.

"Jenn, you promised you wouldn't tell!" Sheila said.

"Don't worry, I won't. Trust me." She gently maneuvered Sheila off the elevator.

As the doors closed, Sheila wanted to cry. Wasn't there anyone she could trust? Now, she'd be going home today. She sat in her office and waited with dread until Jenn showed up.

To make matters worse, Baxter and Paul were talking outside Alessandra's office. Sheila watched them secretively from her office. She had no idea what they discussed but every so often one of them turned the doorknob, which didn't open the door.

When Jenn walked into the pit, she went up to both men causing Sheila to panic.

"Good morning!" Jenn smiled brightly. Baxter and Paul turned, irritated at interruption.

"I wanted you both to be the first to congratulate me! I'm pregnant!" Jenn beamed. "It's still really early. So we've got eight and a half months left. I just filled out my paperwork in HR, so if you have any questions, you can give them a call. Have a great day!"

Sheila ducked out of view and sat smiling at her computer screen. That was brilliant. Everyone knew a pregnant woman couldn't get fired. Jenn had won. An IM popped on Sheila's screen. It was from Jenn.

"*Sorry.*"

"*For what? Now they can't touch you.*" Sheila typed, still smirking with glee for her friend.

"*Yeah. But what about u?*"

57

Ruth's forty-five year old son, Nicholas, opened the door of Ruth's co-op wearing a t-shirt and jeans. He looked different than he had at Ruth's wake and funeral. Without a suit and tie, Sheila could see that Nicholas looked very much like a younger, male version of Ruth.

"Hi." Nicholas smiled apologetically. "The place is a mess, but please come in."

As Sheila walked into the living room, her heart sank. This would be the last time she'd be surrounded by Ruth's life, she realized. "I hope I'm not here at a bad time."

Nicholas moved some boxes from the couch. "I'm glad for the company. Would you like some tea? The water's hot and Mom said you're a fan of her Darjeeling."

"Oh, no. I don't want to take too much of your time —"

"Please." Nicholas interrupted. "I'm grateful for the distraction and I'd love to get to know you a little. My mother raved about you. Your friendship meant a lot to her. Please stay."

Sheila sat in her usual spot on Ruth's red couch while Nicholas went to the kitchen.

"We became close recently. Ruth really helped me through the past few months. She is, I mean was, an amazing woman," Sheila called into the next room.

"Yes, that's an understatement," Nicholas called to her. "She said you are pretty amazing too." He brought the tea tray to the living room.

"That's an overstatement." She laughed. "I wouldn't have made it through the past six months without your mother's help. She had an innate strength that I desperately need to learn. Of course, with all she'd been through in the war and working as a dressmaker, she knew how to survive."

Nicholas drew his eyebrows together. "Well, she did well as a dressmaker, but that was really just the training for her costume designing. I mean, there aren't many women who can say they traveled all over the world as the most sought after costume designer for the opera."

"What?" Sheila said.

"Mom made costumes for some of the biggest stars in the opera. She was in high demand and sat on quite a few swanky boards," Nicholas said. "She didn't tell you?"

"No. She talked a lot about the war and working as a dress-maker when she returned. I guess she had a lot more to tell me." Sheila sat stunned.

"She talked to you about the war?" Nicholas looked surprised. "She didn't like to talk about that time in her life. I mean, I know the stories, but she rarely shared it outside of the family. That is one sign that you were very special to her."

Sheila drank her tea.

"Mom's life was amazing. She was a great mother," he said.

"And a great friend," Sheila said.

"Well, I should get back to packing, but before I do, there is something Mom wanted you to have." Nicholas went to the dining room table and picked up the blue vase Sheila had admired. "Mom said you loved this vase from the minute you saw it. Most people didn't take the time to appreciate the beauty of it, she told me. But you did, so she wanted you to have it."

"Thank you." Sheila took the vase lovingly.

"Thank you for being such a great friend to my Mom." Nicholas's eyes filled with tears. They laughed to ease the tension.

"It was an honor." Sheila smiled and opened the door. As she entered her place, the tears came fast and hard and she hugged the vase to her. There would be no one else she could talk to about Ruth in that way again, nor would Sheila find out about the second part of her life. Standing in her apartment, Sheila suddenly felt completely alone.

58

"**W**ait a second. Your neighbor was Ruth Grey? The Ruth Grey? And you didn't even know who she was?" Susan stared at the obituary on Melissa's screen. "How the hell is it you've survived this long in New York?"

"Even I know that was a missed opportunity." Jenn shook her head.

"She was just a friend in my building." Sheila sipped her latte. "Isn't it enough to just be friends with someone?"

"Not in this town," Mark said. "I mean, it was all very romantic that you were spending time with some old lady, but to know it was Ruth Grey. Aah! She was on the Board of ABT in the seventies! How cool. She must have known Baryshnikov!" He scanned the print-out of Ruth's obituary.

"Plus, you could have used her connections to get a boyfriend. A very rich boyfriend." Susan threw in. "She must have known tons of eligible bachelors, especially if she was on the board at the Met."

"I didn't want her to set me up with bachelors." Sheila was growing tired of the conversation. "I just wanted a friend, which is what she wanted, obviously. Ruth taught me about dealing with life because her problems make all of ours seem like nothing. She survived the war while hiding in the woods and had a very successful career. She's the most fascinating woman I have ever met. Does it occur to any of you to just be friends with someone for the sake of friendship or is it always about getting ahead?"

Mark looked from Susan to Stacey.

"Getting ahead," all three replied.

"I like to be friends for the sake of friendship," Melissa offered with a smile.

"Then you should move to the country," Stacey said.

Shaking her head in disgust, Sheila went to her office.

"You need to send me a picture of the bottom of that vase," Susan yelled after her. "If Ruth was rich, I'm positive it's a Dergen, which you could sell for a lot of money."

Sheila sat staring at her computer, moving the mouse around to look busy. The conversation had turned her stomach. Ruth had been a great friend, which is what Sheila needed. Rubbing her stomach, she considered the shallowness of her co-workers. Yes, this is New York. Yes, every edge counts. But it had been so nice to go to Ruth's apartment and leave that behind. It had been like going home and it was now gone.

Fighting back the tears, Sheila Googled 'Dergen vases.' Photos appeared looking exactly like the vase Sheila now owned.

The Dergen family started the business over two-hundred years ago. Aristocrats and Royalty from all over Europe commissioned the Dergen family to create one-of-a-kind pieces. By the 1920s, the vases were sold in select upscale boutiques throughout Germany. The Dergens were revered as artisans until the war. Being Jewish, the family was forced into concentration camps. The Nazis smashed the remaining stock as the family was marched out of their factory. Not one member of the family survived the war, making all existing pieces very rare. One most recently sold at auction for as high as seventy-five thousand dollars.

Sheila stared at the number. That would be more than enough to take care of her HELOC plus give her a small cushion, but then she wouldn't have anything of Ruth's. She quickly closed the screen when someone walked into her office and the idea flew out of her mind.

59

"**I** refuse to take the blame for this," Sheila stated simply as she sat next to Paul in Baxter's office. Ever since Jenn had announced her pregnancy, Baxter had been calling Sheila with problem after problem, most of them involving Crystal.

"Crystal is your direct report and she's been losing accounts! Why did I have to hear this from Paul?" Baxter was livid.

"You heard from Paul because he took Crystal for a nice lunch. It's not my fault he ran to you in hysterics," Sheila replied.

"I did not run to Baxter. You weren't in, or answering your phone, so I ran a budget analysis and couldn't believe my eyes. I'm at a loss as to what you are thinking here." Paul threw his spreadsheets on Baxter's desk.

"Well, Paul. If you'd ever actually sold anything, you would know we lose big accounts all the time. When competent sales people are on the team, they close new accounts to offset that. As I said, I'm taking care of it." Sheila shot him a dirty look.

"You should have come to me immediately." Baxter stood by Sheila's chair with his hands on his hips.

"I'm handling it," she said again.

"Sheila, this is a very serious matter. I strongly suggest you listen carefully." Baxter was livid now.

"You're right. It is serious. As I said, I am handling it. Now if you'll excuse me, I have a lunch appointment." Sheila looked at him.

"Handling it? How, exactly, are you doing that? Because all I see is a big, fat loss for the quarter!" Baxter yelled.

"Excuse me, but you put a junior person on a major account and she lost it. Not me. Crystal lost it. I am not responsible for that but I will fix it," Sheila shot back.

"So now you doubt my account assignments? Pretty convenient, now that there's a problem," Baxter said, still standing above Sheila.

"I said from the very beginning that Crystal shouldn't have those accounts. I said it to you, Paul, and Alessandra."

"I don't remember that," Paul said.

"Well, maybe you'll remember while I'm at lunch." Sheila couldn't stand because Baxter hovered so close, furiously grinding his jaw.

"I didn't tell you we were finished. A VP is supposed to train their staff, not drop them on their heads. I think I may have to make some changes of my own and it may include talking to Ann Joyce." He leaned over her a bit for emphasis.

"She'll be thrilled to hear from you. Now excuse me, Baxter. You're too close." Sheila moved forward in her seat.

"What's that supposed to mean?" He stepped back.

"It means whatever you want it to, Baxter. I can't be late for this lunch so back up." Baxter took a few steps back, unnerved by Sheila's lack of concern. Paul stayed in his spot, eying her suspiciously.

"This conversation isn't finished. I want you in here tomorrow at 8:00 a.m.," Baxter practically spit.

Sheila went to her office with Paul following close behind.

"I don't know what's gotten into you, Sheila, but you are out of your league here. Ann may like you, but I have connections that go much farther than that," Paul said softly.

"I'm sure those people will give you what you deserve." Sheila grabbed her bag, leaving Paul alone in her office.

Something was going on with her, he thought as he stared at her desk. She was never this gutsy before. He walked to her chair.

"Paul, you really shouldn't be in Sheila's office while she's not here." Paul turned to see Melissa in the doorway.

"Melissa, this really doesn't concern you." He turned back to the desk.

"Yes, it does. I'm her assistant." Melissa walked past Paul and leaned over Sheila's desk. There were three keys in her hand. She had no idea which key locked Sheila's desk but she knew she had to find it. Her hands shook so badly, she dropped one on the floor.

"What do you think you're doing?" Paul came behind her.

"Locking Sheila's desk." She tried the first key.

"Melissa, get back to your desk," he ordered.

"After I do this." Melissa's face was red. She had no idea what had happened with Baxter, but it was obvious that Sheila was in trouble. Sheila had helped her plenty of times. She wasn't about to turn her back on her. She tried the second key. It worked. Filled with relief, she put the other two keys in her left hand and headed for her cubicle.

Paul put his hand to his face. Sheila had something in that desk or she wouldn't be so cocky. He needed to find out what she knew. In a split-second decision, he swung at Melissa's hand when she passed. Melissa gasped as the key flew into the air, landing on the hallway floor. Paul shoved past her and lunged for the key while she stood in horror. Just as he was about to close his fingers on the small piece of silver, he ended up grabbing a large black work boot instead.

"What are you doing, Paul?" Rick stared down at him.

"I dropped something. You're standing on it. Could you move?"

"What is it?" Rick didn't budge.

"It's a key. I dropped it." Paul spat angrily. First, an assistant goes against him and now a maintenance guy. He glared at Rick. "Move your foot."

Instead of moving his foot, Rick crouched down to Paul's level. Since Rick was over six feet tall, Paul had never been face-to-face with the guy. Now they were inches apart. Where Paul always saw an uneducated, dispensable person, he now saw a man with lines of integrity etched in his face. Rick's eyes were clear blue and unflinching because he had nothing to hide and therefore, nothing to fear. He was also a man who knew how to fight for himself and others.

"I suggest you get up, Paul," Rick said.

Paul wasn't street tough but he had been hazed in a fraternity and he had survived years climbing the corporate ladder, which wasn't exactly a picnic. He was not about to lose to someone in a uniform. The two men glared at each other. "You are blocking my way. I will take this to the union if I have to, Rick. Now move your foot."

"That's too bad, Paul. See, I came up here for two things. But since we've got ourselves a problem, I won't be able to unlock Alessandra's door like you asked. Now I have to call my union representative." Rick stood and stepped around Paul, leaving the key uncovered.

Paul grabbed the key and stood. "Wait, Rick. Please. I'm sorry. Really. Everything's fine. I'm just having a bad day and I took it out on the wrong guy. You know how it is." He pasted a smile on his face. "How can I make it up to you?"

"Sorry, Paul. I have to protect myself. But before I go," he turned to Melissa, "I got a call from HR. Seems they missed an important procedure when Sheila was made Interim VP of Sales."

Rick pushed the tool cart into Sheila's office and shut the door. Paul moved forward, listening through the door. Melissa went back to her cubicle. They both heard banging and the sound of pulling metal. Paul stepped back as the door handle jiggered. Rick opened the door within seconds, sliding a brand new lock into the space. He shut the door, making sure everything was secure.

"You see, Sheila needs a lock on her door since she has access to all kinds of important documents." He stuck a key in the lock and turned it. "Safe and secure.

"Now, Melissa. Since you are Sheila's assistant, I would normally give you the new keys to her door and her desk." He smiled at Paul, holding up another set of smaller keys, "From what I've seen here today, I think it's best I keep them. You okay with that?"

"Yes." Melissa couldn't help but smile.

"Great!" Rick said, looking at his watch. "Look at that, it's lunch time. Melissa, do you have plans for lunch?"

"No," she said.

"Well, why don't you come with me? You see, you and I belong to the same union. Since I'm calling my representative, I thought you'd want to join me. They have a very strict rule against physical contact among employees. Which I believe was broken today." Rick stared at Paul.

The color drained from Paul's face. Even his father wouldn't be able to fix a problem with the unions. It would be another failure for everyone to talk about at the holidays. "Melissa, it was a simple misunderstanding." Paul smiled.

She looked at Paul. He was a jerk but she didn't want to make any waves. She just wanted to pretend it didn't happen.

"Oh good, you're here. I need you in my office." Crystal walked past the entire scene while texting on her phone. "Now!"

"I'm going to get lunch." Melissa called to her weakly.

"No, you're helping me. Lunch can wait." Crystal continued texting and laughed at her phone.

Melissa turned to her. Not only did Crystal not care if Melissa was hungry, she was oblivious to the very serious situation taking place right at Melissa's desk. Finished with her phone, Crystal came into the pit and looked at Paul.

"Please tell me you'll deal with this kind of attitude when you take over from Sheila." Crystal threw her hands in the air.

Melissa looked quickly to Paul.

"She doesn't know what she's talking about." His mouth twitched and his breathing was shallow.

"I thought Baxter had his meeting with her. Isn't it done?" Crystal asked incredulously.

"What have you done?" Melissa asked Paul.

He just stared at her helplessly. It was then she noticed the sweat on his brow.

"Hello." Crystal called out. "Is anyone going to answer me?"

Melissa looked at Rick. "Let's go."

60

Later that evening, Sheila studied the markings on the bottom of Ruth's blue vase. It was a Dergen. Filled with awe, Sheila stared at the vase she had admired all these months, wondering what Eliza had thought when she had unwrapped the gift.

She carefully put the vase on a shelf and went to her desk to review the documents from her lunch meeting with Tristan and the packet from Barbara. The lunch had been nice, but strictly professional. When Sheila referred to him as 'Attorney Phelan', he didn't even suggest that she call him Tristan. In fact, he didn't mention anything outside of her case. Not even Morgan and Dylan's wedding, which Sheila now had to start organizing. Sheila sighed. Tomorrow was her 8:00 a.m. meeting with Baxter and she had to decide what to do. Feeling overwhelmed, she procrastinated at her computer, searching for more information that might tell her the exact date the vase was made. Startled by a knock on the door, Sheila realized she had just wasted half an hour.

"Hi." Sheila smiled at Nicholas. "What a surprise. Come in."

"Thanks. I can't stay long. I have another box for you." Nicholas placed a cardboard box on her coffee table. "Working?" He nodded to the laptop.

"No. I was actually looking for some history on the vase your mother gave me." Sheila hoped she didn't sound shallow.

"Did you find anything interesting?" Nicholas asked.

"It's a Dergen," Sheila said. Nicholas shrugged, clearly not knowing the significance.

"The company was destroyed during the war so it's actually very valuable," Sheila told him.

"Really? Do you mind if I look?" Nicholas pointed to the laptop and sat when Sheila shook her head 'no.' "Wow. I'll be damned." Nicholas scrolled through the article.

"Are you going to sell it?" he asked.

"No. In fact, I feel bad having it. I'm not sure Ruth knew just how much it's worth. If she did, she'd want you to have it," Sheila answered.

Nicholas shook his head and smiled. "I'm sure Mom knew exactly what she was doing with the vase plus she left more things for you in this box."

"That's weird." Sheila looked at the box noticing the tape had yellowed with age. "It looks like she sealed it years ago."

Nicholas just shrugged and displayed his ever present smile. "My Mom has so much stuff in there. I can't keep it all straight. But your name is on it, so it must have things she thought you'd like. Since there are no daughters, it's probably stuff for a trousseau. Either way, it's all yours."

After Nicholas left, Sheila became more intrigued when she realized the box was quite heavy. Cutting the tape, she opened the lid and stepped back gasping at the sight of an SS pin. She had never seen real Nazi memorabilia, except in museums. She turned it around and saw a small piece of cloth still attached to the pin. It must be the pin from Irma's uniform, the day Ruth was saved. Sheila stared in awe. Under that was a baby dress of soft faded cotton, muted yellow. Sheila recognized it as the dress Annabelle wore in Ruth's family portrait. It would have been left at their home in New York when they went to Germany. Sheila hugged it gently to her chest, connecting to the soul which had once lived inside. She imagined that Ruth had held Annabelle in this very dress the same way. Moments later, she unwrapped a towel to reveal the small wooden doll that Vincenzo had carved after Annabelle died. Sheila recalled that Ruth said she kept that doll with her every day but Sheila assumed she lost it when she went to the camp. As she looked into the doll's small face, Sheila smiled with pride as she realized that Ruth would have found a way to sew this prized possession into her uniform. She laid the doll on the table to finish going through the box.

Next, Sheila found a small cardboard box from the department store, Jordan Marsh. She sat back on the couch, wondering what this surprise would be, shaking it gently next to her ear. Whatever lay inside was well insulated. Opening the box, Sheila looked in shock at the gold chain that had waited for almost seventy years for its owner to return. Sheila studied the chain delicately. Ruth had it fixed. There was no sign of a break. She put the chain around her neck. It was a little long, but fell nicely against her shirt.

Sheila started to look at all the things in her apartment and realized that she disliked most of them. In fact, most of the stuff had been chosen by Joe or she had chosen it to make Joe happy and here she was, living with it even though he had been gone for six months. Meanwhile, Ruth had surrounded herself with things she loved, which is what made her apartment so warm and inviting.

Looking at the things Ruth had left behind, Sheila started to rethink her current situation. So she might lose her job. She would get another one. It wasn't like her irreplaceable baby sister had died. Joe hadn't been taken from her by Taylor, he chose to leave. For Sheila to waste more time thinking about it made no sense. It wasn't like they were ripped apart by war like Ruth and Vincenzo. Even so, Ruth had gone on to love someone wonderful and have an amazing son. As for the financial problems, Sheila turned back to her desk. There was a solution in those documents; she just had to find the strength to fight. Fingering the chain around her neck, she knew what she had to do.

When she stood, Sheila realized there was still something in the box. It was heavy and fit tightly against the sides, forcing her to turn the box upside down on her sofa. A beautiful, cherry box slid onto the cushion. Lifting it, Sheila saw a key taped to the bottom.

When she opened the lid, her jaw fell. Ruth's diaries were lined up next to one another. Sheila counted ten in all. Each year was marked on the binding, starting from 1947 and ending in 1962. They began where Ruth had left off. Sheila looked back to the desk, knowing that she needed to go through those documents. But first, she needed a little advice from Ruth.

EPILOGUE

Sheila looked at the butter yellow walls of her apartment, remembering her last phone call with Joe.

"I can't believe you're doing this to me! I'm in the middle of buying a co-op and you are destroying everything!" Joe had yelled into the phone.

"Joe, the money belongs to me. Maybe you should talk to your lawyer."

"Now I'll have to sell my boat to get the money for my co-op! And I have to give you half of that, too! You don't want me to be happy," Joe whined.

"It's our boat, Joe. And you know what? Your happiness doesn't concern me anymore. What I want is for me to be happy. Something you never cared about. If you have anything else to say, call my lawyer." Sheila hung up the phone.

Sheila smiled at the memory and silently thanked Barbara for saving all of Sheila's bank statements from the past seven years. Sheila's lawyers used that information to get back every cent that Joe had taken from their account and Joe had to cut a check for half of all the assets he had in his possession including, the bedroom furniture and the boat.

Shortly after Sheila hung up on Joe, she decided to make some major changes, starting with her living situation. Memories of Joe were all around. She might be alone, but it was better to move forward than hold onto bad memories.

Since having good memories around had been the key to making Ruth's apartment a home, Sheila had approached Nicholas with one last request, which he happily obliged. It had given Sheila great pleasure to get rid of the uncomfortable brown sofa and club chair and take ownership of Ruth's red velvet sofa.

Nicholas had even offered to let Sheila buy Ruth's co-op for a good price. Aside from being too expensive, it would have been too full of memories. Sheila had to make her own way and since her confrontation with Baxter, a lot of things didn't seem so scary.

It was nice to wake every morning and know she didn't have to face a bully. But nicer still, Sheila knew that she had stood up for herself and did the right thing.

Sheila had actually felt bad for Baxter when the HR rep told him they were not at the meeting to fire Sheila, but that Baxter was under investigation for embezzlement. Although he deserved everything he got, the look on his face when the police arrived clearly showed that the crime hadn't been worth the risk. Instead of seeing the man who had used her, she saw a little boy who had gotten in over his head as he tried to keep up with his friends.

Paul was arrested at home since he had been fired immediately for hitting Melissa. What made him think his behavior was okay was a mystery. Even Paul's high-powered circle wouldn't back him up for hitting a woman in the office.

Alessandra returned to assist in the deposition and gave Sheila a glowing recommendation prompting Ann Joyce to reward Sheila with a nice bonus and a promotion to VP of Strategic Accounts and an office on the twenty-fifth floor. It's strange how a common enemy can turn adversaries into friends, though not everyone appreciated Sheila's actions. Apparently Crystal's low salary had not been supplemented by her father. Baxter arranged for her to have a huge expense account and free rein to use it anyway she wanted. That was how she could afford her rent and utilities as well as the designer clothes and jewelry she flaunted. When the reports were submitted, Paul approved them and the money was used to repay what he stole. Crystal wore the clothes a few times and gave them to Paul's wife, who either wore them herself or sold them at a local consignment shop and pocketed the money.

Once the embezzlement charges were made, company officials visited Crystal's office to let her know she wouldn't be fired and wouldn't have to pay back the money if she cooperated. It all went well until she learned that all remaining items had to be turned over as evidence, even the Hermès bracelet. She ran out of the office in tears and quit two days later.

*****

The knocking on the door brought Sheila out of her reverie. She opened it to let Rudy and two other men into the apartment.

"Wow, it's empty." Rudy looked around.

"Weird, isn't it?" Sheila let the men set up. It wasn't long before the shelves were on the hallway floor and tarps were all over the place.

"Please be careful of these boxes. Maybe I should put them in the closet." Sheila's stomach started to flutter.

"I'll do it," Rudy said.

Taking a deep breath, Sheila looked around the room one last time. She didn't expect to be this sad.

"You sure you're all set?" Rudy looked at her with concern. "You can still change your mind."

Sheila watched the men cover the yellow paint, erasing years of uneasiness and smiled. "No. Keep going. The deep blue color will look fabulous with my red sofa." She took her suitcase and walked out the door.

As Sheila passed Ruth's apartment, she stopped. She knew the apartment was empty. Nicholas had put it on the market a few days ago. But for a few more moments, Sheila wanted to think that Ruth was on the other side of the door, sitting in her chair, waiting with tea and a story.

It had been six months to the day since Joe had walked out on her and she thought her world had collapsed. But it hadn't. Instead she had been forced to keep going with Ruth pushing her gently, and she became stronger for it.

Every story that Ruth shared in their time together had given Sheila a new perspective because, really, Ruth faced problems that were insurmountable compared with Sheila's. From war to losing her first love, to being in debt and having a crazy boss, Ruth made it to the ripe old age of eighty-six with a life that Sheila hoped she now had the courage to get for herself.

The hardest part now for Sheila was the burden that many bear when someone close dies suddenly. Yes, Ruth had lived a full life into old age, but her spirit was so strong that death somehow seemed far away. If Sheila had thought for a moment that Ruth would be gone and their last conversation was truly their last, she would have told Ruth how much she had meant and how much she had helped her. More importantly, she would have said the very thing that one sometimes only realizes after a person is gone. Although the moment was past, Sheila laid her forehead on the door.

"Thank you, my dear friend, for showing me what love truly is," Sheila said.

*****

As the cab driver put Sheila's luggage in the trunk, her phone vibrated. Instinctively she reached into her pocket to check her messages but stopped herself. Settling into the backseat, she closed her eyes and promised herself she would ignore it. After all, she had earned this two week vacation, which she needed desperately. Work, she had learned, would survive without her.

But the familiar tug of the phone wouldn't go away. After a few more seconds, Sheila decided to check this one last time and turn off the phone. Seeing the tiny email icon, her heart skipped when she saw it was a message from Attorney Phelan. Don't check, she warned herself, but she'd never rest until she knew if something was wrong, so she opened the email and read.

Dear Sheila —

Since we are finished with your legal affairs, I was hoping you might like to check out the fall leaves in the Berkshires next weekend. It may sound corny, but I know a great place we could get lunch and they have a spa and meditation center.

Any interest?

Tristan

As the cab edged away from the curb, Sheila turned back to look up at Ruth's window and smiled.

Dear Readers,

You've just finished reading ***Finding Out***, and now you want to know more about one of your new favorite authors, Sheryn MacMunn?

Well, you can ***find out*** more at
www.SherynMacMunn.com

Come visit and you will get:

∫   More information about *Finding Out*

∫   Sneak peeks at upcoming books

∫   Appearance dates

∫   And more!

You can also:

∫   Like us on Facebook at
www.Facebook.com/SherynMacMunn

∫   Friend us at www.Goodreads.com/MacMunn

∫   Follow us on Twitter @SherynMacMunn

Book Club Guide
FINDING OUT – A NOVEL

1. When Joe leaves Sheila, she is surprised. Based on what you learn about their relationship, do you think Sheila should have been so surprised? If Sheila were your friend, would you have seen that her relationship wasn't as perfect as she thought? Would you have said anything to her?

2. Sheila and Ruth knew each other for years but their friendship had not fully developed because Joe didn't want to spend time with an "old person". Do you feel the same as Joe about talking with an elderly person or do you enjoy it?

3. Ruth enjoys taking care of Sheila and Sheila enjoys being taken care of. Which do you prefer?

4. What do you think drives Alessandra?

5. Speaking of Alessandra, have you worked for someone like her? If you had a boss like her now would you stay or would you quit?

6. Do you think Crystal represents the values of most people her age or is she this way because of her privileged background? Do you think Sheila should have handled Crystal differently? Do you think she could have made Crystal behave?

7. Baxter gave Paul the General Manager position for two reasons: he owed Paul's father a favor, and Paul could help Baxter fix his problem. Do you think Paul has been

311

manipulated his entire life or have his friends and family
been protecting him from his own stupidity?

8. Both Sheila and Ruth work for bossy, harsh women yet Ruth
   demands to be respected. Why do you think Sheila couldn't
   do that for herself? What do you think Sheila's upbringing
   was like?

9. When Ruth's family goes to Germany, the events in Europe
   are unknown to Americans. Do you think that situation
   could happen today? Has the Internet made it possible to
   know everything that's going on all over the world?

10. Ruth's love story with Vincenzo shows Sheila what love is
    supposed to be and how important it is to move on if things
    don't work out. Did you learn anything from Ruth and
    Vincenzo's love story?

11. Was there someone in your life, like Ruth, who was a major
    influence? Who was s/he and in what way?

ABOUT THE AUTHOR

Sheryn MacMunn lives in Connecticut with her family. This is her first novel.

Made in the USA
Charleston, SC
23 April 2014